GHOST HEART

GHOST HEART

The PSS Chronicles: Book Three

RIPLEY PATTON

Shawna,
from my heart
to yours.

Ripley Patton

Cover design by Scarlett Rugers of The Scarlett
Rugers Book Design Agency
Cover © 2014 by Ripley Patton
Edited by Lauren McKellar and Jennifer Ingman
Typesetting and Formatting by Simon Petrie

Library of Congress Control Number: 2014915556
ISBN 9780988491052

Publisher's website: www.ripleypatton.com

DEDICATION

For my lovely readers and all the dedicated bloggers
who have spread the word and fed my heart.
Without you, I'd still be whistling in the dark.

OTHER BOOKS BY RIPLEY PATTON

The PSS Chronicles
Ghost Hand (Book One)
Ghost Hold (Book Two)

Novellas
Over The Rim (Young Adult Fantasy)

CONTENTS

1

THE MAGIC EIGHT BALL

n the early morning after the Eidolon, dark clouds
scudded in, gathering menacingly over Indiana's
Shades State Park. The air grew thick, a few fat,
distinctive drops plopping into the swirling Sweet
Water River. Then, without warning, the world was
nothing but a wall of wet, all individuality lost. The
sky was the air was the water was the river. It was all
one.

The river swelled, kissing its banks, then ravishing
them. Blue water churned to white and brown. The
sun rose, but no one saw it, and the river valley that
ran through the park became a raging flood, every
visible surface slick and wild.

Beneath the turbulence, sitting on a stone shelf

three feet below the water of a deep pool, something lurked, unmoved by this grand display of nature.

It was a black, round ball, and the ledge it was perched on was narrow, but it balanced easily, resting on its one flattened edge. On its top, a white circle encompassed the symbol for infinity, stamped in black, bold script.

The ball knew nothing. It did not know what it was or why it was there. It did not remember the girl named Olivia Black who had yanked it into existence and tossed it aside. It did not know what to do, or even that it could do anything, other than sit on that submerged rock covering its answer-window ass.

But then the pool at the bottom of the cliff known as Devil's Drop began to swirl. The current grew deeper and stronger, buffeting the ball and nudging it closer to the edge of its ledge. Something groaned and creaked and crashed above it, and a huge logjam plummeted into the pool from upriver, displacing everything in its path.

Water surged against the ball, pushing it off its shelf, sending it end over end, roiling in a tumultuous wave of questionless answers.

It is certain.

Don't count on it.

It is decidedly so.

Slowly, slowly, gravity and the current carried it into darkness, toward the calm nether regions of the deepest part of the pool. And the ball sank, still flashing its vague banalities.

Ask again later.

You may rely on it.

Better not tell you now.

Past gleaming grey-green walls of stone and silhouettes of sunken trees.

Yes definitely

My sources say no.

Reply hazy try again.

At last, the ball landed upon another shelf, but this one was not made of rock. It was made of flesh.

The flesh belonged to a young man, his shirt torn to ribbons that floated around him like kelp, revealing a gaping hole in his chest. From the hole, a jagged branch jutted, rising up and through the man from the log he rested on.

The ball rolled gently toward the sloping cavity of the man's chest, its answer window flickering a sweet blue sigh of *YES*.

A shadow passed overhead as a log, like a giant lumbering pool cue, plunged down, cracking into the end of the log the man and the ball sat upon. They both bounced, the ball careening into the man's gaping chest even as his body rose just above the top of the branch skewering him.

There was a flash of light, bright and cerulean.

It washed over the ball, filling it with wonder, as it slipped down through the hole in the man and under him.

The man settled, returning to his stick, his weight pressing the ball against the log's slimy surface and shooting it out into the stronger currents.

Outlook not so good

My sources say no

Don't count on it

Help me. I am Marcus.

The ball, propelled closer to the surface of the pool, rushed downriver, leaving the man on the stick far behind it.

Mostly.

2

PASSION

"It's stopped raining." I turned from the dirty window pane and the grey dripping forest beyond, looking at Jason. "We have to go back."

"Passion," he said, his voice hard but his eyes tinged with understanding. "There's nothing we can do." He was sitting on the edge of the yellowed mattress and rusty metal bed that dominated the one-room cabin we'd stumbled upon as we'd fled downriver last night.

I hadn't wanted to stop here, despite the fact that we'd both been soaked to the bone from our fall into the river, our clothes plastered to our skin. I'd been running on pure adrenaline and the certain knowledge that if the CAMFers took us, they would kill us.

They would shoot us and leave us in pools of our own blood just like they'd done to Yale and Nose. All I'd wanted to do was run as fast and as far away from the Eidolon as I could.

I turned back to the window. They were still out there. The men who had massacred my friends in cold blood. Not just my friends; they'd also mowed down twenty or so others up on those cliffs. I had seen them bleeding, wide-eyed, and floating in the river, and I would never forget it. Never understand it.

I didn't even understand how Jason and I had gotten away. The woods had been teeming with CAMFers, all descending upon the pool at the bottom of Devil's Drop. Jason had dragged me into the woods, and I'd followed him. I hadn't resisted. I'd gone with him willingly, leaving Olivia behind to be taken because she'd told me to. Because I'd wanted to survive. Because I'd become resigned to loss a long time ago.

The Lord giveth, and the Lord taketh away.

That was the comfort my father had offered when we'd lost my sister, as if God were some kind of cosmically fickle Santa Claus. But I didn't want to believe in that kind of god anymore. I wanted to believe in a good god who did good things.

After what I'd just been through, some people might think that was impossible, but it wasn't. God hadn't mowed anyone down with automatic weapons. CAMFers had done that. Stupid, godless, CAMFers. God didn't scare me. People did.

Last night had been the most terrifying thing I'd ever been through, and my life hadn't exactly been a walk in the park. *A walk in the park.*

Yeah, that had new meaning now.

Even so, as I stood at the window in the dim light of morning, the instinct to flee for my life had faded to a faint whisper, replaced by the louder internal voices of guilt, grief and devastation. How could we have left Olivia behind? Or Marcus? How many times had both of them risked themselves, against all odds, to save one of us? We should have stayed and fought, no matter what. If they were captured by the CAMFers, I should be too. How could I possibly live with the knowledge I had abandoned them to save myself?

"Stop torturing yourself," Jason said, seemingly reading my thoughts. "We can't help them."

"You don't know that," I said, facing him, desperation rising up in my throat. "What if Olivia used her ghost hand and got away? She could be out there somewhere, hiding and injured. We can't just leave her." I knew what I said wasn't true, but I wanted it to be. All night, I'd felt the glimmer of Olivia's presence, the connection we had through the dog tags she wore that had been made from my blades. The CAMFers had taken her. I could tell that by her desperate resignation, but my sense of her was fading. I could barely feel her now; wasn't even sure if I was feeling her, or if it was just an echo of what I'd once felt. It was possible she was just sleeping or unconscious. The connection always felt fainter then. Or it could be something worse, and that thought made panic rise in my throat. What would it mean when I couldn't sense Olivia at all?

"We already left her," Jason said, the words cutting into me. "And there's no way, even using her hand, she could have held off hundreds of armed men, especially with an injured knee. They have her now. We have to admit it and move on. Going back just gets us caught, and that doesn't help anyone."

Everything he was saying was rational, and logical, and objective, and I still hated it.

"What about Marcus?" I asked, my eyes pleading. We hadn't just left Olivia at the side of the pool; we'd left Marcus at the bottom of it. I had been the one to stop her from trying to save him. If he was down there still, alone in the cold depths—I had to know he wasn't. I couldn't leave him like that.

"They've found him by now, or he's dead," Jason said, not looking away from me. If saying it bothered him, it was hard to tell. It was always hard to tell with Jason.

"But he can reboot," I argued. "If we could get him out—"

"Well, we can't." Jason's voice plowed over mine, hot and angry, as he stood up. "The pool will be crawling with CAMFers. And even if it isn't, he's too deep. It would take a diver with tanks to haul him up. We would die trying and you know it. You think I want to leave him here?"

"No, I—"

"Then stop second guessing everything I say. What's done is done." He strode to the window to stand next to me, frustration radiating off his body. "What we have to do now is get the hell out of here. We're only a couple of miles from the kill site. They may still come down this far to clean up any stray bodies and check for survivors. The storm bought us some time, but that time is running out."

The kill site. Is that how he thought of it? Is that why he'd been able to lie down on that lumpy bed last night and fall asleep, even in wet clothes, unarmed, with CAMFers all around us? By boxing it neatly in his mind as "the kill site"?

I hadn't slept. Every time I closed my eyes, visions of the Eidolon assaulted me. The sounds of screaming. The sting of the tear gas. The rattle of gunfire and the images of bodies strewn everywhere. If that was the waking nightmare, how bad would the sleeping ones be? Then there was the storm raging overhead, battering against our leaky little cabin. So, instead of sleeping, I'd spent the night curled up in a corner of the mattress holding onto my connection with Olivia. She should be able to feel me too, if she was awake or conscious. The connection went both ways. Besides, how could I sleep with her life in the balance? How could I rest knowing she'd feel me do it and think we'd given up, that we weren't coming for her?

Trying to sense Olivia wasn't all I'd done. I'd also shivered a lot. And prayed. I'd prayed for Samantha, that she would be safe, and for Olivia, that she would be strong. I'd prayed for Marcus, that he wasn't dead, or that even if he were, he'd rise up like Lazarus again. I'd prayed for all the souls lost at the top of that cliff, and all the evil men who had done the deed. And of course, I'd prayed for Nose and Yale, though that had been the hardest prayer of all. "Why?" was the only word I'd come up with for that one; just an empty, pain-filled "Why?"

And had God answered me?

Maybe he had.

Sometime near morning, the paralyzing fear had left my mind and body, replaced with a calmness I did not understand. The grief was still there, an eternal deep hole I'd learned to dance around long ago. Grief was a constant I was used to. People died. People you loved. And yes, it sucked, but that was just how the world worked. It was also why I had to believe in heaven. Otherwise, none of it made sense.

Nose had once asked me how I could still believe in God after the way my parents had treated me. That was when I'd first realized I believed in Him *because* of the way they'd treated me. There had to be a better love than that. A truer Father. A different way than all this nastiness.

"I'm going to get the trunk open," Jason said, turning away from the window. "There might be something we can use."

The trunk was more of a wooden crate with a padlock on it that someone, long ago, had slid under the bed. Last night it had been too dark to see it, but this morning, when we'd first woken up, Jason had made a thorough search of the cabin. He hadn't found much. There was the locked box under the bed, some trash, including three empty, plastic water bottles, a rusty bucket we'd put in the far corner of the cabin, now reeking of urine, and an old short-handled ax, probably for chopping kindling for the cabin's small, black, pot-bellied stove.

Jason grabbed the ax and crossed to the crate.

"I hope there's food," I said, my stomach growling in unison with my words.

"Don't count on it." He raised the ax and pounded on the lock. It only took about five whacks before it fell away. He lifted the lid, the hinges creaking, to reveal some clothes, mostly camo in men's size large, which pretty much confirmed his theory that this was an old hunting cabin just beyond the edge of the state park's boundaries. There were also two pairs of long johns, still wrapped in plastic from the store, and under them some beef jerky, a large can of mixed nuts, and some dried fruit.

"We should wait to eat until we have water," Jason said. "This stuff is salty. It will only make it worse."

"We could eat the fruit, though," I said, hopefully.

"Yeah, okay." He popped open the sealed bag of fruit and handed me some.

As we chewed, he continued to dig, revealing matches in a small watertight tube, water purification tablets, and a fishing kit, complete with a collapsible pole, hooks, lines, lures, and a sharp fillet knife. Last but not least, under the kit was a rifle next to a box of ammo.

"It's a .22," Jason said, picking up the gun reverently. "So, mostly for hunting small game, but it's better than nothing. And everything's in decent shape. This is probably someone's bug-out box."

"Bug-out box?" I asked, raising an eyebrow.

"You know, for a natural disaster, or the zombie apocalypse, or whatever. You have a place like this cabin and this box. If you can hunt and fish, it's all you really need to survive."

"Unless someone takes it," I pointed out, popping another handful of fruit into my mouth.

"Survival of the fittest." Jason shrugged, setting the gun down on the bed. "We should put on some of these dry clothes and get the hell out of here."

"Where are we going?"

"I don't know. Back to Indy, I guess. We'd have some protection from CAMFers there."

My heart soared at the thought of making it to Indy and maybe seeing Samantha, of knowing she was okay. Olivia and Marcus had said Samantha had made it off the cliff to safety, but how could they have been sure in all the chaos? Still, I comforted myself with the fact that I hadn't seen her, or Renzo, or any of those closest to her around the pool. They must have gotten away.

I had to see Samantha again. Our last moments together hadn't been great. We'd fought about the Eidolon. She had completely dismissed my fears, and I'd called her crazy. That's when the truth had come crashing down on me; we barely knew each other. Had I crushed on her so hard simply because she was the first girl who'd ever shown any interest in me? Even now, just thinking about her, the way she tilted her head when she was listening, the curve of her ass in her jeans, it made my face flush and my body feel heavy, something I had never felt for any guy. *Ever.* Like I was a magnet that had finally found true north after seventeen years of facing the wrong direction.

Jason was right. There was protection in Indy as well. Mr. James, Samantha's father, had promised us all safe haven and a future if we joined The Hold. He would take us in.

But Indy, and Samantha, and her father were a long way off. "Indy is fifty miles away," I pointed out the obvious. "How are we going to get there?"

"We follow the river downstream and look for a bridge or road to lead us to civilization. Then we either walk or hitchhike. Walking would be safer. Less chance we'll be spotted."

"Walk fifty miles? How long will that take?"

"That depends on how fast we walk," Jason said, handing me a pair of men's long johns and one of the camo jackets.

We each went to our own corner of the cabin and turned our backs on one another to change into the dry clothes. I hesitated for a moment, feeling the twinge of fear that always came when I knew my arms and scars would be exposed. But it was only a moment. I yanked my damp shirt off over my head, leaving my bra on, which had mostly dried from the heat of my body. In the dim light of the cabin, my arms looked even paler than usual. I always covered them, always hid the evidence away, not just from other people, but also from myself. Olivia had asked me why I cut. So had her mother. I'd given them each a different answer. I had as many answers as I had scars, and as many questions. Was I really done cutting, now that I'd solved the mystery of my weird PSS blood? Had Olivia truly cured me by taking away the blades, or was this just another long reprieve like I'd experienced in the past? Looking at the marks on my arms both shamed and warmed me. But it didn't warm me enough to stop the goose bumps from breaking out all over my skin from the cold cabin air.

I shrugged the oversized camo jacket on and buttoned it up. It hung down to my knees nicely so I wasn't exposed when I took off my pants, which ended up being a lot harder than I'd anticipated. Removing wet jeans requires a level of escapism I'm not sure Houdini could manage. Putting them back on over a pair of dry, oversized long johns is a level up from that. I had to hop and pull and yank with all my might. Even then, everything bunched in all the wrong places, making me feel like a cross between Kim Kardashian and the Stay Puft Marshmallow Man. Still, it was a relief to get the cold jeans off my skin. When I was finally all zipped up and had managed to wrestle the button into the button hole, I turned to find Jason watching me, fully dressed, the .22 slung over his shoulder and the ax tucked into his knife belt.

"What?" I asked.

"Nice pants dance," he said, handing me one of the empty water bottles. "We'll head to the river first to fill these. We can put the water tablets in them, and they should be good to drink in twenty minutes. Put this in your jacket," he instructed, handing me some of the food, the fishing kit, half the water tabs, and some of the matches. "You'll need it if we get separated."

Separated? That one word terrified me. What would I do out here alone? Probably die, and what I could fit in my pockets wasn't going to make a difference, but I tucked the stuff away anyway, humoring him.

Then Jason handed me the fillet knife wrapped in a small piece of cloth he'd cut from the mattress. "And keep this handy, just in case."

"Just in case what? I'm attacked by a fish?"

"In case you need to gut something," he said grimly, turning toward the door. "I'll scout ahead. Always stay at least ten feet behind, but keep me in your line of sight. Don't move until I wave you forward. And if we see anyone, do not engage. Stay hidden and let me handle it."

"Okay." I slipped the knife in my most accessible pocket as he opened the door.

3

PASSION

An hour later, the cabin was nothing but a distant memory in the forest behind us, and I found myself crouched in the mud behind a bush, waiting for Jason to call me forward another ten feet. In front of me, I could hear the river rushing and roaring, so much louder than it had been last night. We were almost there, but I felt like I might die of thirst before we reached it. The sound of the water was maddening, and it taunted me with a freshness I could practically taste in the air. If we were going to make it back to Indy alive, we needed water.

Still, I was torn. Jason had already warned me we'd be exposed and visible on the banks and the flood levels would be dangerous after the storm.

"And there might be bodies," he'd added. "Everything got pushed downriver last night." I didn't want to see those bodies again. For some people, water was a soothing thing, but in my life it had always carried death. A river had killed my sister, Purity. And now this one had taken my friends. I really didn't want to go back to the river, unless I was going back to save Olivia and Marcus.

Jason had made his case. It was unwise, and stupid, and it might get us caught. My head knew he was right, but my gut said otherwise. We hadn't seen any sign of CAMFers since we'd left the cabin. No helicopters. No voices or sounds of pursuit echoing down the valley. I could still feel Olivia's presence, vague and tenuous. I couldn't tell if she was near or far, just that she was alive. But even if the CAMFers had taken her, Marcus was still back there in the pool. Olivia would never give him up, which meant Jason and I were the only ones left who knew where he was. I knew the exact spot. I'd watched him sink away from us as Olivia had struggled against me.

But he wasn't dead. That was the part of Jason's argument I knew was wrong. I'd seen Marcus come back from the dead with my own eyes. It had been like a miracle out of the Bible, except better. Not that I thought Marcus was a prophet or Messiah or anything. He was way too flawed and paranoid. But I did believe he was a sign. A sign that had led me to Samantha, and The Hold, and the new truth I'd only just begun to understand. Marcus was crucial to the cause. Samantha had explained that much to me. Each one of us with PSS was important, but Marcus was essential.

And time was ticking away. I could feel it. Even a miracle like Marcus's couldn't override the forces of nature forever. Jesus had risen after three days, before decay had set in, but he'd been prepped and wrapped and sealed in a tomb. Underwater, Marcus probably had considerably less time than that.

I looked away from Jason, back the way we'd come, an urgency pulling at me. Something was wrong.

Suddenly, Olivia's presence crashed over me stronger than I'd ever felt it before. She was alive and conscious. She was terrified and pissed off. I got a flash of the inside of a car and men—men she loathed with every fiber of her being. The connection had never been this sharp before, this clear. Not even when she'd been in the same room with me. It wasn't strong because she was close. In fact, I could feel her moving swiftly away from me, somewhere off to the west. No, it wasn't her proximity I was feeling. It was her terror.

Oh God, don't let them kill her.

I turned around, pulling myself away from Olivia and back toward Jason. *I can't help her. I can feel her, but I can't help her.*

Jason was waving me forward, and based on his scowling face and the impatient vigor of his gestures, he'd been doing it for a while.

I stood up, moving toward him, one careful step, and then another.

I was halfway to him when pain slammed into my ribs, knocking me to the ground. I writhed in the mud, feeling it squish into my hair and onto my face, soaking cloyingly into my clothes. *Am I hit? I didn't even hear a gunshot.*

"What happened? Did you twist your ankle?" Jason was bent over me, his hand running over my lower legs, feeling for swelling or breaks.

The pain was fading.

Olivia's pain, not mine.

I looked up into Jason's confused face. "No—I—I just tripped." I'm not sure why I lied. Probably just out of habit. I was used to hiding my pain from the world, *my craziness,* as I'd heard my parents refer to it in hushed whispers when they'd thought I was out of earshot. It seemed even crazier to be feeling someone else's pain. But at least there was pain. That meant Olivia wasn't dead. I could still feel her, could still feel the dull ache in my side. "Help me up," I said to Jason.

He held out a hand, pulling me to my feet, and I walked alongside him to where he'd been crouched before. I could finally see the river in front of us, foaming right up against the pale boulders that had once been high on its banks. Downriver was a wall of thick, tangled, thorny brush, virtually impenetrable, beyond which the river curved sharply to left. That was the way we were headed, but it didn't even look passable.

"We're going to have to break cover," Jason said, talking loudly so I could hear him over the roar of the water. "I'll go first, this side of those boulders and then around the bend. As soon as I scout out a clear path and a safe place to get water, I'll come back for you. But you won't be able to see me, and it may take some time. Just be patient and stay hidden."

"Okay," I said.

"Once we're past this, we should be able to move faster," he said, crawled away from me and scrambling through the brush out onto the open rocks. Then, he stood and moved cautiously around the bend, his gun in hand, never giving me a backward glance.

It took a moment for it to sink in; I was utterly alone in the wilderness. And now there was nothing to distract me from the vastness of it except Olivia's panic rising in me like a feral animal determined to scratch its way out. *It's okay. I'm here. You're not alone.* I'm not sure if I was telling her or myself.

They're taking me away. Too far away. That was her. In my head, almost as clear as if she were sitting next to me. She was terrified. An image flashed through my mind—her hurling herself out of a moving car.

"No," I cried. Could she hear me the way I'd just heard her?

Something stung me in the arm, hard, straight through the camo jacket and my shirt, but when I looked down there was nothing there.

And then Olivia faded away to nothingness. I couldn't feel her anymore. At all.

"No, no, no," I moaned. What had just happened? She hadn't jumped out of the car. I definitely would have felt that. Maybe they'd taken the tags off of her. That had to be it. They'd drugged her and taken them off. *She's alive. She has to be alive.* But I wasn't sure. I wasn't sure about anything anymore.

I glanced around, the stillness of the wilderness expanding away from me in all directions. What if Jason didn't come back? What if he'd left me here for the CAMFers to find so I wouldn't slow him down?

Dr. Black had once said something about me having abandonment issues. *"Your sister abandoned you when she died. Your parents abandoned you emotionally out of grief. You even abandon yourself when you cut. No one in your life has been there for you the way they should have been."*

"That's life," I'd shrugged it off. "You can't control other people."

"No, you can't," she'd replied. "But you can be there for yourself. And you can seek out more reliable relationships. They do exist, you know."

And that's exactly what I'd been trying to do, until the CAMFers had shot it all to hell.

Jason would come back. He had to. He was all I had left. I just needed to focus and stop freaking out.

I waited, ten or fifteen minutes maybe, my thirst growing. Not even the faint smell of rotting fish on the breeze coming from the river deterred it. I would drink fishy water. I would drink any water. Jason would be back any minute. *God, please let him come back.*

Something rustled in the brush above my head. It was a red-winged black bird perched on a branch, peering down at me with beady eyes as if to say, *"What are you doing here, human? This is not your place."*

A gunshot pierced the air, and I jumped up, my hand feeling for the fillet knife, the black bird fluttering into the sky.

The sound reverberated, echoing up and down the river canyon. I couldn't even tell which way it had come from. Had it been Jason's .22 or a CAMFer's gun?

I waited, my body braced for more shots, but none came. What did that mean? Could the CAMFers take Jason down with one shot? Surely he'd have gotten one off too? What if they'd shot him? What if I was truly on my own now? I took a deep breath, ready to call out for him. Screw the CAMFers. Screw everyone. Anything would be better than dying in the woods alone.

And then I heard voices, male voices, coming closer, and I ducked down into my little brush hole just before a troop of armed men came around the bend from the direction Jason had gone. There were eight of them, four clumped close together in the middle. When they got to the boulders, they spread out a little, and I could see what they were guarding so carefully.

It was Jason.

The group stopped, and one of them shoved him face-first against a large, flat rock while another handcuffed his wrists behind him. I didn't see Jason's gun, but obviously, he didn't have it anymore. They made him stand and searched him, taking away everything we'd found at the cabin except the clothes on his back. When they were frisking his pant legs, there was a discussion between the two who had bound him and another one, maybe the leader, but I couldn't hear it because the wind had shifted toward the river.

One of the men crouched down in front of Jason and grabbed the bottom of his right pant leg.

Jason kicked, clipping the crouching man in the chin with his boot, sending him sprawling backward onto the rocks.

Immediately, four of them were on Jason, pinning him down spread-eagle, yelling at him with their black guns drawn.

I clutched the fillet knife, the handle digging painfully into my palm. What was he thinking? They were going to kill him for sure now.

The guy who was down staggered to his feet, shaking his head and clutching his jaw. The leader put a hand on his shoulder, asking him something, and when he nodded, they both moved toward Jason, blocking my view of him altogether.

What were they doing? I had to stop them. If I gave myself up, if I stepped out of the woods, it might defuse the situation.

I stood up and took a tentative step forward.

From that angle, I could see Jason's face, his eyes instantly connecting with mine. He was the only one facing me. All the men were focused on him.

"No," he shouted, as the leader grabbed at his ankle and yanked up the cuff of his pants, revealing the glowing blue pulse of his PSS leg. I'd never seen it before, even in all the weeks we'd camped together on the way to Indy. Jason hid his leg the way I hid my scars, and for much the same reason.

His eye bored into mine over the shoulder of the men holding him. His "no" hadn't been for them. It had been for me. I nodded at him and stepped back into hiding, my body sinking soundlessly down the same way my heart was sinking in my chest.

What would they do now? Kill him or extract him? And what could I do but watch? If I gave myself up, they'd simply do the same to me.

Jason struggled and bucked against the men who held him. The leader began to question him, some of it drifting to me on the wind. *Who are you?*

What are you doing here? Have you seen anyone else?
But Jason wasn't answering. Eventually he stopped
struggling, but his lips remained a firm, closed line,
his eyes defiant and filled with determined malice.

They finally gave up the interrogation and the
leader gestured to his men, indicating they should
bring Jason along.

Two of them grabbed Jason by the arms and
dragged him off the rock. Then all of them proceeded
to head upriver back toward the pool, disappearing
into the woods almost before I realized what was
happening.

When their voices had faded, I crawled out of my
hiding place and followed them. They left a fairly
clear trail, a swathe of broken brush and their boot
prints heavy in the soft mud. They didn't have to
travel slowly and stealthily the way Jason and I had
been forced to. They had nothing to fear. No reason
to hide.

After about fifteen minutes, they curved back
toward the river and I was so thankful. I needed to
drink. Badly. When the woods opened up to a small
riverside clearing and a flooded sandbar, I could
barely wait for them to move on before I rushed to
the banks. In the water ten feet from where I filled
my bottle was a black robe, soaked and caught upon
a large rock. I turned away from it and plopped the
purification tab into my soon-to-be drink. Jason had
said to wait twenty minutes, so I would. But I was
pretty sure it would be the longest twenty minutes
I'd ever lived. At least I had the tracking to occupy
my mind.

The CAMFers were staying close to the banks now, taking advantage of the easier terrain, which meant I had to be extra careful to keep cover between me and them. They were moving quickly and I was struggling to keep up.

It seemed encouraging, though, that Jason was still alive, especially after he'd struggled and flipped out about his leg. Considering everyone they'd killed last night, I had no idea why he was still alive. But I was thankful. My guess was they were taking him back to the cliffs, back to the scene of the Eidolon, and I had no idea what they'd do to him when they got there. Not anything good. I knew that much.

They were leading me close to the river, the bank a rocky shelf growing narrower and narrower. The proximity of the raging water was terrifying and I was running out of places to hide. My shoes splashed in a puddle, water caught in the indent of the shelf, and my toes collided with something hard, sending it skidding across the rock.

I ducked down, afraid the noise might have drawn attention, but when I looked up Jason and his captors were nowhere in sight. Ahead, the rocky shelf ended in a sudden drop-off. *They must have cut off into the woods. Either that or they'd heard me stumble and were waiting to ambush me.*

I stood, cautiously, and crept forward, crouching next to the thing I'd kicked. It was nestled in a rounded indentation of the stone shelf, like an egg in a puddled nest. But it wasn't an egg.

It was a ball.

A black gleaming magic eight ball, to be exact.

I reached out and picked it up, turning it in my hands. It felt unusually warm, but maybe it had been sitting in the sun before I'd sent it flying. What in the world was a magic eight ball doing out here in the middle of nowhere? Had it been in someone's pocket last night? Had some poor, scared kid brought it to the Eidolon like a lucky rabbit's foot? *Not so lucky then.*

I put it back down in its rocky nest.

I'd owned a magic eight ball when I was eleven. Well, technically it had been Purity's, but we'd played with it a lot together, asking it questions about all the boys she had crushes on, all the girls who were mean to us. It had been our little secret, because my parents were adamantly against anything with "the appearance of evil" and a ball of divination definitely fit that category. Never mind that it was a dumb toy two girls had giggled and bonded over. At least until my father had found it under her pillow and taken it away.

This one had meant something to someone, too. Plus, it looked so forlorn.

I picked it back up.

"Where did you come from?" I asked, turning it over and watching the blue answer triangle slowly emerge from murky darkness to bump up against the glass.

Better not tell you now.

Oh, yes. How could I forget? The thing had twenty vaguely useless answers and none of them were going to help me get Jason back.

I stuffed it in my oversized jacket pocket anyway and resumed following the obvious trail the CAMFers had left me.

4

PASSION

I was back in the woods now, following a path of beaten down brush and broken branches. The CAMFers certainly weren't trying to hide anything. I could barely hear the river now, but I knew it was on my right, and I was trekking parallel to it and upstream, back toward the scene of the Eidolon. The terrain surrounding me seemed vaguely familiar. Were we back as far as the cabin already? Maybe. Based on the slant of the sunlight through the trees, I was guessing it was early afternoon. At this rate, we'd be back at the pool in half the time it had taken Jason and me last night.

I stopped for a minute and pulled out my water bottle. The purification tablet had dissolved.

Had it been twenty minutes yet? *Close enough.* I gulped down half the contents, hoping it was supposed to taste gritty and stale, and resumed my trek. Shortly after that, the signs of the CAMFers passage seemed to disappear, and I had to backtrack a little and try several rabbit trails before I found it again, the boot prints faint but there.

I stood for a moment, contemplating how this was all going to end when I arrived wherever they were leading me. I didn't have a plan. I had been moving on blind faith and pure desperation. Still, despite everything, I felt calmer and less afraid than when Jason and I had been running away. That didn't make sense, but there it was.

After maybe another half an hour, I stopped to pee, and I took the time to eat and drink, depleting the last of my stores. With the empty water bottle and the purification tablets, I could source more water from the river if I had to. And presumably, with some skill and the fishing kit, I could catch food, and fillet and cook it with my handy knife and matches. Unfortunately, I had no such skill. There was simply no way I was going to make it in the wilderness on my own, or make it back to Indy by myself.

So, I got up and headed down the CAMFer-blazed trail once more, listening carefully for man-made noises in the distance ahead, scanning the terrain for the cliffs I knew would soon rise up on my right. Surely, I was close to the pool and Devil's Drop by now.

Then the trees suddenly broke open in front of me and I was there.

To my right was the river, gushing over rocks and

into a pool I barely recognized. It looked different. Really different. Gone was the tranquil blue water of last night. The huge logjam that had made up the upper rim of the pool was gone as well. No, not gone. The logs had just moved. They'd been pushed right over the top of the rocks and were now jammed at the bottom end of the pool, making it deeper and wider.

The rocks we'd left Olivia on weren't even visible. They were under the new water line.

And what about Marcus? Could he have survived all that turmoil?

God, let him still be alive. Please.

I glanced around, but I didn't see any CAMFers. Or Jason. Didn't hear any signs of anyone or even a hint of the terrible deeds wrought there the night before. The water and the clearing around it looked completely untouched and serene. It was surreal, like the horrors I'd so recently experienced had only been a dream, a figment of my imagination. And where were Jason and the men I had been following? I was standing right on their trail. I could see their footprints mixed with mine. They had definitely come this way, but maybe they'd kept going. But to where?

I raised my eyes, tipping my head back so I could see the top of the cliffs.

The pool might have transformed overnight, but Devil's Drop rose, mighty and unchanging. Up there, the CAMFers had come and mowed us down with their gunfire. We'd had no option but to jump. No choice but the questionable kindness of gravity and water. I could hardly believe I'd plunged from that height, pinned in Jason's arms and the grip of my own panic. But we hadn't fallen because Jason's leg had manifested its power. I wasn't even sure exactly how we'd gotten down—I think I'd blacked out—but I suspected Marcus and Olivia had pulled us. Whatever had happened, we'd all landed in the pool together—I knew that much—the cold smack of the water bringing me back to myself just in time to stop Olivia from following Marcus down into its murky depths.

Jason had a power, and we hadn't talked about it. Honestly, I hadn't even thought about it since then. I guess we'd just been too busy trying to survive. But if Jason had a power from jumping off the cliff, did I?

I pulled up the right sleeve of my jacket, my strange purple veins standing out against my pale skin and the crisscross of pink scars. Was my blood different now? Did it have some miraculous quality it hadn't possessed last night? Samantha had claimed the Eidolon would give us power. Power like she and Marcus and Olivia had.

"You there," a voice called from behind me, slamming be back to the present. "Turn around slowly with your hands up."

I lifted my arms, making sure my empty hands could be seen from behind me as I turned slowly to face the eight men I'd been following for hours.

Jason's grim, disappointed face peered out at me from their midst.

Somehow, I'd gotten ahead of them. That possibility had never entered my mind. It must have been when I'd lost the trail. Maybe they'd veered off somewhere and I'd barreled right past them. But then how could their boot prints be under my feet? Unless they were someone else's.

"Who are you?" the leader asked, coming forward with his gun lowered. "Were you up there?" he lifted his gun a little higher, pointing at the cliffs.

I whirled away, ready to run, but he grabbed my arm.

"Hey, it's okay. We're not going to hurt you."

I turned, looking up into his eyes, expecting to see the lie.

"We're from The Hold," he said. "What's your name?"

I glanced at Jason, confusion warring with disbelief. If these guys were from The Hold, then we were saved. Unless telling me that was just a trap, a ploy to get my guard down.

Jason's eyes drilled into mine, warning, cautioning me, but he also gave the slightest nod of his head.

The man holding my arm didn't miss the exchange. "Do you two know each other?" he asked, looking from me to Jason and back again, his grip on my arm tightening. "What's your name?"

"Passion," I croaked, tears stinging in my throat and behind my nose. "Passion Wainwright."

"Come with me." It wasn't a request. It was a command. "Mr. James will want to talk to you immediately. Both of you," he said, pulling me by the arm into the clearing.

"Mr. James is here?" I asked, relief and skepticism battling it out as I tried to catch up with this amazing turn of luck. "You guys aren't CAMFers?" What was wrong with me? My legs didn't seem to be working.

I stumbled, almost falling to my knees, and I would have if someone hadn't been holding me up. The woods were spinning, dancing around me and coalescing into a black tunnel.

"Are you all right?" the guy's voice called, but I was already gone, falling into cool peaceful darkness.

I came to slowly, black matte not-sky above me, smooth leather beneath my hands. I wasn't outside anymore. I was inside, but not in a building.

"She's coming around," Mr. James's familiar voice said. "Give her some water."

"Here, take a sip." The head of an older blond man who was not Mr. James swam over me and I felt his arm slip behind my shoulders, helping me to a sitting position. "You're a little dehydrated."

I lifted a shaking hand to the glass he was holding to my lips, and our fingers touched. When I'd drained the whole thing and propped myself up against the seat, he moved away and sat back staring at me. Mr. James was staring at me, too. But the two of them were intently NOT making eye contact with each other, waves of tension roiling between the two of them. These two men did not like one another. In fact, I'd have wagered a guess they hated each other. So, why were all three of us in the back of a stretch limo together?

I was sprawled across the longest bench seat with the blonde guy on the bench across from me. Mr. James was on the shorter seat on the end, hunkered over the drink in his hand. He looked haggard and haunted as his eyes settled on me.

"Passion, this is John Holbrook," Mr. James introduced the other man, his voice grinding on the name as if he'd like to reduce it and the man it represented to a fine powder. "His son Luke was up on those cliffs with you last night. Mr. Holbrook and I are going to ask you some questions about what happened, and it's crucial you answer us thoroughly and honestly."

"Where's Jason?" I asked, peering out the limo windows and instantly recognizing the parking lot of Shades State Park. It didn't look much different than it had last night, most of the cars parked right where their owners had left them. Of course they were. No one had come back to drive them home. There were some extra vehicles now too, several military looking trucks and a couple black-windowed SUVs. The spot where Renzo's Mercedes had been was empty, but I could see a team of black-clad soldiers going over the Porsche that Yale, Jason, Marcus and Olivia had arrived in. The doors, trunk, and hood were all open and they were taking out the seats.

"What are they doing?" I asked, turning back to Mr. James. "Where's Jason?" Some unknown fear rose in my heart.

"He's safe," Mr. Holbrook assured me. "I promise you. No harm will come to either of you. But there are kids missing, a lot of them, and that boy refuses to say anything."

"Can you tell us what happened?" Mr. James asked, leaning back, his eyes scanning mine. Something about his bleak calmness compared to Mr. Holbrook's barely-masked desperation terrified me.

"Is Samantha—did she—" I couldn't even ask it.

"My daughter is in critical condition after suffering a gunshot wound to the head," Mr. James said.

"What?" I blurted. No. That couldn't be. Olivia and Marcus had said Samantha had gotten away safely. Maybe she'd been shot after they'd seen her? Oh, God, at least she was alive. Critical condition was bad, but it was still alive. "What about the others? Renzo and Juliana? Eva and Lily and Dimitri? Are they okay?"

"Renzo and Juliana are safe," Mr. James said. "They were the ones who got Samantha to Indy. With her injury so severe, the fact that they didn't linger here probably saved her life. But, for that reason, they couldn't tell us much of what happened. I'm afraid everyone else is still unaccounted for."

"Did you see my son Luke?" Mr. Holbrook asked, lunging toward me. "Did you see what happened to him?"

"John, take it easy," Mr. James said, putting his hand on Mr. Holbrook's shoulder.

"If you were in my position, would you *take it easy?*" Mr. Holbrook snarled, shaking off Mr. James's hand and turning on him. "We've lost our children thanks to you and your carelessness, and here you are protecting a boy and girl who very well could have had something to do with it. Aren't they a part of that feral group Renzo said showed up last week? Who's to say they didn't tip off the CAMFers—"

"That's enough," Mr. James growled, grabbing the other man's shoulder again, and this time I could see his fingers squeeze, digging in, as the two of them faced off.

The back of the limo was suddenly a tiny, cramped vessel of raging testosterone.

"We all want to find them," Mr. James said. "And I will. I promise."

"No, you won't," Mr. Holbrook said, like it was a threat, removing himself from under Mr. James's hand once again. "You had your chance, Alex, and you threw it away. You've thrown away your chance at a lot of things."

Mr. James went perfectly still. He looked at Holbrook, his eyes cold and hard, glinting like shards of broken glass. I had never seen a look like that before, so full of pure malice, like a dangerous predator backed into a corner who has nothing left to lose.

He's going to kill him. He's going to club him to death with his drink glass and I'm going to have to sit here and watch.

But Holbrook glanced away, back at me, pretending he hadn't glimpsed his own murder in Mr. James's eyes. "Did you see my son?" he asked me again. "Do you have any idea where he is?"

"I'm sorry." I shook my head. "I have no idea. There were so many people and I didn't know most of them."

I tried to feel sorry for the guy. I really did. I mean, I could understand his distress, but calling my friends and me feral, like we were stray cats, and blaming us and Mr. James for what the CAMFers had done seemed a little extreme. It didn't make me want to kill the guy, but it didn't exactly warm my heart toward him either.

"You didn't find him up there?" I glanced out the window toward the cliff. "So, that's good, right? That means he might still be alive."

They both stared at me like I'd said something odd. "The only thing we found up there was a little blood and a few bullets," Mr. James said softly. "The area has obviously been intentionally swept clean of evidence."

"Which is exactly why we need some answers," Holbrook insisted.

I looked from one man to the other, a horrible realization dawning over me. *They had no idea.* They hadn't seen the bodies and pools of blood. The CAMFers had spent all night sweeping the area clean with their helicopter and troops. Mr. Holbrook thought he wanted me to tell him what happened, but he really didn't. He didn't want to know his son was probably dead, mowed down by random bullets. And I certainly didn't want to be the one to tell him, given how mad he was just thinking Luke had been taken. How could they not know? Samantha had been shot in the head. *What did they think had gone on after that? Hopscotch and tiddlywinks?*

"Passion, I know this is difficult," Mr. James said gently.

"I think it's obvious by now the two of them were in on it," Holbrook interjected. "We caught them on the run and the boy has been more than uncooperative. Now she won't even—"

"They shot my friends in the back," I said, staring at the man, my rage overwhelming any sympathy I'd ever felt for him. "They came up the stairs and ambushed us. They threw tear gas and shot into the crowd. Some people jumped off the cliff. Many of them drowned, floating in the water with their robes and blood spreading out around them." My voice broke and I felt the tears welling up in my throat. "Your son Luke might have been one of them." I stared into Holbrook's pale face. "Or maybe they took him. But mostly, they killed people."

There was a moment of silence while they both stared at me in horror. Then Holbrook put his head in his hands, moaning, "God, no."

"John, I'm sorry," Mr. James said.

"Sorry?" John Holbrook choked on the word. "You're sorry my son is probably dead? Fuck you, Alex. You let this happen. You allowed your spoiled daughter to play at this Eidolon thing and now everyone is paying for it except you and her. But you will pay. I guarantee it. You're no longer fit to lead The Hold. Everyone knows it's what the new council will decide. I will make sure of that." He pushed past Mr. James to the limo door and shoved it open. When he was clear of it, he slammed it shut so hard the entire vehicle rocked back and forth.

I watched out the window as he stormed up to one of the groups of soldiers and started barking orders. Then John Holbrook pulled a cell phone out of his pocket and made a call.

"I knew that wasn't going to go well," Mr. James said, drawing my eyes back to him. "I didn't want him to sit in on this interview for that exact reason, but he insisted. Now, unfortunately, you and I have very little time. Passion, did you see who shot Samantha?"

"I—no—I wasn't anywhere near her when it happened," I said, more confused than ever. Was Mr. James even the leader of The Hold anymore? Because it sure didn't sound like it. Samantha had never mentioned The Hold having a council. And if Mr. James wasn't in charge, where did that leave Jason and me? Holbrook had practically accused us of inviting the CAMFers to the Eidolon. "Jason and I decided not to jump," I went on. "I didn't want to watch and he wanted to guard the stairs. So, we hung back in some bushes."

"Guard the stairs against what?" Mr. James asked.

"Against CAMFers," I said, surprised it wasn't obvious. "Jason had been feeling paranoid all night. Well, really, he feels paranoid all the time, but he's also frequently right. Then, he thought he heard someone on the stairs. He told me to stay down and he went to check it out. I couldn't see much from where I was hiding, not the stairs or the people jumping. And then there was a gunshot. And screaming. And smoke." I heard and saw and felt it all again, as if it were a high definition video and me the narrator. "Before I knew what was happening, they were everywhere. They were shooting into the crowd. Jason came running back and grabbed me. I don't know how we made it past them, but we did, and we found Marcus and Olivia." I looked down at my hands and was surprised to see them trembling.

"You found them alive?" Mr. James asked, a hopeful catch in his voice.

"Yeah. But Olivia had injured her knee, so Marcus was carrying her. Then Marcus said the only way to escape the CAMFers was to jump. And I didn't want to, but Jason grabbed me and we ran toward the cliff." I didn't have the words to tell him about Nose and Yale. My mind veered away from it. "The CAMFers were getting closer, but we made it to the cliff, and Jason and I jumped first." My mouth and lips had gone dry. I could barely squeeze the words from them.

"Here." Mr. James handed me his drink.

I downed it in one shot, the auburn liquid setting fire to my insides. I had no idea what it was, but it helped.

"You're doing great," he said, taking the glass back. "Please, go on."

"Olivia and Marcus jumped right after us," I said, skipping the part about Jason's power. That was for him to tell, if he ever wanted to. "But when they hit the pool, Marcus sank. Olivia tried to dive after him, but he was too heavy and her knee was messed up. She was going to go down with him, if I didn't stop her." I had kept Olivia from rescuing Marcus, David Marcus Jordon, who also happened to be Mr. James's long-lost nephew. He probably wasn't going to thank me for that, even if it had saved Olivia's life.

"So you stopped her," Mr. James said, his eyes coming back to me, cold and calculating.

"Yes," I said. "I had to. She would have drowned going after him. I grabbed her and got her to the edge of the pool."

"Then where is she?" he asked, confusion in his voice. "Why wasn't she with you and Jason?"

"She couldn't walk. Not with her knee the way it was." The horrifying guilt of leaving her pounded into me all over again. "I didn't want to leave her," I said, feeling a tear leak from my right eye and run down my cheek. "She told us to. The CAMFers were descending on the pool. Jason said we had to go. They would have taken us too if we hadn't."

"Did you see them take her?" he asked, his voice like ice.

"No," I said, a whisper.

"And what about Marcus? Did you see them take him?"

"No."

"But you know where he sank? You remember where it was?"

"Yes."

"Show me," he said, pushing the limo door open and gesturing for me to go first.

I climbed out and he climbed out after me.

"Where the hell do you think you're going?" Holbrook charged up to us like an angry bull.

"My nephew's body is at the bottom of that pool," Mr. James said, staring him down. "And I intend to retrieve it. Do you have a problem with that?"

"The council has instructed me to keep you under my surveillance," Holbrook answered. He wasn't backing down, but there was an uncertainty in his voice.

"Watch me all you want," Mr. James said. "Just get the damn divers in there. Now."

"Okay," John nodded. "Get the divers prepped," he called over his shoulder to one of the men behind him. "But the girl comes with me," he said, his eyes boring into me. "I have more questions for her."

"I need her," Mr. James said. "She knows where the body is."

Great. They were fighting over me.

"My daughter was shot," Mr. James said. "My nephew is dead. You aren't the only one who has lost something here, John. At least let me recover my dead before you throw me under the bus. You owe me that."

They stood there glaring at each other, two desperate men vying for control.

"All right." Holbrook conceded. "You can keep the girl. I've been called back to Indy to report face-to-face. But remember," he said, staring hard at Mr. James, "these men are under council orders to bring you and all the evidence back to the city tonight. This isn't your show anymore, Alex. Don't make the mistake of thinking it is."

"No, of course not," Mr. James said, and as Holbrook turned away he murmured under his breath, "It's your show now, John. All yours."

5

PASSION

There were three divers, two men and one woman. They looked strange all decked out in their black and neon green scuba gear so far from the ocean, and they were serious and quiet, like aliens eager to return to their home world. I showed them where I'd last seen Marcus, hoping with all my heart I'd gauged it right given the changes to the water level.

"Sir," one of the male divers said, turning to Mr. James, "you need to understand that with all this rain and flooding, the likelihood that anything is where it was last night is slim. And we are going to have zero visibility down there."

"Just do your job," Mr. James said.

The diver nodded and returned to his team, some who were setting up lights around the pool because the sun was beginning to set behind Devil's Drop.

It surprised me that the Hold had brought divers to Shades. Maybe Renzo and Juliana had told them about the terrain and the cliff and the river, so they'd come prepared just in case. But was Mr. James prepared to see his long-lost nephew dead? Did he know Marcus could reboot? The way he'd talked to Holbrook about his dead nephew, it sure didn't sound like it.

Three large splashes, one right after the other, brought me back to my surroundings as the divers plunged into the pool, disappearing in a profusion of bubbles, a rope trailing behind each one of them, held by a tender on shore. I stood on a rocky ledge overlooking the pool with Mr. James. The night air grew chilly, but moisture beaded on my face and forehead. This is how I'd imagined it in my mind for years. The edge of a river. My parents standing together, side by side, stoic in their silent prayer as the police divers searched for my sister's body. The broken red rental canoe, like the twisted smile of a giant Cheshire cat, propped up against a tree behind them. Of course, those were only my childhood imaginings. I had been left at home for three days, tended to by an aunt I barely knew, and swallowed by a grief I could not comprehend. Had it been my fault the canoe had tipped? Why had it been me safely trapped in an air pocket under it while my sister was swept downstream? What had my father thought when he'd wrenched the canoe upward with all his strength, practically snapping it in two against the jutting log pinning it down, only to discover one daughter, not two. Had he been disappointed it was me there, and not her?

I would never know the answers to these questions, never have them resolved, even in heaven. Because I would never have the guts to ask them.

We hadn't even had a body to bury and mourn over. When my parents had finally come home they'd simply said, "They didn't find her. But she is gone."

Would Marcus be gone too?

An uncontrollable shiver swept over me, and I jammed my hands in my pockets, trying to get warm, remembering the fillet knife almost at the last second. I shouldn't have worried. The knife was gone. So was the fishing kit with its water tabs and matches. The only thing left was the magic eight ball, nestled in the rag the knife had once been wrapped in, round and solid to my touch.

Of course. They'd searched me while I'd been passed out.

I gave a side-long glance at Mr. James. Had it been his hands that had patted me down while I lay unconscious in his limo, or had John Holbrook done it? Did they think it had been a gesture of goodwill to leave me the toy? I'd thought I'd be safe with The Hold, that Mr. James was on my side, but now I wasn't sure.

"Where is Jason?" I asked, trying to sound casual.

Mr. James looked away from the pool, staring at me. "Holbrook took him back to Indy for questioning," he said. "He suspects Jason disclosed the Eidolon's location to the CAMFers."

"But that's ridiculous. Jason hates the CAMFers. He would never do that. Besides, I thought you were the leader of The Hold, not Holbrook."

"Officially, I am. At least for a few more hours," he said, glancing down at his watch. "But I'm afraid I have little real power left."

I wanted to ask him more, but suddenly bubbles roiled in the pool, and an orange buoy popped to the surface like an oversized fishing bobber.

Did that mean they'd found Marcus?

"They're marking off where they've already searched," Mr. James explained.

A few minutes later, another buoy popped up.

Then the female diver surfaced, accompanied by yet another buoy, but this one had a white mesh bag attached to it with something blue inside of it. A blue tennis shoe. Not Marcus's. I didn't recognize it.

"They're wasting time," I turned to Mr. James. "If he's down there—"

"They'll find him," he cut me off, taking a step closer, his eyes scanning to make sure no one was within earshot. "There's no rush to find a corpse, you understand?" He turned his piercing gaze on me, but I could read the tension in his body. He wanted them to hurry as much as I did. He knew; he knew Marcus could reboot and it was crucial we find him as soon as possible. He just didn't want anyone else around the pool to know.

"I understand," I said. I could keep a secret. But it wouldn't be a secret for long if they pulled Marcus up and he rebooted in front of everyone. Hopefully, Mr. James had a plan to prevent that.

Inside my pocket, I gripped the eight ball, feeling its solid roundness, tracing the circular ridge of the answer window with my fingertips. And I prayed. *Please, just let them find him. Let him be alive and able to reboot. And please don't let him kill me when he finds out I let the CAMFers take Olivia.*

In a flurry of bubbles, all three of the divers came up. They were asking for something, gesturing to the men on shore. In response, one of them picked up a long, rectangular bag made of black mesh with a zippered opening on one end. He quickly attached the bag to a cable and pulley system on shore and reeled out some slack, sending it skimming across the water to the divers.

"What is that?" I asked Mr. James, afraid of the answer.

"They've found him," he said, and I could hear the excitement in his voice. "That's a body bag. A special one for underwater recovery."

The woman diver grabbed it, and all three dove again, disappearing below the surface, the cable snaking after them.

What if, when they pulled it up, it wasn't Marcus?

What if it was Purity?

Don't be silly. This isn't the same river. This isn't even the same state. And that was five years ago.

The body bag rose from the pool, water pouring from it, leaving only the blurry outline of the form cradled inside. The neon gloves of the divers stood out against its black backdrop as they guided it to shore, like the luminous deep-sea hands of bodiless pall-bearers.

I turned away, running to some bushes, heaving up chunks of nuts and fruit and beef jerky as I watched, from under my arm, the divers and men on shore heft the body bag out of the river.

"Here, have some water," Mr. James said, coming alongside me and handing me a bottle. "It will help."

I took a gulp and it did help. A little.

"They're loading the body into the truck, sir," a dark-clad soldier said, strolling up to us.

Wow. That had been fast.

"Good." Mr. James said. "The girl and I will ride with it."

"Um, Mr. Holbrook said you'd both be riding back in the limo." No "sir" this time, but the guy still looked deeply uncomfortable questioning Mr. James.

"And I am telling you we'll ride in the truck." Mr. James dismissed him with a wave of his hand.

I guess I didn't get any say in the matter. The limo was nice, but If Marcus was going to come back from the dead in a body bag in the back of a truck with an estranged uncle he despised, he was going to need a familiar face there to tell him why. And to keep him from killing said uncle. I wasn't sure I could do the latter, but I was willing to give it a try.

Mr. James turned, and I followed him to the parking lot, both of us picking our way between soldiers loading up equipment. It was getting pretty dark and many of them were flicking on the headlamps attached to their helmets. A few glanced our way, their lamps flashing across our faces, but most ignored us.

Mr. James climbed into the back of one of the big army trucks, and held out a hand to pull me up. The interior was big, and sparse, and cold, and it didn't help the ambiance any that the central feature of its decor was a soggy mesh body bag sitting in a puddle of murky water. Other than that, there were two long metal bench seats bolted to the floor along the walls. And at the far back sat a large wooden crate, two strange, red, spray-painted Xs above it spaced about four feet apart.

"Sir, your case from the limo," a voice said. It was the leader of the group that had taken Jason and me. He was standing at the back of the truck, holding up a hard leather briefcase for Mr. James.

"Thank you," Mr. James said, taking it. "You can close the doors now."

"Yes, sir," the guy said, holding up something else. "And here's a radio, sir, direct to me and the driver up in the cab. Just let us know when you're ready to go, or if you need anything en route."

"Thank you. I will." Mr. James said, a look passing between them.

The soldier nodded and swung the doors shut. They clanged loudly as they hit one another, the lock bar slamming into place, metal squealing against metal.

The cargo compartment of the truck went dark for a second, but then a light in the far corner flickered on, bathing me in a sickly yellow glow.

"Take a seat and hang on," Mr. James said, sitting on the bench nearest him.

As the truck engine rumbled to life, I sat on the bench near me, gripping the edge with my hands.

The truck backed up slowly, then surged forward, rumbling and clattering even louder as we hit the questionably paved road leading out of the state park. I could feel the vibrations of it in my bones and water from the body bag seemed to be bouncing across the floor toward me.

We took a hard right, which I thought should have been a left onto the highway back toward Indy, but maybe I'd gotten turned around. Thankfully, the road and the ride smoothed out a bit.

Mr. James had his briefcase open on his lap, and he took out his phone.

"Here, I need you to hold this," he said, tossing it to me.

I didn't exactly catch it. More like it hit my chest and fell in my lap, but at least I didn't drop it.

"Do you see the moving green blip on the map?" he asked, and I looked down to see a GPS tracking grid on the screen. "That's this truck. Now, do you see the red dot to the northwest about two miles from here?"

I nodded.

"I need you to tell me exactly when we reach it."

"Why? What is it?" I asked.

"My last hurrah," he said, taking a large handgun from his briefcase.

I stared at the gun, my limbs trembling, my mind screaming in fear. I would have run if there had been anywhere to run to.

"Passion," he said, glancing from my face to his gun and back again. "I'm not going to hurt you.

There is a chance I can get you, Marcus, and Jason out from under the grasp of John Holbrook and his new council, but we only have one shot at it. Do you understand?"

"No—I—how? You said they took Jason to Indy."

"I lied," he said, nodding toward the big wooden crate.

I looked at it, completely confused.

"Jason is in there," Mr. James said. "He's drugged a little, but he's fine. At least for now."

"You put Jason in a crate?"

Mr. James nodded.

Oh, Jason was going to be royally pissed. But, at least he was still with me, not whisked off to Indy by himself.

And wasn't this a strange turn of events; Mr. James trying to get us away from The Hold, rather than into it? How had things changed so much in one night? The world had changed. Everything had changed.

"How much further?" Mr. James asked me.

I glanced down at the phone. "About a mile."

"Good." He shut his briefcase and lodged it under the bench. Then he got up and made his way carefully to the back of the truck, his gun in one hand, the radio to the cab in the other. He braced himself against the wall and looked at me. "Just tell me when," he said.

The green blip moved closer to the red dot. We were almost on top of it.

"Now," I said.

"Hailing the cab," Mr. James spoke into the handheld radio. "We need to make a pit stop. The girl needs to relieve herself."

There was a moment of silence and then a crackle of static. "No can do," a voice came back to us. "We have orders not to stop until we reach HQ. She'll have to hold it."

"Shit!" Mr. James clicked off the handheld, scowling. "They switched out my man. Holbrook must have gotten wind of something. Looks like we'll just have to do this the hard way. Hold on to something."

I was already holding onto the bench, but I gripped it harder.

He placed the barrel of his gun on the wall of the cab, right over the red X furthest to the right, and he pulled the trigger.

I screamed and covered my ears against the echo of the blast. Before the sound had even dissipated, there were three more in quick succession—four shots total, two into each X on the back wall.

The truck swerved wildly, throwing me off the bench and smack onto the body bag, the eight ball in my pocket digging into my hip. I could feel the wet oozing into me, the clamminess of Marcus's body under me. And even though my brain was screaming at me to get off, I clung to the bag as we slid around the bottom of the truck, me and my soggy sled of death.

And then the truck slowed. The body bag, with me on top of it, came to a gentle rest against the back doors of the truck. We were stopped on a slight slant.

The truck engine sputtered and died.

The yellow light flickered out, plunging us into pitch darkness.

There was a noise outside, a low hum, muffled by the ringing in my ears.

"Are you all right?" Mr. James asked, his voice coming from my left. He'd killed them, the driver and the passenger. He'd shot them right through the cab wall.

"Yeah, I'm okay." I wasn't okay. Not even a little bit. But I wasn't going to tell him that. He still had the gun, and I was locked in the back of a truck with him.

I heard him move, and there was a loud thud. At first I thought he'd tripped, but the thudding continued, growing louder and more frantic, like someone trying to beat their way out of something. Because they were. Jason had apparently woken up in his crate.

"Find my briefcase," Mr. James instructed over the noise. "It should be near you, and there's a small crowbar in it. Oh for Pete's sake," he added, banging the lid of the crate loudly. "Be quiet, or we won't let you out."

Surprisingly, the thudding from inside stopped. Jason wasn't normally that cooperative. Then again, he must have heard the gunshots.

I slid off the body bag, trying not to put my hands anywhere but on the cold metal of the truck floor. When I stood up, the front of my shirt was sopping and my arms felt slimy, but I had no time to be squeamish. From outside, I could hear the unmistakable sound of an approaching vehicle. Someone was coming for us.

I stumbled, feeling my way across the truck bed to the far bench. Amazingly, Mr. James's briefcase was still lodged under it and I pulled it out.

"I've got it," I told him. "I'm bringing it back."

"Good girl. Don't trip on David."

David. Right. Of course Mr. James referred to his nephew by his first name. But I had always known him by his middle name.

"I won't. He slid. He's by the door now." It had been much longer than ten minutes since we'd pulled Marcus from the pool, and he still hadn't rebooted. I didn't want to think about what that meant. I didn't have the luxury.

I could hear muffled voices outside now. "Someone's coming," I whispered as I fumbled my way to the back of the truck feeling for the crate with my feet.

"I know," Mr. James said from right in front of me. "I'm hoping they're my people, but we can't be sure."

"Here's the briefcase." I tried to hand it to him in the dark.

"You'll have to let him out," he said. "If these aren't my men, I'm going to need to be holding this gun. Can you do it?"

"I'll try." I set the briefcase on top of the crate and felt for the latch release. When I'd found it, I lifted the lid and reached inside, my hand landing immediately on the cool smoothness of a crowbar. I pulled it out and latched the case, setting it at my feet. Everything took so long in the dark. The voices outside were closer. They were coming around the back of the truck to the doors.

I felt along the top of the crate and over the edge to the crack between the lid and the container. I slipped the tip of the crowbar into the crack and yanked, hearing the satisfying creak of wood and nails separating. I ran the crowbar along the crack a few more inches and yanked again. It was coming loose.

The voices were closer, maybe right outside the doors.

Metal clanked, the sound of the handles being lifted.

I moved around to the end of the crate. One more yank and the lid came free, moving under my hands as Jason pushed it aside, sending it clattering to the floor.

The voices outside went silent.

Jason's dark form rose out of the crate, and he grabbed me, swinging me around and wrapping his arm around my throat, squeezing, pulling me against the crate, him inside and me outside, the wood pinned between us.

"What the fuck is going on?" he huffed into my ear, his words slurring a little. Whatever they'd given him, it hadn't completely worn off. But his arm was strong, squeezing the breath out of my throat so I couldn't even answer him.

"We're about to find out," Mr. James said, and Jason's arm seemed to relax a little.

The handle to the truck doors screeched and they swung open, light shining in and blinding us.

6

PASSION

"Mr. James?" a voice called.

"Marshall, thank God," Mr. James answered, striding forward. "We were compromised at the park. Holbrook switched out Rodgers, so I had to do a little improvising. I had no idea if he'd caught you in his net as well."

"Never, sir," the man said, looking up at Mr. James reverently. "I will always have your back."

"Did you bring the ambulance?"

"Yes, sir."

"Good. Let's load him up," he said, gesturing at the body bag. "The quicker we're out of here, the better."

Men came forward from behind Marshall and began to carefully lift the mesh bag out of the truck.

"Who are these guys?" Jason asked, his arm around my throat relaxing completely, but he didn't let go of me. "And who's the stiff?"

"That *stiff* is Marcus," I said, stepping out of his grasp. "And those men are the old Hold, the ones still loyal to Mr. James. There was a coup or something, because of the Eidolon, and the new Hold thinks you invited the CAMFers to it."

He just stared at me, his dark eyes blinking.

"They were going to take you to Indy for questioning. That's why Mr. James knocked you out and put you in there."

"I guess I owe him then," Jason said, stepping over the edge of the crate, still a little wobbly, his arm slipping over my shoulder for support. It was certainly better than being choked.

"You two. Come on," Mr. James called. "We need to get out of here."

Jason and I shuffled to the doors, his arm still around me.

Hands reached up, helping us down.

There were about fifteen men stationed around the doors, armed and alert.

We were led to the front of the truck where an ambulance and several SUVs waited.

The ambulance doors were open, two EMTs frantically working over someone on the gurney inside. At first, I thought it might be one of the guys Mr. James had shot. But when we came up to the doors, I realized it was Marcus, the black body bag gone. They had his clothes stripped off and were wrapping him in some kind of insulated blanket, but it was still hard to ignore the gaping hole in his chest. His skin was grey and he did not look alive.

"Get those heat packs on him now. We have to get his core temperature up," one of the medics said, a petite, dark-skinned woman with a nose ring.

The other EMT, a big guy built like a linebacker, started slapping blue heat packs all over Marcus's body: in his arm pits, in his crotch, and across his abdomen.

"You're taking these two as well," the guy behind us told them.

"We don't have room," the woman said, not even looking up from the IV she was inserting into Marcus's arm.

"Make room," the guy said. "Mr. James wants them all in the ambulance."

"Fine." She finally looked up. "What are their manifestations?" Her eyes fell on Jason and then me, inspecting us as if we were petri dish specimens.

"He's leg. She's blood," the guy behind us rattled off.

"Oh, you're blood." She smiled at me like "blood" was my name and she was my new best friend. "Excellent. I've seen your labs. We can use you for a transfusion. Come on. Get in." She moved aside and indicated a seat at the back of the interior.

Jason was still a little wobbly, so I helped him in, the two of us passing so close to Marcus I could smell the dank, fishy heat coming off of him. Could the EMTs really bring him back, and would my blood actually help? I'd never given blood before, for obvious reasons. Samples of it had been taken twice though, once by Dr. Fineman and once by Samantha James. I'd thought Samantha's sample had only been tested at Edgemont High School but, if this woman had seen it, it had obviously made it further than I'd thought.

Jason and I sat down, buckled ourselves in, and someone slammed the ambulance doors closed.

"I'm Reiny." The female EMT introduced herself as the ambulance engine rumbled to life and we began to move. "This is Pete." She gestured at the big guy.

"Um, I'm Passion and this is Jason," I said.

"Great." She smiled. "And now I need some of your blood." She began unwrapping a large needle. "Can you roll up your sleeve please?"

I hesitated—of course I did—and she saw it.

"Don't worry," she assured me. "I do this all the time. I'm really good at it, and we won't take too much."

"No, I—it's fine," I said, pulling up my sleeve.

She was a pro. She didn't even bat an eye at the scars. She wrapped a rubber strap around my bicep, tapped the skin of my inner arm for veins, found a good one, swabbed it with disinfectant, and inserted the needle, my blue and red blood racing through the catchment and down a tube into a waiting IV bag, swirling like purple marble before it began to separate into PSS and blood.

"Are you sure it won't mess him up?" I asked. Didn't blood types have to match? Because I was pretty sure mine wouldn't match anyone's.

"Your regular blood type is O negative, which is the best universal match," she said, like my blood was something to be proud of. "The PSS doesn't change that. Anyone with PSS could take your blood."

It was strange to think having PSS blood might be a perk, rather than a dark secret I must hide.

"What about people without PSS?" I asked.

"I wouldn't recommend it," she said, her eyes glancing away.

There was something there. Something she didn't want to tell me.

When the IV bag was full, Reiny pulled the needle from my arm and slapped a cotton ball and Band-Aid over the small welling of blood.

Then she turned back to Marcus. "His blood is low on oxygen," she explained. "Your blood will help re-oxygenate it, as well as help stabilize his core body temperature."

"So, you can bring him back?" I asked. "Even after all this time?"

"We're pretty sure," she said, attaching my bag of blood to his IV, then gently brushing aside the wet hair that was plastered to his forehead. It was an odd gesture, almost maternal. His bangs fell back, revealing the jagged zig-zag of scars leading up into his hairline, reminding me that Marcus had been seriously dead before. Olivia had told me he'd been killed in a terrible car accident when he was young. If he'd come back from that, surely he could come back from this.

Reiny didn't seem surprised by his scars either. She glanced at them briefly, then looked at me. "We'll do everything we can," she said, her voice confident. "We have a full hospital set-up back at the farm."

"What farm?" Jason asked. "Where are you taking us?"

"To a safe house," Pete answered, clipping some kind of monitor thing onto the end of one of Marcus's prune-like fingers. "A well-armed safe house."

Jason should like that.

We sat together, silently, watching my weird blood flow into Marcus's arm.

I stuffed my hands in my jacket pockets, my knuckles banging up against the hard roundness of the magic eight ball. I'd completely forgotten I had it. Thank goodness I hadn't lost it in the truck.

Suddenly, monitors began to beep like crazy and the EMTs were jabbing buttons and glancing frantically at each other.

"What the hell?" Pete blurted out as the entire inside of the ambulance was plunged into darkness. The overhead lights went out. Every machine fell silent. I could still hear the hum of the ambulance engine and feel us moving forward, but the only light source was the dim red glow of the taillights through the back door windows. Jason was gripping my arm and I was gripping his.

There was a flash, a pulse of blue emanating from Marcus's chest and filling the interior of the vehicle like a strobe. For a moment I could see Reiny and Pete's surprised faces before they flashed back into blackness.

"He's coming back," I said, relief and excitement coursing through me.

"Okay, but what the fuck happened to our equipment?" Reiny asked.

There was another pulse, blue and beautiful, and the equipment hummed to life, the overhead light springing on and blinding us. The machines were still freaking out, beeping and flat-lining, but at least they were on.

The burst of light from Marcus's chest pulsed faster and closer together. It was amazing. I'd never actually seen the process itself, only the results of Marcus dead and then not dead.

The EMTs weren't even paying attention to their monitors anymore. They were focused on Marcus, as transfixed as Jason and I. It was impossible to look away from the miracle happening right in front of us. With each new pulse, his color got better, and his body became more vital looking. And then he gasped, sucking in air and jerking upwards, the blanket and heat packs falling away as he sat up. His chest was whole now, the ugly gaping hole filled with the intricate outline of PSS lungs and a healthy, beating PSS heart.

"You're okay," Reiny said gently, grabbing his arm and steadying him.

"We've got you," Pete said, holding him from the other side.

Slowly, Marcus turned and looked at Reiny, his eyes confused, his face strangely slack.

"Waib—got—nar," he slurred, drool dripping from his lower lip, his mouth scrunching in frustration. "Waib goth ner." He tested the strange sounds again. Louder. Angrier.

"David, it's okay. You've experienced some trauma." Reiny held his bare arm with one hand while she fumbled for a nearby syringe full of clear liquid. "You're going to feel confused. It may take a little while for your head to clear."

"My scissor. Theb goth ner," he said, struggling against the hold of both the EMT's now, his head turning and catching sight of Jason and me sitting behind him. His eyes met mine, but there was no recognition. He looked like a scared animal. Or a confused child.

Reiny sank the syringe into his bicep, and his glance flew to her, bewildered and betrayed as his eyes rolled back in his head and he collapsed into Pete's arms.

Pete lowered him down on the stretcher and pulled the blanket around him again.

"Get him oxygen, now," Reiny commanded Pete. "I'll put the sedative directly into the IV." She grabbed another syringe, prepping it for insertion.

"What's wrong with him?" I demanded.

"Why can't he talk?" Jason fired at them too. "What did you do to him?"

"Be quiet," Pete snapped, strapping an oxygen mask over Marcus's face, "and let us help him."

No, this could not be happening. This was supposed to be our miracle; Marcus fully restored like he'd always been and coming to our rescue. Not this—not Marcus confused and jabbering like an idiot.

"But is he okay?" I couldn't stop myself from asking.

"We don't know," Reiny said. "It's too soon to tell."

"But you have an idea," Jason pressed. "Don't you?"

She turned away from us, exchanging a look with Pete.

"He's our friend," I told both of them. "We want to know."

Pete nodded and Reiny turned to us, her lips pressed into a thin line. "Most likely, he's suffering from cerebral hypoxia," she said. "He went a very long time without getting adequate oxygen to his brain. That can result in temporary or permanent damage. We won't know which until we've run more tests back at the farm. And even then, every brain recovers differently."

"Brain damage," I said, the words sounding all garbled and wrong, as if I was the one who couldn't speak.

"We'll do everything we can for him," Reiny promised, putting her warm brown hand over mine.

But it didn't comfort me. If Marcus was broken, damaged beyond repair, Olivia would never forgive me. I would never forgive myself.

No, God. Please, no.

As I prayed, my thoughts nothing but a desperate plea, the ambulance drove on into the night, Reiny and Pete watching their monitors with guarded expressions.

Jason sat silently next to me.

I don't know how long we drove. It seemed like forever. From what I could see out the back window, it looked like we were taking back roads, not the highway.

Then we turned off onto a dirt road, dust billowing behind us, illuminated by the taillights.

A wooden sign flashed past us, disappearing into the dark, something about it vaguely familiar.

The ambulance turned sharply and slowed, pulling to a stop.

"We're here," Pete said, getting up to unlatch the doors and swing them open. He hopped out, ready to receive the gurney.

Reiny attached Marcus's IV to it before they lowered it out, popping the wheeled legs down and rolling it to the side so Jason and I could climb out.

Jason stepped down first, his boots crunching in the gravel, and I stepped after him. Pete and Reiny were pushing Marcus toward one of the buildings in front of us. It was a huge farmhouse, another long, low building to its left stretching off into the dark fields of rural Indiana.

We were back at The Warren Gun Club.

I'd never expected to see the man who had taught me to shoot a gun ever again.

I'd certainly never expected to be sitting around a table with him, his two brothers, and Jason, downing the best fried chicken and garlic mashed potatoes I'd ever had.

Apparently, Bo, the guy Olivia had always referred to as Shotgun, was an amazing cook. His brothers, Bruce and Butch, the one who'd been my shooting instructor, were just good eaters.

Jason and I ate and drank, our eyes flicking between each other and the three burly men. And they weren't the only men here. On the way into the farmhouse from the ambulance, I'd seen the yard full of tents, groups of men sitting around low, glowing campfires. Jason has seen it too and given me a quizzical look. Something was going on here, a gathering of some kind.

When we'd first arrived, Reiny and Pete had taken Marcus upstairs, and occasionally Pete would pass through the dining room, bringing yet another piece of monitoring equipment in from the ambulance. I wanted to ask him what was going on. I wanted to ask one of the three Bs, but I couldn't work up the nerve. Still, I could guess. It looked like Mr. James wasn't abandoning The Hold quite as easily as it had abandoned him. It looked like he was amassing a following out there, maybe even an army.

As if he'd heard me thinking about him, Mr. James entered the room, coming down from upstairs.

"How's Marcus?" I blurted. I didn't care if it sounded rude. It had been a rough night.

"He's stable," Mr. James said. "His body has made a remarkable recovery already. He's a quick healer. It runs in our family. You'll see that when you go up to visit Samantha."

"Samantha is here?" My fork fell from my hand and clattered onto my plate. "Shouldn't she be in a hospital?"

"I'm afraid the reports of my daughter's demise were greatly exaggerated," Mr. James said, his eyes flicking to Jason for a moment. "Thankfully, the shooter wasn't as proficient as he could have been. Her wound was only a graze to the ribs, not a shot to the head."

"She's okay?" I pushed back my chair and stood up, glaring at him. "Then why did you tell me she was almost dead?"

"That bit of untruth was for the sake of Mr. Holbrook and his new council, I'm afraid," Mr. James explained. "I needed them to think I was at their mercy.

That I wouldn't act against them. With Samantha fatally injured and immobile, they believed exactly that. But she was already here, safe and sound, when we found you two. My apologies that you had to take part in my little subterfuge."

"She's upstairs?" I asked, still in shock, barely believing it was possible. "Are Renzo and Juliana here too?"

"No," he shook his head. "They're somewhere else, but safe."

"And Samantha—she's fine? Can I see her?"

"Of course," Mr. James said, gesturing to the stairway behind him.

I circled the table and hurried past him, barely holding myself back from a run. I bolted up the steps, taking them two at a time, my heart in my throat. She was here. And she was okay.

At the top of the stairs, I paused, wondering if I should go right or left. To the right was a shorter hallway, leading to one door. I was pretty sure that was where they'd put Marcus. The left had a longer hall with several doors off of it and one at the end.

Just as I stepped off the landing to head left, I heard Mr. James's voice from downstairs, a low subdued rumble. "You did well," he said. "You're as good as Bruce claimed you were. And no one saw you, you're sure?"

I couldn't make out what Jason answered in response. He was too far from the stairwell. But I recognized the timbre and cadence of his voice. He answered Mr. James and they both laughed.

I had never heard Jason Williams laugh.

I stopped stock still, straining to hear more, but they were moving away from the stairwell, their voices fading.

As far as I knew, Jason and Mr. James had never met before today. So, why had they become buddy-buddy the second I'd left the room? And what had Mr. James been talking about? What had Jason done so well that no one had seen?

I looked down the hallway.

Whatever it was, I would deal with it later.

Samantha was in one of these rooms, and the one on the end would be the largest, so she was probably there. I ran down the hall, but stopped just outside the door, suddenly shy and terrified to see her. What if she was still angry about the things I'd said at the Eidolon? Was I still angry at her? No. I reached down and turned the knob, stepping into a brightly lit room filled with old fashioned furniture and dominated by an out-of-place hospital bed with Samantha propped up smack in the middle of it. She was wearing a downy white robe and reading a book like she'd just had a day at the spa.

She looked up at me and a smile blossomed across her face. "What took you so long?" she asked, as if I'd arrived late to some high school party, instead of barely escaping a massacre. "I've been hearing all three of you since you came in."

Of course she had. Samantha heard PSS as music.

"You're alive," I said like an idiot, feeling strangely angry. Even with the happy PSS orchestra playing in her head all the time, how could she smile after everything that had happened? Did she know Marcus might have brain damage, or that Olivia had been taken? Did she know Yale and Nose were gone? How could she be here, practically unscathed, when I felt like the walking wounded, like damaged goods that could never be restored to their former state?

"So are you," she pointed out. "And your PSS has changed." She furrowed her brow and turned her good ear toward me, listening. "You have a power," she said, smiling.

"I do? What is it?"

"I have no idea. I can't hear what they are, only that they've manifested."

So, the Eidolon had worked on me. But what good was a power if I had no idea what it was or how to use it?

"Don't worry," Samantha said, as if reading my mind. "It will show itself when you need it. Will you come sit by me?" She patted the edge of the bed. "I want to see you. I need to know you're okay."

I crossed to the bed and sat down, painfully aware I was filthy and stinky and probably looked like something the cat dragged in.

"I should have listened to you," she said, and I could see the pain and guilt swimming in her eyes. She hadn't gotten away from the Eidolon unscathed. Not by a long shot.

"What happened up there wasn't your fault," I told her.

She threw herself into my arms, or I threw myself into hers. I'm not sure which and it didn't matter. We held each other, and she cried, and her hair smelled like shampoo and sunshine. Her hands crawled up my back and clung to me, as if she would squeeze what she needed right out of my body. My hands rubbed and soothed in return, stroking her back, feeling the thick bandages under her shirt where the bullet had skimmed her ribs.

God, thank you.

"Lay down with me," she whispered, and I did, curling myself around her and pulling the covers over both of us. She was so warm and soft, my breasts pressing into the curve of her back.

"Um, is that something in your pocket or are you just happy to see me?" she asked, sounding amused.

"Oh, that's my eight ball," I laughed, pulling the camo jacket out from between us and digging the thing out of the pocket. "See?" I handed it to her, using it as an excuse to drape my arm around her. "I found it along the river bank."

She took it, turning the ball and waiting for an answer to float to the top.

"What did you ask it?" I whispered into her hair.

"If everything is going to be okay," she said.

7

MARCUS

old.
Pain.
Water.
Darkness.
Time runs through me like a river of death.
I move in eddies and swirls of nothingness, going nowhere.
Dying isn't supposed to take this long.
I should know. I've done it so many times before.
But it has never been like this.
Something is wrong.
The deep water moves around me. Tugging. Lifting.
A dark sphere descends, flashing answers that mean nothing.

It falls into me.

Light pulses.

A moment of life.

It passes through me.

I'm underwater oh my God I'm stuck can't move can't swim can't think can't live where is she fuck this.

Help me. I am Marcus.

Cold.

Pain.

Water.

Darkness.

I float through wordless dreams for days. How many days? What are days?

I wake. Sometimes in light. Sometimes in darkness. In a room I've never seen before. With people I don't know. In a hospital bed, but not in a hospital.

I think I'm drugged.

Words are so hard.

Remembering is even harder.

Something about a girl, though, lingers like an echo. Like a ghost. Her hand touches me, reaching right into my chest and clutching my heart until it feels like it will burst.

I dream that a lot.

It is terrifying.

And I like it.

The door to my room creaked on its hinges, and I opened my eyes to bare slits, feigning sleep even though I was more awake than I'd been in days.

My head was finally clear, words and ideas colliding together like magnets of meaning. The light streaming between the curtains was dim. Either it was morning or overcast, I couldn't tell which. The house was quiet, the only sound the girl's bare feet as she padded to my bedside, peering down at me.

She was not the girl from my dreams. She was blonde and taller, and her clothes were rumpled, as if she'd been sleeping in them. She did not look happy.

She sat down at my bedside, pulling her legs up into the chair and resting her chin on her knees. She glanced at the door nervously, then back at me, and whispered, "I wish you could hear me. I'm not supposed to be here, but I'm tired of waiting, Marcus. We need you."

I focused on keeping my breathing steady. If I showed her I was awake, she'd expect me to respond. To talk. To answer her need. And there was no way I could do that. I didn't even know where I was or how I'd gotten there. Then again, I was used to waking up in some weird situations after a reboot. The girl sounded desperate, and she'd called me by my middle name, which was odd. Did that mean something? Maybe she could be an ally. Maybe we could help each other.

"I don't know what to do," she went on. "Jason has been acting strange. He spends most of his time out at the shooting range. It's like he's suddenly become one of them. I think he's avoiding me and then there's the thing I heard your uncle say to him. It just doesn't make sense unless they somehow knew each other before. And if they're working together, I don't even know what that means, but it can't be good.

I'm such a chicken. I haven't told Samantha what I heard. I don't want to make her mad at me again. She worships her father. Actually, everyone here pretty much worships him."

My uncle. And Samantha. What the hell? They were here in this house? They were the ones holding me? Why? How?

"Then this morning, I woke up and felt Olivia," the girl said, her voice cracking on the name. "After days of nothing, I got a flash of her so clear it was like she was in the same room with me. She was touching the tags, brushing her fingers over them, but it wasn't good. She's in pain. They've been hurting her. They're doing something awful to her. And I feel so bad because I was glad it was only a flash. If it had been constant, I don't think I could have taken it. I don't know how she can take it." The girl was crying now, her head bowed and her shoulders shaking. I wanted to reach out and touch her. I wanted to comfort her and help her, except she sounded a little crazy. That, and I had absolutely no idea what she was talking about.

"No one has even mentioned rescuing her," the girl said, her voice growing hard and angry. "It's like they don't care. I know the CAMFers took her west. I could probably lead us right to her if she keeps touching the tags. But I don't think anyone else would go."

CAMFers? My heart raced at the word. They were the enemy. They'd hurt my sister. They'd handcuffed me to a car while they made her scream. The memories were right there, open and raw and alive. My wrist felt the cut of pain as I yanked against the cuffs, metal ripping into flesh. They had her. It was my fault.

I had to save her.

"Danielle!" The word exploded from my lips as I sat up, grabbing the girl sitting at my bedside.

My hands were on her shoulders, digging in.

My face was in hers, but she didn't resist or try to get away.

"The CAMFers have Danielle," I said, the words slightly slurred, but words. Real, understandable words. "We have to get her back."

"Marcus," she said gently, her voice quivering. "Danielle is—they don't have her anymore. Don't you remember?"

"No." I shook my head. "They took her. They have her."

The door flew opened and a petite woman and a burly guy rushed in, followed by my uncle.

"What are you doing in here?" Uncle Alex demanded of the girl. "What did you say to him?"

The woman was moving toward my IV, a look of determination on her face, and I knew what that meant. More drugs.

"Don't," I said, shoving myself off the bed and yanking the IV out of her reach. My legs were wobbly and I clung to the IV pole just to hold myself upright, my body between it and her.

She stared at me, our eyes locked. "That was very clear," she said, surprise in her voice. "Your language faculties are coming back quickly."

"No drugs," I said, still a little slurred. "They— make it—harder."

"Okay, but you need to get back in bed before you fall down."

"Promise," I said. I knew it didn't matter. She would probably lie to me, and as weak as I was, I wasn't going to make it out of this bedroom on my own. But the power of speech had returned to me and it felt damn good to use it.

She glanced at my uncle and he nodded.

"No more sedatives," she agreed. "But there are other drugs that will help you heal without clouding your mind. Now, please get back in bed before you fall on your face."

"What happened to me?" I asked, leaning back against the bed.

"You experienced a traumatic event," she said, "and we're all here to help you recover. My name is Reiny and this is Pete," she gestured at the big guy. "We're both EMTs and certified nurses."

"What traumatic event?" I pressed her.

"What's the last thing you remember?" Pete asked, a look passing between the three adults.

I didn't want to tell them. My uncle was a man I hadn't seen for ten years, and last time I'd seen him he'd killed my parents and left me for dead. Reiny and Pete obviously worked for him and had kept me sedated against my will. But at the moment, it looked like I was at their mercy. And my uncle might be a psychotic bastard, but he was a powerful psychotic bastard. I had no idea what he was doing here or what he wanted from me, but if anyone could help get Danielle back, he could.

"Danielle and I went out in—a car." I spoke slowly, the words like pieces of a puzzle I had to find just the right spot for. "Some men stopped us.

They were—cops—bad men—CAMFers. They hurt her." I tried to block the memories out of my mind this time, just focusing on the words, but the images kept rushing at me, jumbled and confused. "We fell off—we fell down—and they took her. I don't know—the rest. I think they left me in the water. I remember a lot of water."

"And that's your most recent memory?" Reiny asked.

"Yes."

I heard the girl behind me make a noise, a tiny moan as if she'd cut herself. I'd almost forgotten she was there.

"Okay. That's fine," Reiny smiled, taking my arm and helping me back into the bed. I didn't resist. I was suddenly exhausted, barely able to keep my eyes open, my legs like noodles.

"Let's go," Pete said, leading the girl from the room, her expression haunted and hopeless. I'd disappointed her somehow, and it made me feel sad.

The last thing I saw before I shut my eyes was my uncle standing over me.

8

PASSION

I walked away from Pete down the hall, trying to keep my disappointment from crushing me to the floor.

"Hey," he said, "wait."

I turned and looked at him.

"It's short-term memory loss," he explained, sympathy written across his face. "This kind of thing is common in cerebral hypoxia patients."

"Short-term?" I said, the words sticking in my throat. "He doesn't remember the last eight months. He doesn't remember *his sister is dead*. He doesn't remember Olivia, or Jason, or the Eidolon. He doesn't even know who I am." I had seen it in Marcus's eyes twice now—that complete and utter lack of recognition.

It was like being erased. We were all being erased. First Nose and Yale, then Olivia, now Marcus, and with him, the rest of us. He had been the backbone of the PSS Campers, the hero who had rescued us all and knit us into some sort of weird PSS family. And I had been waiting for days for him to wake up and tell me what to do.

"Look how fast he's recovered his speech," Pete said. "We never expected him to improve this quickly. That means his brain is healing, his nerve cells are rerouting themselves around the damaged areas and making new connections. If his speech has come back, it is likely his memory will as well. It's just going to take time."

"How long? How long will it take him to remember?" I didn't want to cry in front of Pete, but seeing Marcus like that, seeing him helpless and confused, it had been horrible.

"There's no way to know for sure. Based on his rate of recovery already, I'd say a month. Maybe less."

"A month before he remembers anything, or everything?" It was too long, either way. Olivia didn't have that kind of time. Whatever the CAMFers were doing to her, it was bad. I'd never felt her like this before. It was as if she were shrinking deeper and deeper into herself, as if she was shriveling and burying herself behind some kind of wall. And there had been pain, not just physical. She wasn't okay. She was dying inside. And the CAMFers had only had her for a few days.

"Every recovering brain is different," Pete was saying. "Sometimes memory comes back in pieces;

other times all at once. And I want to be honest with you, sometimes it doesn't come back at all."

That was not what I'd wanted to hear.

The door to Marcus's room opened, and Mr. James came out, shutting it carefully and quietly behind him.

"What were you doing in there?" he demanded of me again. "I thought I'd made it clear he was not to be disturbed for any reason."

"He's my friend." I raised my chin and glared at Mr. James. "I was worried about him." *And you aren't the boss of me.*

"It's okay," Pete said, coming to my defense against his boss, which surprised me. "That was a significant breakthrough for your nephew in there, and her presence seems to have triggered it. In fact, it might not be a bad idea to have her and Sam spend a little time with him every day. If nothing else, it will help facilitate his speech recovery."

"Well, if you think it would help," Mr. James said, but he didn't sound convinced. "But didn't you say it could be dangerous to jar his memory? What if the conversation strays to things it shouldn't?" What was Mr. James afraid I'd tell his nephew? That he and Jason had secretly been working together?

"It is best if it comes back on its own, yes," Pete said. "Dumping the last eight months on him all at once would do more harm than good. His brain knows exactly what he can handle both physically and psychologically. It will mete out memories as he's ready, but I'm sure the girls will be sensitive to that, won't you?" he asked, turning back to me.

"Yeah, sure," I said.

"Good," Mr. James said, his eyes assessing me. "I'm glad I can trust you." He turned to head down the stairs.

"When are you going to get Olivia back?" I asked, stopping him in his tracks. "It's been days and you haven't done anything." I was probably pushing my luck, but it seemed like the right time to push it.

"I am working on it, I assure you," Mr. James said, staring at me over his shoulder. "But the current priority is the recovery of Samantha and David."

And the recovery of The Hold. It was obvious that was a priority. People, and troops, and guns had been in and out of the farmhouse over the last forty-eight hours like it was Fort Knox. Mr. James had a room set up downstairs full of maps and plans that was even more off-limits than Marcus's room. Mr. James wasn't just waiting for his daughter and his nephew to recover. I didn't buy it. Even weirder than that, where was Samantha's mom? Whenever I asked, Samantha looked uncomfortable and immediately changed the subject. I was beginning to think Mrs. James was a figment of everyone's imagination. And what about Olivia's mom? Where was she in all of this? Was she still back in Indy wondering where her daughter was and expecting Mr. James to find her?

"What about Dr. Black?" I asked Mr. James. Might as well get it all out while I had his undivided attention. "She paid you to find Olivia. She gave you all her husband's paintings *to find Olivia*."

Pete shot me a warning glance. I was pushing my luck and I knew it.

"I no longer have that payment, it seems," Mr. James said, his cheek twitching in annoyance. "Perhaps the new Hold will help her out, but I doubt it."

"So that's it? You just left her in Indy at their mercy?"

"As a matter-of-fact, I didn't," he said. "I've been in contact with Dr. Black, and my people are keeping her safe there. But it's much too dangerous to try and get her out at the moment. It would only draw unwanted attention to her."

The door to Marcus's room creaked open and Reiny poked her head out. "Would you please keep it down?" she growled. "My patient is sleeping without a sedative, which I have promised not to give him, but I may have to inject the three of you." She glared daggers at us.

"Our business is done," Mr. James said, straightening his suit jacket and heading down the stairs.

Reiny gave a final glare to Pete and me and tucked herself back into Marcus's room, shutting the door softly but firmly behind her.

"Be careful," Pete said, practically a whisper, his eyes glancing down the stairs. "That is not a man you want to challenge."

"I know." And I did. How could I forget the moment in the back of that truck when Mr. James had killed two people without hesitation? He was a dangerous man. Marcus had once tried to tell me that, but I hadn't wanted to believe him. Now, I was beginning to.

"And if the CAMFers have your friend," Pete said, "he may be one of the few people alive who has any chance of getting her back. So, don't go doing anything stupid, you hear me? Bide your time, and be smart. You understand?"

"Yeah, okay." I wasn't sure why he was going out of his way to warn me.

"Good. When Marcus is awake again, Reiny or I will come get you. Will you let Samantha know?" He nodded toward her room at the end of the hall.

"Sure," I said, turning away from him.

Samantha would be thrilled. She'd been asking to see Marcus.

And then I remembered she didn't know about his memory loss yet.

Great. I guess I got to tell her that part too.

"So, what are you implying?" Samantha asked, glaring at me, her face pale and angry.

"I'm not implying anything," I said. "I'm just telling you what I heard."

Crap. This was exactly what I'd been afraid of.

I was standing at the end of Samantha's bed. She'd taken the news of Marcus's memory loss really well. Then again, she hadn't been a huge part of his last eight months. Samantha and Marcus had been reunited at the Eidolon, so for her it was the loss of one night, one night all of us would have gladly paid to forget.

But the topic of the connection between her father and Jason? That wasn't going so well. I'd told her what I'd heard. I'd also mentioned, as delicately as I could, the men her father had killed in the truck and the interrogation I'd received at the hands of both him and John Holbrook.

As soon as I'd said Holbrook's name, all the blood had drained from Samantha's face. Something was going on here. Something no one was telling me.

"Who is Holbrook anyway?" I asked. I figured I'd come this far, I might as well push all the way. "You've never mentioned him, or a council. It's like they just appeared overnight."

"Well, they didn't," Samantha said, pain and anger flashing across her face. "He's been around for a while, chipping away at my father's power. They used to be best friends." Her hands were clutching at the blanket on top of her.

"Why didn't you ever mention him?" I was trying to understand. Hadn't Samantha herself been chipping away at her father's power? That's what the Eidolon had been. Didn't she realize that? It was almost enough to make me feel sorry for Alexander James—both his best friend and his daughter had been trying to overthrow him at the same time.

"You really want to know who John Holbrook is?" Samantha asked, turning away from me to look out the window. She was blinking back tears and her jaw was clenched. "He's my mother's lover." She turned back to me, letting out a shaky breath. "My mother hasn't been away on business. She's been away on pleasure. Well, maybe part of it was business. My father suspected that John was after more than my mother's heart when she started bringing up the idea of a council-led Hold. They fought about it all the time.

Probably more than they fought about the fact that she was sleeping with someone else. But I didn't really think she'd betray him like this. I didn't think she'd leave us." Samantha's voice had grown small like a heartbroken child's. She looked back out the window again, and I could see the tears running down her face.

I didn't know what to say. No wonder the animosity between the two men had been so thick, and no wonder Mr. James was scrambling. His wife had cheated on him and left him for a man who wanted to take his place in more ways than one. And I'd thought my family was messed up.

"I was stupid enough to think I could rescue The Hold from all three of them," Samantha said bitterly. "I thought if I could get the Marked on board, if I could give them more of a sense of power and ownership, then we could save it from the dickishness of adults. I was sick and tired of them fighting over it like it was their plaything." She wiped the tears from her face with the back of her hand, strength coming back into her voice. "It doesn't belong to them. They don't get to destroy it along with everything else."

"I'm so sorry." I didn't know what else to say. Samantha had already felt betrayed by both her parents, especially her mother, and then I'd come along spreading more doubt about the one parent she had left. "I mean, I could have misunderstood," I backpedalled, wanting to wipe the agony from her face. "Maybe he wasn't even talking to Jason. I was at the top of the stairs, and everything was muffled."

"No," she said, turning back to me, her voice defeated. "I'm sorry. You could be right. My father has a lot of connections through The Hold. If it sounded like he knew Jason already, he probably did. Tell me what they said again."

I had never wanted to be less right in my life, but I couldn't shake the feeling this was important. "Your father complimented Jason on doing a good job and said something about him being as good as Bruce said he was. Then he asked Jason if he was sure no one had seen him. Jason said something back, but I couldn't quite hear it, and then he laughed."

"It sounds like Jason knew Bruce before too, not just my father," she pointed out.

"Well, yeah, Jason and Bruce met on the way to Indy when we stopped here to learn how to shoot. I mean, Jason was already pretty good, but the rest of us—" I stopped, my mind catching up with what I was saying. Bruce had been in Jason's lane when we'd trained at the gun club, but Jason hadn't needed much instruction. He'd already been a good shot. Is that what Bruce had told Mr. James—that a bunch of PSS kids had stopped by for guns and ammo and one of them was an accomplished marksmen?

"What?" Samantha asked, scanning my face.

"The only thing Bruce really knew about Jason was that he could shoot," I said. "Maybe that's what he told your father."

"So, the 'good job' was the shooting he did at the Eidolon to save you," Samantha said, her voice full of relief. "My father was just thanking him."

"Maybe, but it doesn't explain the last thing he said about no one seeing it. If he was talking about saving me at the Eidolon, why would that matter?"

"I don't know," Samantha snapped. "You're determined so see my father as some kind of villain, aren't you? I know you think he's terrible, but he's not. What he did in that truck saved you, Jason, and David. Sometimes he does things that seem awful, but it's always to protect The Hold and what it stands for. He would do anything to protect the people under his care. I don't know why you're making such a big deal out of this, when all he's ever done is help you. I thought you'd be grateful. You could have been taken by the CAMFers if it wasn't for him. Instead, you're here, safe, with me. I don't understand why you're trying to smear him like this."

"I'm not trying to smear him," I protested. "I'm just trying to figure this out." She was hurt. She was pissed at me. I'd messed everything up. Again. Maybe I just wasn't cut out to have a relationship with anyone.

"Why don't you go ask Jason, then," she said, "instead of dragging me into your conspiracy theories and trying to get me to take your side against my own father? I'm sure Jason will be happy to explain everything to you." She was dismissing me, turning her back to me even as she said it.

"Samantha," I pleaded. I'd come seeking her help, and instead I'd destroyed everything we'd had.

"Leave me alone, okay?" she said, still not looking at me. "I just need some time to myself."

So, that's what I did.

I left Samantha alone.

9

OLIVIA

"**W**ake up," a voice commanded.

Instantly I was awake and alert, every muscle and nerve in my body wired. But I didn't show it because the owner of that voice fed on my fear. It was his aphrodisiac. His tool. His weapon against me.

Instead, I opened my eyes and stretched my arms over my head, ignoring the pain and smiling sleepily. In my imagination, I was in my bed at home, not on a slab of cold stone in a prison cell. In that safe place where I hid myself, there were still such things as a snooze alarms, warm coffee in the kitchen, and my mom griping about me being late for school.

"Get up, bitch," Anthony said, his nostrils flaring.

He reached out to grab me and I let him, let myself pretend I had a choice. He pulled me against him, his cigarette breath huffing in my face like the stench of death. "The doctor has some tricks for you today, and this time you'd better perform."

My ghost hand was pinned between us, the metal cuff they'd put on my wrist digging into my chest. I'd experimented with the cuff, doing everything I could to get it off, but the closer it got to my PSS, the more it resisted, like they were two magnets with the same pole. And I hated it, because without it I would have reached into Anthony right there and eviscerated his psyche without a second thought. I would have found his deepest, darkest secret and stripped him of it, then used it to destroy him. I found it funny that there had been a time, not so long ago, when I'd been afraid to use my hand. In a few short days, all that had changed. Now, I constantly fantasized about showing my enemies, *firsthand*, exactly what I was capable of.

"Let's go." Anthony shoved me toward the door. It was open and I could see down the well-lit corridor of metal and stone.

The compound must be underground. It was the only real explanation for the lack of windows or outside sound, or the way the temperature stayed the same, day and night, without any visible heat source. It all added up; everything I'd been able to observe and notice on my way to my daily visits to Dr. Fineman's lab. I'd even begun to map the corridors and doors in my mind for when I escaped. Not if, but when.

Just the thought of it made me giddy, and I darted past Anthony toward the threshold of the cell, my bare feet padding softly on the smooth floor. I'd made it my habit to push the boundaries and test his limits, just like I'd done with my last guard, Felix. They'd taken my boots away after I'd kicked Felix in the balls. Then they'd replaced him with Anthony, which I hope meant I'd ruptured something important.

"Not so fast." Anthony grabbed my arms, pinning them behind my back, twisting a little to remind me who was boss. He propelled me down the corridor in front of him, and I kept up my fake limp. It bothered me that my knee and ribs had healed so quickly. They had both been badly injured. I remembered the raw pain, the inability to move. I should have still been hurting, but I wasn't. It made me wonder if the CAMFers had drugged me more than I'd realized, or if I'd been their prisoner much longer than I thought.

Anthony and I took a right, then a left up a flight of stairs. Finally, we entered another corridor ending in the familiar double lab doors with their rounded windows.

He pushed me straight through, using my face and chest as his personal battering ram. The doors swung open, revealing the crisp pure white and gleaming metal of a large research laboratory complete with all the fixings; whirling complex-looking machines, busy lab techs in white coats, and racks of rats in glass cages. Everything a mad scientist could ask for.

Dr. Fineman wasn't anywhere in sight though, and Anthony led me past all the science stuff to the interrogation room. It was grey and drab, with a table in the middle of it bolted right into the floor like I'd seen on a million cop shows. It had a metal chair too and, of course, the obligatory two-way mirror built into the wall.

Anthony escorted me inside and left, locking the door behind him. They'd make me wait a while before they did anything or anyone came in. It was all part of the game. Except this time, something was different. There were things on the table. Things I recognized.

I glanced at the mirror, my own reflection staring back. My hair was a mess. My clothes were filthy. My face was dirty. They'd promised me a shower once I cooperated, like I'd really want to take a shower with Anthony watching.

I raised my hand and waved at Dr. Fineman, sure he was behind the glass and hoping it would piss him off. Then, I crossed to the table and looked down at what was on it.

There were four items set out for me, all neatly in a row.

First in line were the dog tags Marcus and Yale had made for me out of one of Passion's blades. They'd once protected me from Dr. Fineman's minus meters and kept me hidden from him. But I was done hiding. If I ever got away from the CAMFers, I wasn't going to cower and run anymore. I was going to come for them the way they'd come for me. I was going to wipe them out.

I looked up at the two-way mirror. Did Dr. Fineman know what else the tags did? Did he know they provided a connection between Passion and me?

Maybe it was a trap, but it was worth the risk, so I slowly reached out and touched the metal tags, rubbing my fingers across the engraved letters of my middle name. They were watching me from behind the glass, so I didn't linger or let my face change expression, but before I pulled my fingers away, I felt her. I got a flash of Passion on a comfortable bed in an old-fashioned looking room. She was okay. They didn't have her. She was alive and safe, probably still back in Indy. She had gotten away, and hopefully Jason with her. And maybe they'd gotten Marcus out too. Surely they would have.

I stifled the smile of victory rising inside of me. The next item on the table was Dr. Fineman's cube, the one I'd pulled out of him back in Greenfield that had sent him into a coma. The cube had Jason's bullet in it. The two of them combined had saved us all from the giant minus meter the doctor had set as a trap, though he'd since claimed it had been a fake.

I stared down at the cube, my heart beating faster and faster. This cube had once jumped me forward in time three days, simultaneously transporting me three miles away. It had whisked me to safety — and not just me, but everyone touching me. If it still worked, I could escape, right now, simply by touching it. And I wanted to so badly, I could taste it. I wanted out of this hell-hole, and it didn't matter where I went, or how I got there, or what I lost in the process. But that would only happen if the cube still worked, which I seriously doubted. Combining the bullet and the cube had been a fluke, a hare-brained idea I'd tried on a whim. But my gut had been telling me ever since that it had been a one-shot deal, like a bulb that blows in a sudden flash when you turn on the light, and then fades forever. Sometimes the big magic only works once.

And Dr. Fineman had put it in front of me for a reason. He wanted me to touch it.

The man had already revealed his agenda for keeping me alive. He wanted me to solve the mystery of the cube, put it back in him, and become his personal PSS pickpocket, yanking things out of people at his command. But I would never forget what he'd done with Passion's razors in the room under Mike Palmer's house. He had no conscience. No hesitation in creating experiments that tortured and killed people.

The items on the table were obviously some kind of test. If I touched the cube, it would establish a connection between the two of us. He wanted me to fall for his little trick so he would know things about me. So he could get inside my head.

My fingers trembled, but I didn't touch it, and my eyes moved past it to the next item on the table. It was Mike Palmer's matchbook, the one he'd left as a warning for us not to go to the Eidolon. Or as a way to entice us to go. I still wasn't sure which. The gasoline soaked message once written on it was unreadable now, smeared into oblivion.

I had thought a lot about that matchbook and the weird actions of Palmer. Why had he come to the house in Indy and not burned it to the ground when he could have? Why had he warned us away from Shades? Why had he said that strange thing in the car to me about Marked brats never listening? Referring to us as Marked was not CAMFer terminology.

It was something someone from The Hold would say. But there was no way Mike Palmer could be from The Hold. If he was a double-agent, then I was the fluffy pink princess of Unicorn Land. I just couldn't believe that. My mind wouldn't bend that far.

I had no idea why Fineman had included the matchbook in this line-up. Maybe just to confuse me.

The fourth item on the table was a small knife. Why would they give me a weapon? I could use it to stick anyone who came into the room. I could use it to fend off Anthony. But then what? They were watching me from the fucking mirror. I was underground in a heavily guarded building, and there were surveillance cameras in every room and corridor. There was no way I'd get out.

The knife was useless to me and they knew it. Still, why put it in a row of things that had belonged to me? I didn't own a knife, had never really wielded one in my life.

Except once.

And then it all came rushing back.

I had pulled a knife from a CAMFer on the night of the Eidolon. I had used it to try to get away from them, and I'd been brutally beaten for it.

So many of my memories from the night of the Eidolon were a blur, like some nightmare I'd stuffed down deep inside of me.

When I was awake, it was easy to focus on the here and now. My cell. My survival. These men. My hatred and determination to thwart them. I did not think about what had happened to my friends. I did not let my mind wander to Nose and Yale, and Marcus sinking away from me. I couldn't let myself. It would undo me. And so, I hadn't thought about this knife either. I'd taken it from inside one of them, and they'd taken it back, and that had been the end of it.

What was Dr. Fineman up to, presenting me with this line of items?

Dog tags.

Cube and bullet.

Matchbook.

Knife.

One of these things was not like the others. Three of them my ghost hand had taken from inside people. Four, if you counted the cube and bullet separately. That much made sense. Dr. Fineman was desperate to understand my power and use it for himself. He'd already grilled me about what I'd done to the two men at the pool; the one kid, Paulie, I'd pulled that useless magic eight ball out of, and the other guy, Gary, who I'd only felt up. Fineman had even brought them into this room with me and tried to make me reach into Gary again. And I'd laughed in their faces.

Presenting this lineup to me was probably just another attempt to get me to demonstrate my power, but why include the matchbook? It wasn't from inside anybody. Then again, maybe Dr. Fineman didn't know that.

"What do you think of my little peace offering?" he asked, making me jump and yank my hand away.

I whirled around to find him coming through the open door.

Behind him came Anthony, a smirk on his face and a gun in his hand, which did not bode well for me.

"These are your things, are they not?" Dr. Fineman asked, coming toward me. "Some important to you. Some important to others."

I moved around the table, putting it between us, my hands clutching the back of the metal chair so they wouldn't reach out and strangle him.

He stopped on the other side, looking down at the contents lined up across its dull surface. "Now, now. No reason to be frightened of me as long as you cooperate," he said, smiling in a way that made me want to curl up into a fetal position. "How about a little trade? You tell me about each of the items on this table, and I'll tell you something you want to know."

"You're a psycho and a pathological liar," I said. "That's all I really need to know."

"You think I've lied to you?" he asked, tilting his head to one side and examining me. "Perhaps I have, but not nearly as much as some. And I assure you, I do have information you want and need. I have been researching PSS for the last twenty-three years. I know more about how it works and what it can do than any human being on this planet. There are things I can tell you about your hand that no one else can."

"If you know so much, why ask me about the things on the table? Can't you go poke them in your lab and figure it out yourself?"

"Stubborn girl," he said. "I've already studied and tested every one of these objects. Of course, you already know where each one came from, what poor soul they belonged to before you so kindly relieved them of it. What you probably don't know is that each of these items has a unique PSS signature."

I tried not to show my interest, but he must have seen it in my eyes.

"Oh yes, they all resonate PSS." He reached down to pick up the dog tags. "Take these, for example. Their signature is a match to the razor blades I took from you in Greenfield." He rubbed the tags between his long, pale fingers. "They also match the PSS signature of the blood I took from your classmate, Miss Wainwright. Of course, because of this, it was easy to conclude they were made from the blades. And I already know what they can do. It is what your hand does during the extraction process that I'm most curious about."

Wait. Something he'd just said didn't make sense. All of these items resonated PSS? Even the matchbook? I hadn't taken that out of anyone.

"How does it change the very nature of what you take?" He droned on. "How does it bend their signature to your will? That is what my lab won't tell me."

"And neither will I," I said. *Because I don't know, you pompous ass. But even if I did…*

"Oh, you will," he said, dropping the tags back on the table with a clatter, his eyes falling to the cube. "Otherwise, you are of no use to me, and a scientist has no room for things which do not serve his research or his purpose."

"I'm not going to put that cube back in you. It's not gonna happen."

"No, no, of course not. That would be unwise."

His eyes came back to me. "Especially after you've so carelessly put something inside of it which shouldn't be there. We will have to find some other means of experimentation." Was that fear in his voice? Was he afraid I'd try to put the cube back in him against his will? What would happen if I did? Would he become trigger-happy like Jason on top of his mad-scientist psychosis? Would he fall into a coma again?

"We must narrow down our options," he said, picking up the cube and tucking it in his lab coat pocket. "We must select the best possible test subject."

"That's not what I meant, and you know it. I'm not sticking my hand into anyone for you." *Until you take this cuff off and I skewer you and Anthony like a giant CAMFer shish-kabob.*

"We could bring in your friend, Passion," Fineman threatened. "She might be willing to volunteer if Anthony was convincing enough."

"Fuck you! You don't have Passion. I saw her get away."

"How do you know we didn't pick her up after that?" His eyes bored into mine.

I couldn't help myself. My eyes darted to the tags. I glanced away quickly, but not quickly enough. He'd noticed and he picked them up again, holding them out and swinging them in front of me. "You can feel her through these. Can't you?"

I looked over the doctor's shoulder and saw Anthony smirking.

"Anthony," Dr. Fineman said. A word. A name. A threat.

I tried to run. I bolted away from the table but

Anthony was on me, seizing me by a fistful of my hair. He yanked me back and slammed me down into the chair, twisting my left arm behind it. Cold metal gouged into my wrist and I heard a handcuff click into place. Then he grabbed my right arm and pinned it to the table, forcing my ghost hand palm up, the control cuff they'd put on it scraping the table, metal against metal.

Dr. Fineman dropped the dog tags into my hand, curling my fingers around them, squeezing them into a fist.

I couldn't stop him, couldn't phase my fingers through his or anything. With the control cuff on, my ghost hand was useless.

But I tried not to think of Passion. I didn't want her to feel this. In my mind I imagined a two-way mirror, just like the one in the room, but I was the one standing behind it, separate and only an observer.

"Where is she?" Dr. Fineman demanded, putting his face in mine. "What do you see?"

"What?" I sneered "You're not a fucking mind reader? Too bad for you."

Anthony's fist crashed into my right ear, sending my neck whipping to the side, pain thundering in my head.

It broke my concentration and, for a moment, I saw Passion clearly in a different room than before. She was sitting next to a hospital bed with monitors and machines in the background.

The person in the bed was Marcus.

Marcus was alive.

He wasn't stuck at the bottom of the river where I'd left him.

And he certainly wasn't on a mission for the CAMFers because they had Danielle. That had just been another of Fineman's lies.

Marcus was alive and safe.

I didn't feel the throbbing in my head anymore. I didn't care about the pain or the trickle of blood down my neck. I didn't even feel the next blow from Anthony, or the next.

If Marcus was alive, he would come for me.

He would get up out of that bed, and he would come.

This must be the same CAMFer compound they'd held him in, so he'd know exactly where to find me.

All I had to do was wait and survive until he did.

10

MARCUS

"So, how are we feeling today?" Reiny asked in her chirpy nurse voice.

I wasn't really awake yet. I'd been dreaming about a girl with a PSS hand who was definitely NOT my sister. This girl was dark and mysterious. She wore black lipstick, had a killer curvy body, and a challenging gleam in her eyes. And her PSS only went up to her wrist, not to the elbow like Danielle's. In the dream, we'd been in a bathtub together, the girl's bare legs pinned between mine, her wet T-shirt clinging to her—

"It looks like you're feeling much better," Reiny said, glancing down at the bed sheet.

Fuck. I was tenting it like a big top at a three-ring circus. I quickly rolled onto my side, staring out the window and trying to think of something else, anything else, plus ignore the fact that a pretty nurse had just commented on my morning boner.

"It's nothing to be ashamed of," she said. "It means your blood is flowing to all the right places again."

Shut up. Now. Please.

"Were you thinking of something in particular? A memory, maybe?"

"No," I said, desperate to distract her from that particular topic of conversation. "What day is it?"

Someone had pulled the curtains aside a little, and the trees outside were stark and bare, just a few brown leaves clinging to limp stems.

Limp stems. Think about limp stems. There, that was better.

"It's Thursday," she said, crossing my line of vision and casually pulling the curtains all the way closed.

There was something about the way she did it, as if she didn't want me to look outside. There hadn't been anything out there except the bare, brown trees. Why wouldn't she want me to see them? I was used to decoding the most subtle passive-aggressive cues. You didn't survive the foster care system without learning to decipher the dark secrets every human being was trying to hide. And Reiny was definitely hiding something.

"Your speech is almost completely back to normal, which is extraordinary," she said, coming to the side of my bed and checking the IV bag plugged into my arm. "And your vitals are all improving by the hour. I've never seen anyone heal this quickly."

I'd always healed fast, even when I hadn't had Danielle's help. But after the accident, it had gotten even faster. Thanks goodness I wasn't in a normal hospital, or they'd be calling in the government by now. Reiny seemed surprised, but not freaked out, and she worked for my uncle, so he'd probably schooled her in keeping the family secrets.

I hadn't noticed her nose ring before, but it made me wonder how old she was. Thirty, maybe, but it was hard to be sure. She was petite and pretty, and I was guessing she was of Native American descent. The silver ring in her nose stood out against her smooth brown skin.

Fuck. I looked past her to the window again, trying to think of anything NOT related to attractive women.

"So, you work for my uncle," I said. My uncle. Just the topic I needed to dampen my enthusiasm. "How'd you land such a great—" I couldn't think of the word. It just wasn't there. I knew what I meant. I just didn't have the word for it.

"Job?" she tried to fill it in for me.

"No," I shook my head. "More like music."

"Aha, gig," she said, smiling. "You still have a few gaps in your speech, but don't worry. It will come back. The less you think about it, the easier it will be. And if you lose a word, just skip over it. You're doing amazingly well, considering."

"Considering what?" I asked, since she seemed so talkative. "What happened to me?"

She stepped back and set my chart aside, looking at me, evaluating me. Not my health. She was weighing something else.

"You were found at the bottom of a river," she said finally, her directness surprising me.

"You'd been clinically dead for more than seventeen hours, and we had to get your body back to normal levels of oxygenation, warmth, and blood flow before your chest could initiate its natural reboot."

"I was in a river?" The water. I remembered the water. "How did I get there?"

"We aren't sure," she said, but now she was lying. She obviously knew more than she was letting on.

"How did you find me?" My mind raced with questions, but I'd have to be sly about how I approached this. Sometimes, if people didn't want to tell me something directly, I could come in from the side and get them to tell me indirectly.

"The girl that was here in your room yesterday," Reiny said, "her name is Passion, and she found you. Then your uncle had you brought here for specialized care and recovery."

So, what was the connection between this girl Passion and my uncle? How had she known who I was, and who he was, or that we were related? My Uncle Alex hadn't shown the remotest interest in me since he'd killed my parents for leaving The Hold. Why the sudden benevolence now? He must want something from me. That was the only reason I could think of. And how had Passion found me at the bottom of a river? Maybe the CAMFers had dumped me, thinking I was dead, and she'd witnessed it. What if she knew what had happened to Danielle? I needed to talk to her. She might have a clue about where they'd taken my sister.

"Can I talk to her?" I asked. "I mean, it sounds like she saved me, and I'd like to thank her."

"I think that would be fine," Reiny said. "The more you converse, the more your language skills will come back. But you need to understand you've suffered something very similar to a stroke. You not only lost language function, you also have some short-term memory loss. This is a common side-effect of the time you spent without normal brain function, and we expect it to come back gradually on its own. In fact, it's best that it comes back naturally. You shouldn't force it by asking too many questions."

The memory loss thing didn't surprise me. Everything was pretty jumbled in my head, and as hard as I tried, I couldn't piece together the details of what had happened after the cops had caught me and Danielle. Sometimes I got flashes of people and events, like waking dreams with no context. The most frequent one was the girl with the PSS hand, but there were others. Other people my age with PSS, on a camping trip or something. And then in a big, fancy house. But if Danielle had been taken, and the CAMFers had tossed me in a river, thinking I was dead, how much memory could I have lost? There was no way those flashes could be real. What if the CAMFers had done something to me before they'd thrown me in the river? What if they'd fucked up my brain on purpose? What if they'd taken memories out and put false ones in? Shit. How could I trust anything I remembered?

"I won't force it," I agreed, the lie coming as easily to my tongue as the truth. Probably easier.

How convenient for my uncle that I'd lost my memories and shouldn't ask about them. Now his people could tell me whatever they wanted, and I'm sure he'd be the hero of it all and I'd be the ungrateful nephew.

"Would you like to see your cousin, Samantha, too," Reiny asked, "or would that be too much?"

"I would love to see Sam." The words burst out of me. My little cousin, Sam, the skinny girl who'd followed me around asking questions about *everything*. I hadn't seen her for ten years.

"Okay then." Reiny took hold of my arm and began removing my IV. "I think we can take this out so you can move around a little."

"Thanks," I said, turning my head away so I didn't have to watch her pull the needle out.

"Remember, try to focus on the here and now." Her cool fingers pressed a cotton ball and Band- Aid to my inner arm. "If you start to feel overwhelmed at any point, just let them know or push this, and I'll come running."

I turned to see her pointing at a nurse-call button attached to the bed.

"Oh, and are you hungry?" she asked. "I could have someone bring up some breakfast."

"I'm starving," I said, recognizing the smell drifting up to the room from downstairs. It was bacon. Frying bacon.

"Good. That's an excellent sign too. Oh, and I thought you might like to put on some real clothes before you have guests, so I brought these." She pointed to a neatly folded pair of boxers, jeans, and a T-shirt on the stand next to the bed. "Do you need help getting dressed?

"No," I blurted. *God, no.* But I couldn't wait to get out of the hospital gown I was wearing. There was a serious draft up my ass.

"Okay. I'll give you some time before I send anyone in then."

"Thanks," I said.

"Of course, Marcus," she said, turning toward the door.

"Not Marcus," I corrected her. "*David.* Marcus is—" I couldn't find the words again.

"Marcus is your middle name, but I thought you preferred to go by it."

"No," I said. Except Passion had called me Marcus too. Why was everyone calling me Marcus and why did I feel that when Reiny had done it, it had been some kind of test?

"Right. My mistake. David it is." She smiled as she slipped out into the hallway and shut the door behind her.

Ten minutes later, I was dressed and pacing in front of the window, the curtains pulled back.

When I heard the door open, I turned to see Passion come in first, followed by a willowy gorgeous girl I could barely believe was my little cousin Sam. But it was. There was no mistaking those eyes and that smile.

"David," she said, rushing to me and throwing herself in my arms almost before I could open them.

I crushed her to me, feeling the strongest sense of déjà vu I'd ever experienced. Had we done this before? No. I hadn't seen Sam since she'd been six and I'd been seven. But we had been close back then; Danielle and Sam and I had been like the Three Amigos.

Now, holding her to me and inhaling the smell of her, it was like those ten lost years were nothing. This was Sam. She knew me. I knew her. And I could trust her.

"Um, you're hurting me," she squeaked, pulling herself out of my embrace, and that was when I noticed she was holding herself oddly, favoring one side of her body almost as if she were protecting it.

"What's wrong?" I asked, reaching out and pulling her shirt up without giving it a second thought.

"Hey!" She smacked my hand away and yanked her shirt back over the bandages wrapped around her ribcage. "Watch it, Cuz. I'm a big girl now."

"You certainly are," I said, grinning. "But it looks like you're still getting into—" What was the word? I couldn't find it, so I rushed on. "What happened?"

"I got shot," she said, "but it's just a graze. Nothing too serious."

"You got shot?" I asked, incredulous. She had to be pulling my leg. "Yeah, right. Who shot you? And why? I thought your dad had super security covering your ass all the time."

"Yeah, well, I sort of ditched all the security," she said, looking chagrined. "Not the wisest thing I've ever done, I know, but I had my reasons."

"Was it a guy?" I asked. Sam had always been strong-headed, an extreme extrovert, and she loved to be the center of attention. I could totally see her shaking my uncle's security to sneak out and meet up with some love-sick admirer.

"No, it wasn't a guy," she scoffed, punching me in the arm. "And it wasn't a girl either," her eyes flashed to Passion and away again, but not before I noticed the other girl blushing. "I was trying to save The Hold, you jackass."

"Save The Hold from what?"

"My parents," she sighed. "Mom is having an affair, and her new fuck-buddy and Dad are fighting over The Hold like it's the one ring to rule them all."

"Shit. That sucks. I mean, the affair part." So, my aunt and uncle were having marital problems. That didn't exactly surprise me, but I still felt bad for Sam. As for The Hold falling apart, that was the best news I'd heard in a long time. "But why save The Hold? If they want to destroy it, why not let them?"

"Listen, I know why you hate The Hold," Sam said, crossing to a chair and sinking into it. "I get it. I really do. But it doesn't have to be like that. We could change it. We could make it better. We could make it our own."

"And by 'we'—you mean the Marked?" The title was like a bad taste in my mouth. "We aren't better than anyone, Sam, just because we were born with PSS." I didn't want to believe she'd become like my uncle. I needed her not to be. I needed an ally.

"I know that," she snapped, heat in her voice. "It isn't about being better. It's about being united." Her eyes rose to mine, pain spilling out of them. "It's about never losing anyone ever again."

"That's noble," I said. She was talking about me and Danielle and my parents. "But it's also naïve," I added. "Whenever people form a group based on an 'us and them' mentality, someone gets lost." The girl with the ghost hand flashed into my mind. She was grinning at me. Like she was proud.

"They said you were having trouble talking and thinking," Sam grumbled, looking accusingly at Passion who was still hanging back by the door as if she might bolt. "You seem just as articulate and stubborn as ever to me."

"You're right," I said, grinning. "I wasn't even thinking about it and all the words were right there."

"And what about your memories?" Passion asked cautiously, coming further into the room. "Are they coming back too?"

"No." I shook my head. "I get flashes sometimes, but they don't make any sense. Reiny said you found me at the bottom of a river, but I have no idea how I got there. Did you see anything? Did you see them take Danielle? And where the hell are we? It doesn't look like Oregon out there." I gestured at the window. "Where are all the evergreens? It doesn't even look like spring. It looks like fall." Fuck all Reiny's dire warnings about me pushing too hard. I needed to know what the hell was going on. "How long was I out before I rebooted? What's the date?"

"It's Friday, October 28th, and we're in Indiana," Passion said, her lips trembling, her eyes full of sympathy. "You were only out for seventeen hours, but you've lost your memories of the last eight months."

"Passion!" Sam said angrily, standing up and grabbing my arm to steady me. "We aren't supposed to tell him. He isn't ready."

"He can see out the window with his own eyes," Passion said. "You know him. Do you really think he's just going to let that go?"

Eight months. How could I have lost eight months? *Oh God, what could have happened to Danielle in eight months?* I had to get out of here. I had to go after her. But I wasn't even in Oregon anymore. How had I gotten to Indiana?

The door to my room swung open and my Uncle Alex came in holding a tray of food.

Passion and Sam turned and looked at him.

"Is it a bad time?" he asked, looking from Sam to me and back again.

I shook off Sam's hand and launched myself at the man who had taken everything from me. Again.

This time I was going to kill him for it.

11

MARCUS

Slamming into my uncle was more satisfying than I'd imagined, and I'd imagined it a lot. I reveled in the look of fear on his face and the way the breakfast tray went flying, bacon and eggs erupting into the air around us.

I pressed my arm into the cartilage of his windpipe, pinning him to the door. My other hand found the lock, turning the deadbolt into place. No one was going to come rescue him now, none of his bodyguards or entourage. It was him and me, man to man. I wasn't a defenseless little boy anymore. I was bigger than he was. Younger. Stronger. All the weakness in my legs was gone. I had saved a life's worth of strength for this one moment.

"David, no!" Samantha cried, moving toward us. Out of the corner of my eye I saw Passion grab her hand and hold her back.

"They need to settle this," she said to my cousin. "You need to let them."

Nice sentiment, but it wasn't going to happen. There was nothing for me and my uncle to settle. I was going to hurt him the way he'd hurt me and Danielle and my parents. I would run him over, leaving him mangled and abandoned beside a road somewhere. I would make him feel pain, endless, insatiable pain.

"You killed them," I spat into his face. "You ran us into a fucking train, your own family, your own sister."

"No," he squeezed out, trying to shake his head.

"Yes!" I pressed my arm even harder into his throat. He didn't get to say no to me. Not ever again.

"David," Samantha pleaded behind me, "don't do this. Let him explain."

"There's nothing to fucking explain," I snarled at her, never taking my eyes off of him. "I was there. I know what happened."

His face was turning red and his eyes were bulging a little. He was running out of air.

Footsteps pounded up the stairwell beyond the door. Someone downstairs had heard the noise, and they were coming to save him. Too bad there was a solid oak door between him and his lackeys.

"David, please," Samantha said, laying her hand gently on my bulging bicep. "He's my father."

I turned just enough to look at her.

Passion was standing behind her, still holding her other hand.

I looked back at my uncle.

I could kill him. It would only take a little longer. He was gasping for breath now, struggling weakly under my arm.

I looked back at Sam, her eyes full of fear and pain, so like Danielle's.

"Fuck!" I roared, pulling myself off my uncle and pacing to the window, my back turned against all of them. I was too weak. I couldn't do it. Not in front of Sam.

My uncle was coughing and hacking, trying to catch his breath.

There was a loud banging at the door and the knob rattled frantically. "Everything okay in there?" a man's voice boomed. "Mr. James, are you all right?"

"Yes, I'm fine," my uncle called back hoarsely. It was hardly convincing.

"Sir, do you need assistance?" the voice persisted.

"No," my uncle said, louder this time. "I'm fine. Stand down."

"Yes sir," the voice said, but I didn't hear the guy go back downstairs. He was waiting out there for me. I'd lost my chance, my only chance. My uncle would open that door, and I'd never be alone with him again. I'd never get the satisfaction I'd yearned for all these years.

I turned and looked at him, a pompous man in an expensive suit with yellow flecks of egg in his perfectly kept hair. God, I hated him and the look of self-righteous pity in his eyes. How could he pity me when he was the one who'd fucked up my life in the first place?

"Why'd you do it?" I asked. I couldn't murder him in front of Sam, but I could expose him. It wasn't anything compared to what he'd done to me, but it was still something. "I want to know, really. What's your justification for killing me and my parents? I'm dying to hear it."

"I didn't kill them," he said, moving away from the door into the middle of the room, a hand still rubbing his neck. "That is something I've wanted to explain to you for a long time. Will you at least sit?" He gestured at the nearest chair. "You haven't been well."

"No," I said, crossing my arms over my chest. "I'll stand."

Samantha and Passion sat though, each taking a chair near the bed within reach of each other. Sam was chewing her bottom lip nervously, looking back and forth between her father and me. I had a feeling she didn't know what he was about to say any more than I did.

"I understand why you believe what you do," my uncle said, spreading his hands in a gesture of peace, "and I deeply regret you've been led to believe it all these years. Yes, I was in a car following you and your parents as you fled The Hold that night. But I wasn't chasing you. I was escorting you."

"Escorting us?" I asked, my voice dripping with sarcasm.

"Yes." He said. "I was trying to ensure your escape. I would never hold your mother to something against her will. She was my sister, and I loved her. When she told me of her plans to flee The Hold, I offered my help, and I wasn't alone.

Bo, the man standing out in the hallway right now, was a childhood friend of mine and your mother's, and he was with me that night. If you don't believe me, you can ask him."

"Yeah, right," I scoffed. "Because he's likely to tell me the truth. Did your plan to 'escort' us also involve escorting us right into an oncoming train?"

"No." He shook his head, pain flaring in his eyes. "That was a terrible accident."

"I bet it was," I mocked him.

"It was," he said, his voice growing cold and hard. "The Hold sent someone after you, just as we'd feared. The plan was for Bo and me to act as the buffer between your car and theirs, and that's exactly what we did. We held the pursuers back, running them off the road into a deep culvert. But we didn't want to hurt or kill anyone, so we stopped to make sure they were all right. When we saw them crawling out of their car, we got back in ours and raced to catch up with you. To this day, I have no idea why your father felt compelled to try and beat that train. It makes no sense. You weren't being chased anymore. There was no reason for it. When that whistle started blowing and blowing, I didn't understand. Not until we heard the terrible noise and came upon the crash a few minutes later." My uncle stopped, rubbing his hand across his eyes.

"Even if any of that is true," I said, "which it isn't, you left us there. You turned and ran. How can you possibly justify that? You left your sister's body lying in the dirt and—"

"No!" he snapped, glaring at me. "I didn't leave her." And then, more softly, "And she wasn't dead."

"What?" My whole body went rigid, my mind spinning. What did he mean? Had he spoken to her? Had this bastard been the last person on earth to speak to my mother? No—he didn't deserve that. It should have been me. Why couldn't it have been me?

"When we came upon the scene, she was badly injured," he choked out, as if it hurt him, as if he were the one who'd just been gutted by the promise of a dead mother come back to say her last words. "Your father was—he died instantly. We couldn't find Danielle. As for you—we thought you were gone, but your mother knew better. She told me about your ability, and Danielle's. It was the main reason she'd run from The Hold. She didn't want them to find out and exploit both of you."

"That's bullshit, and you know it," I said. "She left because they were going to force her to divorce dad and marry someone with PSS. She told us that." He was trying to put this on me and Danielle, make it our fault instead of his. What had she really said to him before she'd died? Had she asked for us? Had she asked for me?

"I know that's what she told you, but that was only part of it. Her last request," he said, fake tears rolling down his fake face, "was that I let you go. She wanted me to go back to The Hold to lead it, and change it. But she wanted you and Danielle to have the freedom to decide for yourself. She made me promise not to interfere. She made me swear on my life to protect you from The Hold, and I kept my promise. I've kept it for ten years."

No. That could not be true.

"You're a fucking liar," I told him, turning my back so he wouldn't see the tears on my face. Oh, he'd reeled me in good. He'd taken me back to that night, to the broken, devastated child I'd been, enticing me with my mother's last words. But there was no way in hell her last request had been to abandon me and Danielle to fend for ourselves as wards of the state. I would never believe that.

"I'm not lying," he said, "and I'm still keeping that promise, even though it's cost me dearly."

"Cost you?" I laughed, an ugly choking laugh, and wiped my sleeve across my face before turning back to him. "What has it ever cost you? Danielle and I grew up being tossed from family to family. They tried to split us up, over and over again. Do you have any idea what they did to us? What they did to her? Don't talk to me about what it cost you."

"You're right," he said. "That isn't fair of me. We've all paid the price, you and Danielle most of all. I promise you, your mother never anticipated that. She loved you both deeply. She wanted the best future possible for you. She couldn't have foreseen how difficult it would be, or how much the climate would change toward children with PSS in such a short time."

How dare he throw me that bone? *Your mother loved you, just not very well.* Fuck him.

"So, you made her a promise, and you left her to die," I summarized. I wanted his story to be over. I wanted him out of my face, so I could get the hell away from him and everything he stood for. The security on the farmhouse wasn't tight, and my window wasn't too high. I was pretty sure I could jump out of it without hurting myself, and the bedroom we were in faced a wooded area, so it would be easy to escape unseen.

"I didn't leave her to die," my uncle said, rubbing his hand across his face again. "We made her as comfortable as possible and called an ambulance. Bo went to try and find Danielle. We thought with her ability, she might be able to help, but he couldn't find her. He did find you, however, though you hadn't rebooted. Your head injuries were severe. Neither of us thought you would make it, despite what your mother had told us. And then she—passed—before the ambulance got there. And yes, we left, and I assure you it was the hardest thing I've ever done in my life. But we thought all of you were dead and staying would only have complicated things."

"Yes, well, we wouldn't have wanted things to get complicated for you," I commented snidely. I was so over this.

"You think they didn't?" he asked heatedly. "I had to tell Samantha you were dead," he looked at his daughter, a haunted look in his eyes. "I have never seen a child so devastated. She thought it was her fault. She even stopped eating and drinking. We were afraid we were going to lose her too."

I had actually forgotten Samantha and Passion were still in the room. That's how much he'd gotten to me. And I didn't like what I saw as I looked at them. Both their faces were wet, but where Samantha had pity swimming in her eyes, Passion had a look of naked understanding. When she caught my eyes, I looked away. I didn't want to be seen by those eyes. Not right now.

"When I discovered you and Danielle had survived," my uncle droned on, "I didn't know what to do. I'd made a promise to your mother, but I almost didn't keep it. I almost came for you. Maybe I should have. I still don't know. I took leadership of The Hold a year later, and I moved the headquarters to Indy to give you both space. Since then, I have dedicated my life to making sure no member of The Hold ever feels in danger of being trapped or controlled the way your mother did. But now that's out of my hands. When I was given the choice to fight for The Hold or protect you from it, I chose my promise to her. I will always choose that promise. You are no prisoner of The Hold here, David. I am no longer its leader."

"What a nice loophole for you," I said.

"It's no loophole," he said. "If you want to leave right now, you can. I hope you'll stay, at least until you're fully healed, but the choice is yours."

Outside in the hallway, I heard voices. Reiny was questioning the guy out there, and she didn't sound happy.

"Gee, thanks for the permission I didn't need," I told him. I wanted to leave. Every instinct in me said to flee. But I was going to stay, at least until I could source more information about Danielle and what had happened to her. Still, I wasn't going to kiss his ass. "As for the rest, I don't buy a word of it. My dad conveniently drives into a train. My mom makes you promise to abandon us. And you're the hero of it all, protecting the innocent. That is NOT my fucking life story. I may have lost my memory, but I'm certainly not going to fill the holes in it with that crap. But nice spin.

I give you an '*A*' for effort. Unfortunately, you get an '*F*' for believability."

"I understand," he said, sounding sad and resigned. "It's a lot to take in, and you're still recovering."

God, he deserved an Emmy.

"What the hell is going on in there?" Reiny yelled, banging on the door. "Unlock this right now. Goddammit, I take one small break— you better not be upsetting my patient."

"I'll leave you alone," my uncle said, turning to the door and unlocking it. "But if you ever want to talk, I'm here." He opened the door, slipping out past Reiny who glared at him on her way in.

"What happened?" she demanded, looking at the breakfast all over the room, her eyes roaming over Samantha and Passion and finally settling on me. "Did you remember you didn't like eggs?"

12

OLIVIA

When I came to, I wasn't back in my cell. I was still handcuffed to the chair in the interrogation room with Dr. Fineman and Anthony. I was slumped over the table, my hair wet with blood from my ear. It wasn't crusting though, which meant I'd only been out a few minutes.

"Welcome back," Anthony said, grabbing my hair and lifting my head up, leaving a brownish-red smear on the table where it had been. "No time for naps. We're not done with you yet."

My head was spinning, and I felt like I might throw up. If I did, I would aim for the doctor.

And that's when I noticed the new guy in the room. He was a CAMFer soldier, an older guy I didn't recognize with a prominent scar across his right cheek, running from eye to chin. I did the best I could to pretend he wasn't intimidating, but he was. I had a bad feeling the torture was about to ramp up a notch. Great. Something to look forward to.

"This is Major Tom," Dr. Fineman introduced him, smiling. "And he has somewhat of a bone to pick with you."

Really? Major Tom? Was that his real name or was he just a huge David Bowie fan? Either way, I was pretty sure I'd never met the guy. And if he was out to get me, he should probably get in line.

"You see," Dr. Fineman said, "The Major had a reputation as one of the best knife fighters on this continent. I say 'had' because it was somewhat ruined when you stole a knife from his person and used it to stab three of his men."

Shit. This was the guy who'd been carrying me the night of the Eidolon. I hadn't seen his face because I'd been slung over his shoulder. But I had reached straight into his back with my ghost hand and pulled out a knife, the same knife that was still sitting on the table in front of me. My eyes flashed to it.

"Yes," Dr. Fineman said, smiling at me. "Now you understand." He turned to Anthony. "Let's have the other hand for this," he directed.

Anthony fumbled at my flesh hand, unlocking the handcuffs. Then he yanked my left arm onto the table, pinning my hand palm-up, just like he'd done before with my ghost hand.

I didn't struggle. It wouldn't do any good. Anthony had proved many times he was stronger than me.

Still, sometimes I could outsmart him if I was patient enough. He wasn't the brightest crayon in the box. For example, he'd just forgotten to recuff my ghost hand to the chair, and it was now tucked in my lap, hidden under the table.

Dr. Fineman picked up the knife, turning it in his hands. Then he lowered it gently, setting it in my open palm, handle-first.

I was never willingly going to do what they wanted me to. They were going to have to force my hand every inch of the way.

Anthony squeezed my wrist even harder as Dr. Fineman closed my fingers around the knife.

Suddenly, I was standing at the door, huge and looming, looking at the pitiful, bloody, minus girl. *No, at me. I was looking at me.*

"She's in my fucking head," I—he—Major Tom said, stumbling back toward the door. "I can feel her there. I can feel where she is."

"Hold your ground," Dr. Fineman barked at me— *no, him. I wasn't him.*—and I held steady at the door, remembering my training and honoring my rank. This little cunt wasn't going to embarrass me a second time.

What the fuck? That hadn't been my thought. It had been his thought in my head.

I looked down at the knife in my hand and tried desperately to unclench my fingers, but Dr. Fineman squeezed them even harder around it.

"Tell me what you feel," he ordered, but he wasn't talking to me.

"I can feel—where she is," Major Tom stammered, sounding confused. "But it's never been this strong before. Usually, I just get a sense of where they are and how they feel. I've never heard thoughts before."

Fuck. Those weren't his words. They were mine. He'd just voiced exactly what I was thinking.

"Apparently, I am a mind reader," Dr. Fineman whispered in my face, his breath hot and sickeningly sweet.

"How?" I asked him, trying to fend off the assault of Major Tom's thoughts. "What did you do to the knife?"

"Just a little enhancement of its PSS signature in my lab," he said, grinning. "I wasn't sure it would work until now, but it never hurts to experiment a little."

"I don't want her in my head," I told him, the words on my lips like a foreign language. "Let me kill her."

"Don't be silly," Dr. Fineman said, looking over his shoulder at Major Tom. "I have so many things planned for her first."

"Like Operation, the wacky doctor game?" Major Tom asked, his expression growing puzzled. "Or Twister? Or should I go play with my small dick in the hallway until you let her mindfuck me again?" He threw his hand over his mouth, his face turning bright red. Then, he lowered it, balling it into a fist as he stepped toward me.

Now he knew how it felt to have someone else put their thoughts in your mouth.

"Major, you are dismissed," Dr. Fineman said, letting go of my hand and pointing at the door.

But I didn't let go of the knife.

Or Major Tom's mind.

If Dr. Fineman liked experiments so much, surely he wouldn't mind me conducting a little one of my own.

Run. Now. I screamed in my head.

Major Tom charged forward, crashing into Dr. Fineman and the table like a linebacker, sending everything on it flying.

Dr. Fineman was on the floor, Major Tom on top of him.

Their impact against the table had shoved my chair back, slamming it into Anthony and knocking him down. Thankfully, I was relatively unscathed.

I pulled my ghost hand out from under the table and flipped Major Tom's knife into it. I couldn't cut my way out of the room, not against three men plus the guards outside, but I had to try something. This was my chance to thwart Dr. Fineman by doing something he'd never expect.

Do it. Put it back. The last thing you want Fineman to have is a fucking mind-reading knife.

I leapt over the table, my arm raised, and plunged the knife down into Major Tom's back.

It sank through his clothes and skin like they were nothing, smooth and easy, going in up to my hand on the hilt and further. My ghost hand slipped into him too, into the space that is nowhere and everywhere. I felt a familiar zap run up my arm, almost like an electrical shock, and the knife finally found its place in Major Tom's psyche, a perfect knife-shaped hole in his soul.

She did it. She put it back in me just like he said. And I'm still alive.

Not my thoughts.

Oh, shit.

I yanked my hand out of the Major and my eyes fell on Dr. Fineman, still pinned beneath him.

He was looking up at me, a smugly satisfied smirk on his face, the controller for my cuff held out in his hand.

"You fuck," I said, just as my arm grew numb and flopped to my side.

"Now, now," he said, as Major Tom climbed off of him and they both got up. "No reason to be crass. That went nearly as well as I'd planned." He brushed himself off, checking to make sure his precious cube was still securely in his coat pocket. "And now we know you can put things back into people without harming them. Very good work for the day. Very good work indeed."

He had planned this entire thing.

And I'd fallen for it like an idiot.

I wasn't even sure if the idea to put the knife back in the Major had been mine. Why would I do that when I knew it was exactly what the doctor wanted to find out? I wouldn't. It must have been Major Tom's idea, his thought influence. They'd gotten in my head, literally, and I'd panicked, and I'd played right into Dr. Fineman's plan.

"You were saying something earlier about mindfucks, I believe," Dr. Fineman said, dragging me to my feet and handing me off to Anthony. "Take her back to her cell, and give her extra rations.

She's been such a good girl today."

"Yes sir," Anthony said, shoving me toward the door.

Back in my cell, I touched my ear tentatively. It had already scabbed over, and my headache was gone too, so I just brushed away the dried blood, watching it fall in brown flakes onto my dingy clothes.

Anthony had left me a tray of food, piled high with mashed potatoes and gravy, juicy meatloaf, and green bean casserole. It even included a tall glass of lemonade with ice, plastic utensils, and a napkin. My stomach clenched and groaned just looking at it. The smell was amazing, like the food was floating in the air around me, but I'd been resisting my urge to devour it.

They were rewarding me for my cooperation, feeding me because I'd been stupid enough to play right into their hands, and that pissed me off. But did it really matter? The food didn't know the difference and neither did my hunger.

I picked up the plastic spork and started shoveling stuff into my mouth.

God, it was delicious, and warm, and the best thing I'd ever tasted.

Within seconds it was gone. Even the lemonade, which I'd guzzled so fast I'd spilled it down the front of my shirt and gotten a brain freeze.

I then licked the tray clean, setting it down on the cement slab next to me and belching like a sailor.

Almost miraculously, my head began to clear. How long had it been since I'd had a real meal? I couldn't remember. It was kind of amazing how having a full belly made everything a bit more bearable.

I looked around my cell, really taking in the details of it for the first time. It was small, maybe eight feet square, with no windows and one heavy metal door. The floor was cobbled stone, worn smooth by years of wear, and there was a metal toilet in one corner. The walls were made from rough-hewn stone, not brick or cement blocks, and there were cracks between them where old mortar was beginning to crumble. In one wall, near the ceiling, there was a metal vent, probably for air flow, but it was way too small for me to fit into, so I wasn't getting out that way. Assessing what I saw, I wasn't getting out any way at all. At least, not directly from the cell.

But I'd seen Marcus. He was alive, and he would come for me. As long as I was here, he'd know where to look. This had to be the same place they'd kept him and Danielle. Dr. Fineman had a big PSS lab here, just like Marcus had described. Plus, it was in Oregon.

How had Marcus escaped? I mean, I knew they'd extracted his PSS and not realized he could reboot. Then they'd left him for dead in a room by himself, unsecured, and he'd gotten away. But how had he gotten out of the compound itself with all its cameras and security? Now I wished I'd asked more about the details of that.

Either way, the question remained; should I stay put and wait for rescue or try to find a way out?

Maybe the answer was both. Even when Marcus did come for me, we'd need a new way out. The CAMFers had amped up security since he'd been here last, even more so since the Eidolon and all their new captives.

All their new captives.

That phrase echoed in my head, sounding strange and surreal.

Where had that idea come from? Had I seen any evidence the CAMFers had taken anyone alive but me?

No. But I knew there were others, as surely as I'd seen them, because I'd seen them in Major Tom's thoughts.

Oh my God.

I racked my brain for details. How many others were there, and where were they being held? But I got nothing. Either Major Tom hadn't known, or I hadn't accessed that part of his thoughts. Still, at least I knew I wasn't alone. I'd heard muffled voices coming from outside my cell a couple of times, but I'd just assumed it was Anthony or another guard. Who knew how big this place was or how many cell blocks it had? If there were other captives, I couldn't just leave them. When Marcus came for me, we'd need to get everyone out.

I had to figure out a way to get more information and see more of the compound.

I looked down at the spork in my hand, then over at the food tray and the cup, now drained of lemonade.

My stomach rumbled, warning me the rich food I'd just eaten wasn't going to come out quite as gently as it had gone in.

My eyes wandered to the metal toilet, a beautiful, devious plan clicking into place.

I turned my back to the camera in the corner of my cell, using my body to block what I was doing as I slammed the tray against my cement sleeping slab. It cracked on the first blow. A few more hits and it was reduced to shards in my hand. Thank goodness the cameras didn't have audio. I'd learned that little tidbit when Fineman had showed me the video feed of Danielle in her cell.

I kept whacking the tray and then the cup, breaking them into pieces. When I was done, I gathered the mess of plastic into the fold of my shirt, making sure each shard was small enough to fit down the toilet drain, yet large enough to give the interior plumbing a difficult time.

Then I walked over to the toilet and sat down, pants still up. I spread my legs, letting go of the cuff of my shirt and listening to the splash as the plastic cascaded down into the bowl. For good measure, I spun out a large handful of toilet paper and put it in as well. The way my stomach was sloshing and cramping, it wouldn't be long, and by then the toilet paper would be good and saturated, jamming whatever cracks and crannies the plastic hadn't filled.

I stood up and walked back to my slab, laying down and putting my face against its cool impassive surface, a smile blooming on my lips.

They had rewarded me with food.

Soon, I would reward it right back to them.

13

OLIVIA

The toilet trick worked like a charm; a very messy, foul-smelling charm.

I had to flush about five times before it got really good and clogged. That was before I deposited my personal contribution to the project and flushed a few more times.

It overflowed, of course. I'd planned that.

What I hadn't really thought about, though, was how long I'd have to wait in my shitty cell before someone came and discovered it.

The answer ended up being "all night."

After a couple of hours, I debated signaling the camera and waving frantically at the toilet, but decided against it. I wanted it to look like a plumbing issue, not sabotage. I wanted them to think I'd given up, that I was so downtrodden I didn't even have the guts to complain about a night spent wallowing in my own waste. I wanted them to move me to a new cell and forget about me.

The stench was pretty bad, though. I wasn't sure I'd be able to sleep, but it's kind of amazing how your senses become dulled to a smell eventually. Still, some part of my subconscious must have been aware. I had my usual swimming dream. The one where I start out as Marcus and then I'm trying to swim down to him, except this time I wasn't Marcus or myself. I was a giant sewer rat wearing a sombrero and an apron. Dreams can be fucking weird sometimes.

I woke up when Anthony rattled my cell door. It felt like morning, but I couldn't be sure. As I sat up he was coming in, an even nastier gleam in his eyes than usual. He looked like shit. Like maybe he'd slept less than I had and had woken up on the wrong side of his evil lair. But he only made it about two steps into the cell before the stench hit him.

"God! What the fuck?" He stopped mid-stride, throwing his arm over his mouth and nose as he turned toward the toilet in the corner, eyeing the thick puddle around it. Slowly, he turned back to me, disgust mixed with the usual hatred reflecting in his eyes. And there was something more. Fear. Under it all was a raw fear I'd never seen in him before.

That was when I noticed the handcuffs in his hands and the gun at his belt. He usually left my hands free when he manhandled me in the morning.

It seemed to make him feel more like I was a willing victim. And he saved his gun as a special show of threat when I was in the interrogation room with Dr. Fineman.

Maybe the thing with Major Tom had freaked him out more than I'd realized, and that was bad. I didn't want him to be on guard this morning. I wanted him to dismiss me, to forget I was any kind of threat.

"I guess my stomach wasn't ready for meatloaf," I said as timidly as I could.

"They don't pay me enough for this shit," he said, glaring at me and backing out of the cell, slamming and locking the door behind him.

"Hey, no. What about the toilet?" I called, but I could already hear his footsteps retreating down the corridor. He'd seemed really upset, disproportionately so, given the situation.

Great. What if he decided to just leave me there to suffocate in that smell? It had gotten worse overnight—decidedly worse—and my bladder was painfully full. I was going to have to pee soon, which would only make things worse.

About a half an hour later, Anthony returned, but he wasn't alone. Mike Palmer came into the cell right behind him, his eyes falling on me, the many scars on his face standing out under the pale fluorescent light.

I found myself plastered against stone, my back jammed into the corner of the bed slab, making myself as small and inaccessible as possible. This was a man I had tortured, and I was pretty sure payback was going to be a bitch.

Anthony had his gun in hand, ready and pointed in my direction, his fingers twitching to use it.

"Put the gun away," Palmer said, frowning at him. "She's not gonna hurt you."

That was the last thing I'd expected Palmer to say. He'd once been terrified of my PSS, just like Anthony was.

Anthony obeyed, reluctantly, slipping his gun back into its holster, but he didn't take his eyes off of me.

Palmer, on the other hand, completely ignored me. He crossed to the toilet and looked down into its ruined innards. "Nope," he said. "This won't be a quick fix. This place has ancient plumbing embedded in even older stone masonry. Doesn't take much to gum it up. We'll probably have to tear this floor out to get to it. Maybe even this whole wing, depending on where the clog is. In the meantime, we're gonna have to move her," he added, nodding in my direction.

Score one for me. At least that part of my plan had worked. No one had even noticed that the plasticware from last night was mysteriously missing.

"Fine," Anthony said, coming at me and grabbing me by the hair to pull me out of my hidey corner. "Where do you want her?"

"You enjoy beating up on young, defenseless women?" Mike Palmer asked, his voice low and mean. I was so startled I tried to lift my head to look at him—to see if he, of all people, was seriously coming to my defense—but my movement only made Anthony tighten his hold.

"If they're young, defenseless minus bitches, I do," Anthony growled. "It's better than she deserves. She's defective." He let go of me, shoving me back into my corner for emphasis. "You want her fuckin' mutation getting into your family line? Because it will if we let her live and breed."

"I'm not afraid of a bunch of kids with PSS," Mike Palmer said, which was pretty impressive, given what we'd done to him. "As for the breeding part, there's always sterilization."

Gee, thanks, Palmer. Way to be on my side. I loved being talked about like I was a stray cat, instead of a human being sitting right there in front of them. But I bit my tongue and shriveled back into my corner. The goal was to get into a new cell and see more of the compound on the way, not pick a fight with two of my worst enemies.

"You hear about what happened last night?" Anthony asked, his voice pitched low.

"Yeah," Mike answered, his face suddenly somber. "Such a shame. I still can't believe he'd—"

"He didn't," Anthony cut him off. "She did something to him." He jabbed a finger in my direction. "He was with her just hours before. That's how dangerous this one is. She's not like your little pet—"

"Shut up!" Mike Palmer snapped, stepping toward Anthony menacingly. "You need to learn when to keep your mouth shut, boy. And when not to." He looked at me, and Anthony's eyes followed. "If she did what you claim, *something* needs to be done."

A look passed between them, some silent message I couldn't decipher.

What were they talking about? What had happened last night, and who had it happened to? Dr. Fineman? Major Tom? Was that why Anthony had been acting so weird today? And what had to be done?

"Take her downstairs," Mike Palmer said. "Find her a cell down there while we deal with this mess."

"Sure," Anthony said, grinning wickedly. "And on the way we can stop in for a little visit with Major Tom." He meant it as some kind of threat, something to strike fear in my heart.

Instead, my heart soared.

If he took me to Major Tom, it would be an opportunity for me to see more of the compound. Unless he was just taking me to the interrogation cell again, but it didn't sound like it.

Mike Palmer frowned and turned back to the toilet I'd destroyed. Apparently, he was a CAMFer, a fireman, and a plumber. Who knew he had so many hidden talents?

"Come on, let's go," Anthony said, grabbing me and pulling me up.

As soon as my bare feet hit the cold cement, my bladder went into warning level urgent, but there was no way I was going to ask Anthony or Mike Palmer for a potty break. Not with them there, watching. And not with the state the toilet was in. I'd just have to hold it.

"Give me your hands," Anthony said, wheeling me around and handcuffing them behind my back.

He pushed me out the door and into the corridor, and I breathed a sigh of relief. Palmer hadn't enacted his revenge. In fact, he'd seemed almost docile. Maybe Fineman had forbidden him to mess with me. God, I hoped so.

Anthony took me the usual route at first, pushing me ahead of him, but instead of going left and up the stairs to the lab, we took another right, then another, and then I was being shoved through the open doors of an old elevator. Anthony wouldn't let me turn to see the buttons or the floor indicator, and the back wall wasn't reflective enough for me to see anything clearly in it, but I did notice there weren't any cameras. I tried to count the seconds as soon as I felt us start to descend. Unfortunately, the sensation also made me feel like every organ in my body had ganged up on my bladder and sucker-punched it.

I pressed my thighs together and shuffled my feet, something my mother had once designated "the pee dance."

"Hold still," Anthony barked, shoving me up against the back wall of the elevator, my face smashing against it. His whole body was pressed against mine, grinding into me. I could feel his dick against my ass through our clothes. In the past I'd seen him want me, seen him take advantage of a chance to brush against my breast or place a hand near my crotch. He'd never been as bad as Felix, my first guard, but he'd been working his way up to it. Yes, Anthony liked to hurt me, but he usually waited for Dr. Fineman's orders to do any serious damage. Because I was a prize. Because I was a potential tool.

But there in that elevator alone with him, something had changed. I could tell he didn't just want to hurt me. He wanted to kill me.

"I'm going to piss in here," I said, desperate, my fear making it that much more urgent. "You need to get me to a bathroom if you don't want another mess to clean up."

"Another mess?" he hissed in my ear, pressing the cold circle of his gun barrel into my temple and cocking it. "How about I make you the mess, you little whore? After what you've done, that's exactly what you deserve."

He was going to do it. I could feel the need seeping out of his pores. I was going to die right there. Somehow, I'd misread everything. I'd made some crucial error and I didn't even know what it was. Maybe this had never been a trip to see Major Tom. The elevators didn't have cameras. Anthony could claim I'd attacked him and he'd simply killed me in self-defense. What had Palmer said to him? *Something needs to be done.* If that something was killing me, would Dr. Fineman really be upset? Would anyone? Maybe Marcus, who was lying in a hospital bed somewhere. Maybe Passion. But they would be the only ones. My mother had probably given up searching for me by now. Fuck this. Fuck them. I didn't want to die.

I released my bladder, opened up the gates and let it all run free. It ran down my legs, soaking warm into my pants, splattering my bare feet and filling the elevator with spritz-o-urine. It soaked into Anthony too, where he was pressed against me.

"What the—you little—" He pushed himself away, smearing me into the wall, but at least he was off me and the moment had been diffused. His gun wasn't pressed to my head anymore.

The elevator stopped, chiming cheerily as the doors slid open.

Anthony yanked me out into a dim foyer and I almost fell, my feet slipping in my own warm piss.

He hauled me down an even dimmer corridor, my wet footprints trailing behind us, to two metal doors with rubber stripping running between them. He got out his keys, fiddling with them, and then the doors were open and he was shoving me into a large, cold room, bathed in florescent light.

I stopped in the doorway, cool air rushing over me and freezing my insides.

This was not Major Tom's office. This was not my new cell. This was not anywhere I wanted to be.

It was a morgue.

"What's the matter?" Anthony whispered in my ear. "Not what you were hoping for?"

"I thought you were taking me to Major Tom?" I blathered, almost a plea. Across the tile floor in front of me were two large white tables. Beyond that was the wall full of metal drawers, all of them closed and shut tight. But my imagination was already filling in the contents. And I was trembling.

"Come on now," Anthony teased, running the end of his gun along my cheekbone. "I thought you were a Goth girl and all that. Isn't this the kind of place that turns you on? Isn't this what you wanted when you got into Major Tom's head and did what you did to him? Didn't you know it would all end up here?"

Shit. He was going to kill me. No one would hear me scream down here. The mess would be easy to clean up, and he wouldn't have to carry my body anywhere. It was the perfect place to murder someone.

"Anthony," I said his name for the first time, hoping to tap into his humanity if there was any left.

"You don't want to do this. You're not a killer."

"I'm not a killer?" He laughed in my ear. "That's funny, coming from you." He shoved me out of his arms, then grabbed me and propelled me past the tables to the body drawers. "I told you I was taking you to Major Tom and here he is." He yanked one of the drawers open, the body under the white sheet scrolling out before me.

I stared down at it, not understanding until Anthony reached out and pulled the sheet back.

Major Tom lay there, pale and blue and naked, his throat cut in a long gaping slice from ear to ear. There were other cuts on him as well, as if he'd been in a knife fight with a real pro, someone who'd been testing him, teasing him, whittling him down and making the agony last as long as possible.

"Oh my God," I blurted, turning my head away.

"Look at him!" Anthony put his hands on either side of my head, forcing me to. "We found him early this morning in his office with a knife in his hand. We've checked all the camera feeds. No one was in or out all night. He did this to himself after you put the knife back in him. This man was a warrior and a soldier. He didn't have a suicidal bone in his body until you got inside his head, and now he's dead."

"No—I—" That couldn't be right. Major Tom had been fine yesterday.

"I know you did this, bitch, even if the doctor won't admit it," Anthony hissed. "He didn't want you to know. Thought it would scare you out of using your hand for him again. Plus, he knows there'd be a lynch mob taking a visit to your cell if anyone else knew what you're capable of. So, if you tell him I brought you down here, or say anything at all, I'll be sure we make this trip again. Except next time you'll stay. You understand me?"

"Yes," I nodded. *He wasn't going to kill me. Not today. Not now.*

"And if you ever come at me with that hand of yours, I'll end you." He pulled the sheet back over Major Tom and shut the drawer.

Then he escorted me to my new cell.

I tried to pay attention, but my mind was reeling. Major Tom was dead. Had I done that? Had I killed him? Is that what happened when people got their burdens back? I kept seeing him alive in my head, then grey and dead in that drawer, a gaping red cut across his neck.

Anthony and I hadn't taken the elevator or any stairs. I knew that much. That meant I was still on the same level as Major Tom and the morgue, most likely the basement of the compound.

Anyway, it didn't matter. My plan had utterly backfired. I hadn't seen anything helpful, and I was probably further from anyone or anything else than I'd been before.

My cell was almost exactly like the previous one. Same camera in the corner. Same cement slab bed. Same metal toilet and single receding light in the ceiling.

I crossed to the slab and collapsed onto it, tears pricking at the corners of my eyes.

I wasn't a killer.

There had to be another explanation.

But I honestly couldn't think of one.

14

OLIVIA

There were rats in my new cell, or at least they were trying to get in, scratching and scrambling at the crumbling mortar.

Maybe they were drawn to the sound of my crying, so I tried to keep it down. I couldn't stop the tears, but I could bite back the sobs.

I slept a little. Dreams of Marcus and the pool were now a welcome escape from images of Major Tom's smiling neck wound. Besides, I knew Marcus was safe, with Passion at his side. Most importantly, he wasn't working for the CAMFers. I clung to that fact, chanting it in my head, making it my mantra. Marcus wasn't one of them. He couldn't be, or everything was lost. Especially me.

I don't know how much time passed. A day and a night? Maybe two? The urine on my clothes dried, making them crusty and rank. I didn't get hungry, but someone had left me a plastic pitcher of water and I drank it all. When it was gone, I began to wonder if they'd just left me to rot down in the depths of dirt and stone. My cell felt like a tomb, but it was better than the morgue. It was better than being noticed by them. I thought that for a while. And then I got angry.

I paced my cell. I cursed and flipped off the camera. I tried to tear it off the wall, but it just ended up dangling at an odd angle from wires I couldn't cut. I contemplated smashing the cup and pitcher and clogging my new toilet, but I didn't know where they'd put me next. There was no going down from here, except perhaps in a drawer next to Major Tom. Anthony had told Palmer I'd done that. What if the rumor spread? What if they convinced Dr. Fineman I was too much of a liability? What if I was too much of a liability?

I lay down and cried again, and the rats become more frantic.

There was a crumbling pile of mortar near the floor now, more dust cascading down. Then something pink, like the tip of a nose, poked through.

Shit.

I scrambled back, fleeing to the corner as far as I could get from the hole. Normally, I wasn't afraid of rodents. Rats were fine with me, in pet stores, or labs, or cages, or even on the street. I'd caught several mice that had found their way into my house, caught them humanely and released them back out into the woods behind our place. But that nose had been large, and I was less than thrilled about being trapped in a small room with a rodent of unusual size.

If I only had a weapon of some kind. Maybe I could trap it in the pitcher, but then what? I'd have a giant, scrambling, angry rat in a plastic pitcher and it would chew its way out eventually.

More mortar crumbled and the pink thing jutted out further.

It wasn't a nose at all.

It was someone's finger, poking through the wall, then quickly retracted again.

I jumped off the slab and threw myself on the floor, putting my mouth up to the crumbling wall. "Hello? Who are you?" I began digging frantically at the wall with my own fingers, brushing away the dust. "Hello? Are you there?"

I glanced over my shoulder at the camera, but thanks to my earlier rage it was now slanted away, pointing to the far corner of the room.

"They can't see us or hear us," I told the wall, almost yelling now. "Why won't you answer me?"

I jammed the index finger of my flesh hand between two stones, breaking through to the other side. I wiggled it, attempting to make an even bigger hole I might be able to see through.

Something touched my finger and I froze. It was the gentle rub of a fingertip against mine, running over my jagged, dirty fingernail, then under as if memorizing the lines of my fingerprint. Human contact, so gentle and wholly unexpected in that deepest, darkest place—I cannot explain what it did to me—but I burst into tears, sobbing and hiccupping and heaving, with my finger stuck in a hole in the wall.

Then, the other finger was gone and I cried out, "Wait. Don't leave me."

I waited, holding my finger still, then wiggling it. How do you make the tip of your finger look inviting, friendly, hopeful, needy, desperate? I knew it was silly, but I was afraid to pull it out. What if that other finger took it as a sign of rejection? What if it never came back? What if the person who belonged to that finger had weighed my finger and found it wanting? Thank God I hadn't used a ghost finger.

"Please, come back," I begged.

And it did, touching me firmly, pushing and nudging my finger back through the hole. I slipped my finger out and her finger came through, but only for a moment, and then it was gone.

I heard a sound, like the crinkle of paper, and I bent down, peering through the hole. Something was coming through, something small and folded. Oh my God. It was a note.

As soon as the edge of it passed the threshold of the hole, I snatched it. "I've got it. I've got your note. Thank you," I said, unfolding it as quickly as I could.

It was the page of a book. Page 113 of some book titled *The Bone Road*.

I turned it over, looking for handwriting, and there it was, scrawled between the lines in faint pencil.

I am your friend. Don't cry. I will help you.

I immediately disobeyed and burst into a fresh round of tears, leaning against the cool wall, my ribs heaving.

"Hello?" I gasped when the sobs had subsided. "My name is Olivia. I'm a prisoner here.

Are you a prisoner too? What's your name? How long have you been here?"

But there was no answer.

"Why won't you talk to me?" I took a deep breath and tried to pull myself together. She'd told me not to cry. Maybe she was pissed because I had anyway. "Hello?" I called through the wall. "Are you still there?"

I heard the rustle of someone moving away. She was leaving. She was abandoning me.

I got down on all fours and smashed my face to the floor, trying to get a look through the hole, but all I could see was a small circle of light.

I tried to dig away at the opening more, but all the loose mortar was gone and what was left was gritty and sharp, biting into my fingers and making them bleed. I might have made it a little bigger, but not much.

I crumpled the book page in my hand, blood from my fingers smearing onto it. Then I opened it up again and smoothed it against my leg, reading the words carefully and slowly, savoring their promise.

I had a friend who wanted to help me. Obviously she wasn't a captive, or she wouldn't have access to a book or a pencil. Maybe someone had been coming and she'd had to leave. Maybe, for some reason, she couldn't talk. And what made me so sure she was a she? The finger had been slender, smaller than mine even. The touch had been feminine and so was the handwriting.

The page blurred as my eyes filled with tears again, but I held them back.

Don't cry. That's what she'd asked of me.

I picked myself up off the floor and moved away from the hole, taking page 113 with me. I needed a place to hide it. There was a crack in the wall on the other side of the cell and I folded the page carefully, slipping it in, making sure to block the camera's view while I did it.

An hour or so later, Anthony came for me.

He handcuffed me and took me back up toward Dr. Fineman's lab, reminding me again on the way that if I said anything about our visit to Major Tom, he'd kill me.

The interrogation room wasn't empty when we arrived.

Dr. Fineman was already there.

And there were others. Five others. Standing in a row along the far wall like a criminal line-up.

I almost cried out when I saw them.

They were teenagers, and captives, just like me.

They were also handcuffed and chained together at the ankles, their demeanor completely beaten down, their shoulders slumped, their clothes filthy, their eyes staring at the floor. Worst of all, each of them was gagged with one of those ball gags, a black strap tight around their heads, sporting a red ball stoppering their mouths as if they'd bitten off an evil clown's nose.

I looked at Dr. Fineman and he smiled.

What a sick fuck.

I turned back to the captives. I vaguely recognized one or two from the crowd at the Eidolon. There were three girls, one blonde and two brunette, bookended by two guys. The guy closest to me was short and stocky with black hair. The guy on the end was tall and ripped, his brown hair flopping over his face.

He flexed his shoulders and looked up at me, blue eyes locking onto mine through the veil of his bangs. I bit down on my lip and looked away, my heart plummeting in my chest.

It was Grant.

Grant was here, his blond hair so dirty I'd mistaken it for brown.

That was why we'd never found his body up on the cliffs. Why no one had seen him escape.

Grant was a captive of the CAMFers, and he didn't even have PSS.

He was here because of me. Because Dr. Fineman, who'd lived in my hometown and dated my mother, knew exactly who Grant was to me. He was my childhood crush. My next-door neighbor. My best friend's brother. And when I'd gone missing, Grant had suddenly decided he loved me and then he'd forced a kiss on me at Shades. Dr. Fineman probably didn't know that part. But it didn't matter.

Grant could not be here. I needed him NOT to be here, because even though he'd been a dick at the Eidolon and I didn't care about him in that way, I still cared about him. He was still Emma's brother and my friend, and I was terrified of what they'd do to him.

And yet, my fear was mixed with an uncontrollable surge of joy and hope.

Grant was here standing in front of me.

I wasn't alone.

"As you can see," Dr. Fineman purred, sidling closer to me, "I brought you some new test subjects. I thought we might conduct a little experiment on what happens when you put an item back into a subject from which it did not originate."

I stared at him, not understanding his words. He was pointing at the table again, the table in the middle of the room with the dog tags and matchbook on it.

No.

An image of Major Tom laid out in the morgue flashed in my mind. He was dead by his own hand, or mine, and that knife had come from him. I didn't even want to think about what would happen if I put something somewhere it didn't belong.

"No way," I said, shaking my head. With the cuff, Dr. Fineman could keep me from using my ghost hand on him and Anthony, but he couldn't make me use it on someone else.

"I thought you might feel that way." The doctor slipped his hand into his lab coat pocket and pulled out his silver cube. "As we learned with Major Tom, telepathy and mind-control are wonderful new side-effects of the enhanced PSS signature of these items. If I put this in your hand and Anthony makes you hold it, I could make you do exactly as I wish."

"Or I could make you do what I wish." I smiled wickedly. "Why don't you ask Major Tom how that worked out for him?"

Even as I said it, Anthony squeezed my arm, his fingers digging in and bruising me, but I didn't care.

Dr. Fineman turned pale and put the cube quickly back into his pocket. He was afraid of me and what I'd threatened. What if I could get my hand on that cube? Would I be able to mind-control my way out of here, or would he control me? Or we could just go back and forth, taking turns controlling each other the way Major Tom and I had. Would it be worth the risk?

"Well," the doctor said, clearing his throat, "if you will not cooperate willingly, then I suppose we will have to hurt one of these other guests until you become more cooperative."

"What? No!" I cried, but Anthony was already dragging me to the table. He shoved me into the chair and unlocked the handcuffs, pulling my arms through the metal slats and relocking them so I couldn't move.

One of the girls in the line-up began to shake and sob.

I looked at Grant and his eyes caught mine, his head shaking slightly. It was the barest of motions, but I caught it. I just had no idea what it meant. Don't give into them? Don't let them hurt us?

Anthony stepped in front of the table, his back to me, and pulled something from his pocket. It was a small boxy gun. Was he going to shoot one of them? No, it wasn't a firearm. This was something else. Maybe a new minus meter design or some kind of stun gun.

He strode up to the line of captives, stopping a few feet in front of the dark, stocky boy.

The boy lifted his head, eyes almost as wide as the red ball in his mouth. He tried to shuffle back, away from Anthony, his chest heaving and drool running down his chin.

Anthony lifted the device in his hand.

"Don't," I shouted. "I'll do it. Just don't hurt him. Please."

Anthony turned and looked at Dr. Fineman, a question in his eyes.

Grant took that moment of distraction to charge forward, barreling into Anthony, the other captives yanked off their feet and dragged across the floor behind him.

Anthony was down, Grant solidly on top of him, but with his ankles, hands and mouth bound, all Grant could really do was lay there.

I tried to jump up and nearly pulled my arms out of their sockets. Someone had bolted the damn chair to the floor.

"Get the fuck off me," Anthony bellowed, shoving Grant aside and sinking the gun thing into him.

Grant gave out a muffled groan, the sound squeezing past the ball in his mouth, and he began to flail on the floor, his arms and legs spasming, his face turning bright red, all his muscles clenching and unclenching. I'd seen it before, when we'd used Yale's homemade stun gun back in Greenfield. I knew it wouldn't kill Grant, but watching him contort in pain because of me was almost more than I could take.

Five seconds later he lay still, panting and puffing, Anthony standing over him.

"You little prick," Anthony said, hauling back his booted foot and kicking Grant in the ribs. "We were saving you for later, but you just couldn't wait, could you?"

I wanted to yell, wanted to tell Anthony to leave him alone, but I could see Dr. Fineman watching me, gauging my reaction and undoubtedly calculating how he could use Grant against me. So, I sat back in my chair and watched Grant try to roll away from the second kick.

The other captives picked themselves up off the floor as best they could, the girls huddling up around the dark boy, all of them kneeling because they didn't have enough slack in the chain to stand.

"So, since you volunteered and all," Anthony said, pulling out a key and bending down to unlock Grant's ankle chains from the rest of them, "how about we see if your little friend here can put something in you?" He grabbed Grant by the arm, pulling him up and propelling him toward me at the table. "And if you do give us anymore trouble, I can always hurt her," Anthony added, nodding in my direction.

Fuck. This wasn't good. It had been bad enough when they'd just had me. Now they could hurt all of us, use us against one another. Now they could make me do their bidding and they knew it.

"Okay. I'll do it," I said, looking down at the items on the table. The matchbook. The dog tags. Which would be worse to put inside Grant? "Unlock my hands and turn off the cuff so we can get this over with," I said to Dr. Fineman. He had a theory about all of this. Well, so did I. Time to do a little test and see who was right.

Grant's blue eyes fixed on me as Dr. Fineman took the keys from Anthony to undo my handcuffs.

The doctor crossed behind me and when I felt the restraints fall away, I pulled my arms from between the chair slats, my muscles twinging with painful pleasure at being set free.

"Put your hands on the table, slowly, where we can see them," Dr. Fineman said. "And remember, I can disable your PSS hand in an instant, so don't try anything funny." He circled around in front of me, keeping a safe distance, withdrawing his hand from his lab coat pocket to show me his finger on the cuff controller.

I placed both my hands on the table, palms up. "I'm not going to try anything funny," I assured him. "But I need to reach for the matchbook and you need to bring him closer." I nodded at Grant.

"Fine, fine," Dr. Fineman said eagerly, gesturing Anthony and Grant forward.

As they approached, I reached out and touched the matchbook. As soon as I picked it up, it crackled in my hand, sending a tingle through my ghost fingers and up my arm.

Whoa. It had never done that before.

I stared down at it.

Oh my God, had it come from inside Palmer? No, that couldn't be. I certainly hadn't pulled it out of him. I'd wanted to. I'd felt something in him that day outside of Greenfield when we'd had him tied to a tree. But I hadn't done it.

Or had I?

Marcus and the guys had said he'd screamed, but I hadn't remembered it. I'd blacked out or something. Could I have pulled something out of Palmer without even realizing it?

No, that still didn't make sense.

They would have told me. Marcus would have told me if I'd pulled something out of Palmer. Besides, if I had, I'd be able to feel where he was whenever I touched it. I'd especially be able to feel him now that Fineman had enhanced the PSS signature. Yet, all I felt was the faint buzz.

I hadn't pulled the matchbook out of Palmer.

But Dr. Fineman was convinced I'd pulled it out of someone, and now I was going to have to try and stuff it into Grant. He was standing in front of me, pressed up against the table, Anthony holding him from behind.

"Take his gag off," I said.

Dr. Fineman nodded to Anthony and he unstrapped Grant's gag, tossing it on the table in front of me with a wet splat.

Grant's jaw tightened and he looked down at me, resignation in his eyes. "It's okay, Olivia," he said, his voice hoarse from lack of use. "Do what you have to do."

It almost undid me, hearing him say that, as if he thought I was going to hurt him, maybe even kill him.

I looked up into his blue, blue eyes, begging his forgiveness as I stretched out my ghost hand, the matchbook folded in my fist.

Then I slipped it straight into his chest.

My hand went into him easily. It sank through his clothes and skin, through flesh and muscle, right up to my wrist stump. There was no urgency like there'd been the other times I'd reached into people. No strange sensations. No sense of needing to find something and pull it out. It just felt like my hand was inside someone's chest, as if it belonged there.

Dr. Fineman glanced from me to Grant and back again.

Anthony stared over Grant's shoulder, his eyes boring into me, full of hatred.

Grant's eyes never left mine. He didn't even look down at my hand inside of him.

For a moment, nothing happened, all of us poised in a strange Mexican standoff. Then the matchbook fell from Grant's shirtfront, fluttering down to the table and landing with a soft slap.

Dr. Fineman frowned.

"Well, that didn't work," I said, slipping my hand out of Grant and trying to hide my relief.

"Try it again," Dr. Fineman commanded, picking up the matchbook and handing it to me.

I tried three more times, all of us standing there watching as I reached into Grant and the matchbook went fluttering to the table.

After the third attempt, Dr. Fineman picked up the matchbook, clutching it in his hand. "Where did you get this?" he asked.

I thought about telling him the truth. Maybe it would get Palmer in trouble. Maybe it would put them at odds. But it would also solve a mystery that was driving Fineman crazy, and I needed every advantage I could get.

"Some random guy at the Eidolon," I lied. "He wanted to see what my hand could do, so I showed him."

"Impossible," Fineman snapped. "This item doesn't match any PSS signature I have on record."

"Yeah, so?" What was he saying? That he had a PSS sample of every Marked kid at the Eidolon? How was that even possible? I mean, I knew he was a collector of PSS. He'd told me that fun fact back in Greenfield, but how would he have gotten access to the members of The Hold?

I looked up at Grant.

He didn't have PSS. And they hadn't killed him.

In fact, at the Eidolon, the CAMFers had specifically targeted and killed the Marked, which made no sense. Marcus had thought Dr. Fineman's intention was to harvest PSS as a renewable energy source, but maybe that wasn't what he'd been doing at all. Or maybe his plans had changed after I'd taken the cube from him. What if all the death and destruction up on those cliffs had somehow been my fault? What had the CAMFers said when they'd captured me? *Hold your fire. He wants her alive.*

I glanced over at the group huddled near the wall. They had no signs of PSS that I could see. Of course, I'd learned from Passion and Samantha that PSS could be deep inside someone, manifesting internally, not externally. But did Dr. Fineman know that? Had he let these four and Grant live because they didn't have PSS? Or did they have PSS he simply couldn't detect?

"Here," Dr. Fineman said, holding the dog tags in front of my face. "Try to put these in him."

I hesitated, feigning reluctance. This is exactly what I'd hoped he'd do.

I reached out and took the tags in my ghost hand, feeling the familiar tingle.

Passion, I screamed in my head, *I'm in the compound in Oregon. Grant is here too. Tell Marcus. Come get us.*

I didn't take time to feel her presence. If she was asleep, that should wake her. If she was awake, it might give her a headache. I didn't really care, as long as she heard me.

"Hurry up. What are you waiting for?" Dr. Fineman prodded me, his voice full of suspicion.

I obediently stuck my ghost hand into Grant and the tags clattered to the table, refusing to go into him just like the matchbook had.

"Good. Excellent," Dr. Fineman said, a smug smile on his face.

Why did he look so satisfied? It hadn't worked. His experiment had been a flop.

My eyes drifted to the square bulge in his pocket, the cube with Jason's bullet in it. He wanted me to put it back in him, and now he knew exactly what would happen to Jason's bullet if I did.

Shit. I'd just shown him how to separate the bullet and the cube.

And with the hostages and Grant as leverage, he could probably make me do it.

God, I was an idiot. I'd played right into his hand, just like last time.

Still, there was the issue of Major Tom. The returning of his knife hadn't gone so smoothly. I suppose if Dr. Fineman wanted to risk death by cube, he could go for it. He was a determined man. Not to mention, he was completely insane. Sooner or later, he would figure out how to counteract whatever had happened to the Major, and then he'd make me put the cube back into him.

That thought chilled me to the bone.

"Take them back to their cells," Dr. Fineman told Anthony, gesturing at the captives behind us. "But put these two together," he said, looking at Grant and then leering at me. "She deserves a little reward for all her hard work."

I wanted to break his nose again. I wanted to sink my ghost hand into him, the cocky bastard.

But he was going to put Grant and me together, and I wanted that more.

I looked up at Grant and I could see it in his eyes, too. Hope, quickly masked. But hope.

"Yes, sir," Anthony said as Fineman exited the interrogation room and several more guards came in to wrangle up the other captives.

Anthony shoved the ball gag back in Grant's mouth, strapping it around his head and pulling it so tight it dug into Grant's temples and cheeks. Anthony was pissed. I could practically see the rage radiating off of him as he circled behind my chair and handcuffed my wrists behind me, then yanked me up. He didn't even undo the shackles that chained Grant's ankles together before he grabbed him as well, shoving us out the door.

It was a slow shuffle to the elevators, Anthony seething all the way. Was he still mad about Major Tom, or was he pissed that Grant would be in my cell with me, a place he considered his dominion?

When we got to the elevators, he shoved us in.

The doors closed and he slowly turned, his gun in his hand.

"What I would really like to do right now is shoot you both in the head," he said. "But I wouldn't be able to explain that to my employer, would I?"

I just stared straight ahead, trying to look scared and non-threatening, which wasn't hard.

Grant shuffled his feet, his shackles clanking together.

"You two make quite a pair." Anthony laughed. "And you're in luck," he said to Grant. "She gives a decent hand job."

I felt the blood rush to my face. I had never—the bastard—someday he was going to pay for those words.

The doors chimed open behind him, and we stepped out into the dim corridor that led to my basement cell.

When both Grant and I were inside and Anthony had locked the door behind us, we stood, waiting, listening to his footsteps fade away into the distance.

He hadn't taken off our handcuffs, Grant's shackles, or the ball gag.

15

PASSION

Three days after the blowout between Marcus and Mr. James, things weren't any better.

Yes, Marcus was recovering physically, but they'd been guarding him like a hawk. They let me and Samantha see him every day, but always with Reiny in the room. Obviously, they weren't happy about what I'd told him, and they didn't want me to tell him anything else. Our conversations were pretty stilted, but at least we got to see him.

Marcus refused to talk to his uncle or even allow him in his room. The guy was seriously sulking, and I'd been depressed enough myself to recognize his downward spiral in that direction. The Marcus I'd known had been replaced by someone else, someone named David who was sullen, and confused, and helpless. I'd lost my sister once. I couldn't imagine losing her twice in one lifetime. I felt for him. I really did, but I also desperately needed him to get over it. And so did Olivia.

I was tired of being Reiny's personal pincushion, too. She'd come to my room with her needles and taken three test tubes of my blood. When I'd asked her why, she'd said she just wanted to run a few more tests.

"Tests for what?" I'd asked. "If something is wrong with me, you'd tell me, right?"

"Nothing is wrong with you," she'd assured me. "You're perfectly healthy, but your blood has taken on some unusual qualities, and we're trying to figure out exactly what that means."

"Taken on?" I asked. "You mean it's changed? Since when?"

"The sample I took in the ambulance differed significantly from the one taken at Edgemont High."

This was about my power. It had to be. Samantha had said the sound of my PSS had changed, and this was proof my blood had changed as well. But Reiny wouldn't say more, even when I pressed her. That didn't seem right. It was my blood she was taking. It was my body and my health. If I had a power, I had a right to know what it was. Then again, at this point it looked like my power was alienating everyone around me.

Samantha would barely talk to me outside of our visits with Marcus. There was a wall between us now, a barrier I couldn't get around. In her mind, I'd called the integrity of her father into question and apparently that was unforgiveable.

We were all a mess. Every one of us walking wounded. Even Mr. James had been thrown off his game. He didn't seem to know what to do, other than amass men and weapons. It was obvious the confrontation with Marcus had taken more out of him than he'd ever admit, and maybe the loss of his wife had finally hit home.

I hadn't talked to Jason about what I'd overheard. I'd almost done it a couple of times, but I could never get him alone. Every day more and more men arrived at the farm, setting up tents all around the house and grounds, practicing at the firing range, and Jason seemed to have finally found his niche amidst an army of Holders. I saw him at meals, but only occasionally, because now, with so many people to feed, there was a rotating eating schedule. He hadn't even come up to see Marcus. Not once. It was like he'd forgotten us completely. Like he had never really been one of us at all.

Plagued by the unrelenting boredom and tension of the farmhouse, I'd gotten into the habit of hiding in my room, questioning the magic eight ball. I should have been praying, and sometimes I did, but God seemed far away and intangible. The ball, on the other hand, was solid and present and felt warm and tingly to the touch, a sensation I found strangely comforting.

It was late one evening and I was in bed, rolling its smooth black roundness in my palms, staring at the dark eight in the white circle.

"Should I try to tell Marcus more? Should I tell him about Olivia, even if it gets me banned from seeing him for good?" I asked, flipping it over to the window side.

Very doubtful

"Should I confront Jason like Samantha suggested?"

Yes definitely

"When? Right now?"

It is decidedly so.

"But how? I don't even know where he is."

You may rely on it.

Okay then. That seemed pretty clear. Purity had always insisted that when the magic eight ball agreed with itself three times in a row, you had to listen.

I got up from my bed, glanced out the window, and there was Jason, alone, striding across the well-lit yard of the farmhouse toward the front door. He had a towel slung over one shoulder. He was probably on his way in for a shower since everyone had been put on a rotation for those too, just like the meals.

I looked down at the eight ball in my hands. How had it known?

I put it reverently down on the bedside table and slipped out of my room, silently heading down the hall to the upstairs bathroom. There was a piece of paper taped to the door, a crude sign-up sheet with times and names scrawled across it. I ran my finger down it and there he was. *Jason Williams, 11:30 p.m.* This was my chance, and a rare one at that, because I knew how little Jason showered. But if I talked to him out in the hallway, someone might overhear us. I put my ear to the door. I didn't hear anything, so I opened it. The bathroom was steamy and warm, but empty. I shut myself in and, a minute later, someone knocked.

"Anyone in there?" Jason asked.

I opened the door a crack, peeking out.

"Oh, Passion, sorry," he said, looking embarrassed.

"Get in here." I opened the door wider and looked up and down the hall. "I need to talk to you."

"Um, okay." He came in and I closed the door, locking it behind him.

It was a small bathroom, only a few feet between the sink, the toilet, and the shower.

"Sit down," I said, gesturing toward the toilet seat.

"No, that's okay," he said, frowning. "Listen, is this going to take long? Because I only get twenty minutes to shower."

"I don't know," I said, floundering. How was I even supposed to broach the subject? Olivia would have just asked him straight out, but I wasn't Olivia. "The thing is—I overheard something the night we got here," I ploughed on. "I was on the stairs, and I heard Mr. James say something to you."

"I see," Jason said, his eyes and his face closing up, his body gone rigid and tense. "Whatever you think you heard, you don't want to go there. Trust me on this, Passion. Leave it alone."

"No," I said, shaking my head. "I can't. You knew Mr. James before this, and he knew you. How can I possibly trust you knowing you kept that a secret from all of us?"

"You should never trust anyone," he said, his voice low and dangerous. "Haven't you learned that by now?"

I spun toward the door, but he was there before me, blocking it with his body, his hand on the doorknob.

"I thought you wanted to talk." He gestured at the toilet seat behind me. "So sit down and we'll talk."

I sat down and glared at him.

"You shouldn't have overheard that," he said, leaning against the door. "It complicates things and puts you in more danger than you're already in. But I can see if I don't tell you something, you're gonna storm out of here and get us both in trouble, so here it goes. I met Mr. James a long time before you did. I met him at my father's game preserve a few weeks before Marcus showed up and got me out. He was there negotiating something between The Hold and the CAMFers. The two sides have meetings like that a few times a year, but that was the first time Mr. James had ever come himself, so it must have been something big. But it didn't go well. My father was in a drunken rage for days afterwards. Mr. James wasn't happy either. Before he left, he found me and told me my father had put me on the CAMFers' extraction list, and someone would be coming to take me away soon. He said I had another choice though—that three guys with PSS would show up and when they did, I should go with them. He promised it would save my life. And that's exactly what happened."

I sat there, stunned, my mouth hanging open. There were a lot of things I'd imagined Jason telling me, but none of them had prepared me for this.

"The CAMFers and The Hold meet? Why would they do that?"

"It's like any other war or conflict." He shrugged. "Politics under the table is always part of it."

"And you trusted Mr. James, knowing he was negotiating with CAMFers?"

"I told you, I don't trust anyone," Jason said. "But he told me someone was coming and they did. I'm not sure I would have trusted Marcus enough to leave if I hadn't had the heads up. And it's worked out for me so far."

"Wait, how would Mr. James have even known Marcus was coming?"

"He's his nephew. You really think he wasn't keeping tabs on him?"

"Tabs like you?" I asked. "Have you been reporting to Mr. James this whole time?"

"No." Jason scowled, his hackles up. "I didn't tell him anything. Are you calling me a traitor?"

"So, he just helped you out of the kindness of his heart, no string attached?" I didn't buy it. There was something Jason wasn't telling me. The Mr. James I knew used every resource at his disposal. And the Jason I knew wouldn't have trusted Mr. James so easily, not even to save his own skin, unless there had been the promise of something else, something more significant. It had been stupid to ask Jason. By his own admission, he didn't trust anyone, including me. He was probably lying straight to my face.

"Let it go, Passion," Jason said, staring down at me. "It's not your concern."

"But I—" I felt a surge of adrenaline pump through me, as if my life was suddenly and inexplicably in danger. And then Olivia was yelling in my head. *Passion, I'm in the compound in Oregon. Grant is here too. Tell Marcus. Come get us.*

I jumped up from the toilet and sprang toward Jason.

"Get out of my way." I shoved at him. "I need to get out of here. Now."

"Hey, settle down!" He grabbed my arms. "You can't tell anyone what I—"

"Let go of me!" I lifted my knee, jabbing it into his crotch as hard as I could.

He went down fast, straight onto the tile floor, curling up into a ball and groaning. When I pulled the door open it banged into his head, and I didn't even care. I was channeling Olivia, her voice and urgency still ringing in my head, and I'd gotten more than a voice this time. There had been an image too, a vision of her in a small room looking up at Grant Campbell. A Grant all grungy and abused with a ball gag in his mouth, but it was definitely him. And it had been horrible.

I raced down the hall toward Marcus's room.

There wasn't any question anymore. I had to tell him.

I threw open the door and charged in, then skidded to a stop when I saw the witch sitting at Marcus's bedside, holding his hand in hers.

There was another one standing at the end of his bed.

A second witch.

They were two grown, middle-aged women, decked out in black flowing dresses, with pointy shoes and hats, fake eyelashes, and caked on makeup, each one with a bulging wart on her nose. Their wigs were awful, both long black hair, one streaked with purple, the other with red, looking all wind-blown as if they'd just ridden in on their brooms.

As soon as I burst in, all eyes were upon me.

The witches stared, and Marcus glanced up.

"I—who—what is going on?" I asked, looking from Marcus to the witchy twins.

"Passion!" the one at the end of the bed cried, rushing at me and crushing me in a crinkly black embrace before I could do anything but gape. "I'm so glad you're safe. Chloe assured me you were, but I had to see for myself." She was babbling, and she might have even been crying a little.

"Dr. Black, what are you doing here?" I gasped, melting into Olivia's mother's arms. As soon as I'd heard her voice, I'd recognized her, even decked out as a witch and looking much thinner and frailer than I remembered. "I thought you were in Indy?"

"Well, we were," she said, gesturing at the other witch who was still sitting with Marcus. "But Chloe needed to see her nephew, and when she told me you were here, I knew I had to come too. When Olivia left Greenfield—I had no idea you two were together and heading to The Hold. It's such a relief to know you're okay. How are you, really?" she asked, gripping my arms gently and holding me away from her to look me up and down. She cared about me. I knew that. But I wasn't who she'd really wanted to see. I wasn't her daughter.

"I'm good," I said, glancing from Olivia's mom to Marcus's aunt, my head still reeling. Samantha's mom was here. What did that even mean? Had she left John Holbrook and the council to side with her husband again? There were so many questions swimming around in my mind I latched on to the most crucial one, of course. "Why are you dressed like that?"

"Oh, this," Dr. Black grimaced, looking down at her odd get-up. "These are our disguises. What better way to escape the watchful eyes of a tired surveillance team than to go out on Halloween in the most popular mom costume there is? They had no chance of tracking us in that onslaught of witches."

Was it Halloween? I did the math in my head and realized it was. How could I have forgotten my family's least favorite holiday? That wonderful night every year when we turned off the porch light, put out the "No trick-or-treaters" sign, barricaded ourselves inside the house, and spent the evening praying and fasting for all the poor souls being lost to Satan through his evil minions: Mars, Nestle, and Hershey.

Then again, no one had dressed up at the farmhouse or even mentioned what day it was, unless you counted everyone being dressed up like G.I. Joe.

I looked over at Marcus. He was holding his aunt's hand, and there was finally a glimmer of hope in his eyes. I glanced at her. "But I thought you were—" I started to say, but didn't even know how to finish the sentence.

"I was," she said, her eyes measuring me. "And I still am. But the new Hold is, unfortunately, a mass of disorganization. So many parents grieving, and none of them thinking. It's going to take a long time for anything useful to formulate out of that chaos, and I just don't think we have the luxury of that kind of time."

"We don't," I said, my eyes sliding back to Marcus. Had she told him? Did he know what we were talking about?

"Well, if there is one thing I know about my husband, he gets things done," she added. "That's why I'm here. Why I brought Sophie. We need to locate these missing kids and get them back. There is nothing more crucial than that. Nothing."

It's what I'd been waiting to hear for days.

"I know where they are," I said.

"What?" Marcus blurted, sitting forward in his bed. "You know where they're holding Danielle?"

"No—I—"

"Calm down and let the girl speak," Mrs. James said, stroking his arm and soothing him.

"I—It's a long story, but I have a connection with Olivia," I explained. "I can sometimes sense where she is and I get images, sometimes even words and feelings."

"Oh my God," Dr. Black exhaled next to me, clutching my hand. "Is she—okay? Can you feel her right now?"

"No, but I did just a minute ago. That's why I ran in here. I've felt her a couple of times before, but this time it was really strong. And it was a message, like she was talking in my head. She told me where she is. And that Grant's with her. She said we should come for her."

"Grant Campbell?" Dr. Black asked, surprised. "He was at the Eidolon?"

"Yes." I nodded. "He came with some girl from The Hold named Eva."

"Did Olivia mention any others besides Grant?" Mrs. James asked.

"What about Danielle?" Marcus demanded. "Did she mention Danielle?"

"Calm down," his aunt told him. "If we find Olivia and Grant, it will lead us to knowledge of Dani as well."

I stared at Samantha's mother. Did she really believe her niece was still alive, or was she just protecting Marcus until his memory came back? I was beginning to see why the old Marcus had been so calculating and wary of trusting his family. Hanging out with them was like swimming with sharks.

"So, what did Olivia tell you?" Mrs. James asked impatiently. "Where are they?"

Crap. How long had I been standing there staring at her and comparing her to marine life?

"A CAMFer compound in Oregon," I said, and Marcus's head snapped my direction. Was that a memory being jarred? No, he was just fixated on Danielle and Oregon was where he'd last seen her. Olivia was counting on him to know exactly where the compound was. Unfortunately, he didn't even know he'd been there. And Oregon was a big state. Once we got there, I might be able to hone in on Olivia's position, but only if she touched the tags again and kept touching them. So, all my information, all my great news about Olivia yelling in my head might be completely useless. Marcus's memory was the key we didn't have. "She thought we would know where it was," I explained to Mrs. James.

"We'll find it," Mrs. James said, sounding sure of herself.

"But how long will that take?" Dr. Black asked, a desperate catch in her voice.

"Not long," Mrs. James assured her. "Alex and I have many contacts in the Pacific Northwest. The Hold's headquarters was there years ago, and we still have friends and connections in the area. When we get the information we need, we'll hunt these CAMFers down like the dogs they are and take our children back."

Whoa. And I'd thought Mr. James was the ruthless one in the family.

"I'm going," Marcus said, crossing his arms over his chest.

"So am I," I added. "The closer I am to Olivia, the more likely I'll be able to pinpoint her location."

"And, of course I'm going," Dr. Black said.

"Of course." Mrs. James nodded.

"And Mr. James will be okay with that?" I asked, incredulous.

"I will," Mr. James said, slipping into the room but staying near the open door, obviously wary of Marcus's reaction. "I thought it might come to this. It's obvious it's our best option, once both David and Samantha are recovered enough to travel."

"Then it seems we finally agree on something," Mrs. James said, smiling wryly at him.

"It seems we do." He smiled thinly back. Then he turned to Olivia's mother. "I promised I'd find your daughter and return her to you, and I have every intention of doing so."

"Good," she said, her eyes boring into him.

"Shall we go downstairs and iron out the details?" he asked, gesturing the ladies toward the door. "Or perhaps you'd like to get out of those costumes first."

"No," Mrs. James said, patting Marcus's arm and rising from her chair. "I believe we are appropriately attired for the task at hand. Come, Sophie. Let's give this rescue plan a woman's touch. And David," she turned back to her nephew, "get some rest. You have a long hard journey ahead of you. We all do." Her eyes fell on me, the cold, calculating look in them sending a chill through my bones.

16

MARCUS

"No." I grabbed my aunt's arm gently, holding her back. "I'm done resting. If you're going to make plans, I want in on it. And I want answers."

She looked at my uncle, a glance passing between them. Samantha claimed they'd been fighting, that my aunt had cheated on my uncle and left him for some other guy who'd been trying to take over The Hold. But that one look made me doubt everything she'd said. Separated, broken couples did not exchange collusive glances like that. Maybe my aunt had slept with some guy. Maybe it had been the only way she and my uncle could maintain their hooks in The Hold. But they weren't truly at odds, that much I was sure of.

As for my aunt suddenly showing up to take my side and champion a rescue? Yeah, they weren't fooling me. Still, if it got me to Oregon and closer to Danielle, I'd play along with them. For now.

"Fair enough." My aunt sat back down in the chair next to my bed. "What do you want to know?"

"Chloe," my uncle said, feigning concern and stepping further into the room. "They've warned us not to overload him."

"I'm not a fucking computer," I snapped. "I think I can handle it."

"It could make things worse," he said.

"Like how?" I laughed bitterly. "I'm not going to forget more. I've already got Swiss cheese for brains. Besides, as you pointed out earlier, I'm not your captive. And I'm not a minor. Legally, I get to decide my own course of treatment and recovery. Don't I?"

"Technically, yes," my uncle answered, his lips pressed together in displeasure.

"Technically?" I echoed, glancing around the room. Passion. My aunt. The woman who'd come with her who was apparently a doctor. Were any of them allies? Passion had at least told me the truth about my memory loss, but at the moment she seemed to have about as much power as I did. Still, I could use the presence of my aunt and this doctor to my advantage. My uncle always liked to look like the good guy. He'd proven that earlier with his whole revised history of my parents' deaths. Now we'd see how committed he was to maintaining that image.

"So which is it? Am I your prisoner, your patient, or your nephew?" I pressed him.

He gave a side-long glance at Dr. Black. "You are my nephew and my patient," he answered. "And yes, you have the right to dictate your own treatment."

"Good," I said. "Then I want to go to Oregon on this rescue mission. And if I'm going to do that, I need to know who this Olivia and Grant are. How did they get taken by the CAMFers and what is their connection to me and Danielle?"

There was a long pause. Everyone seemed to be waiting for someone else to answer. The expression on Passion's face looked pained, like my question had somehow hurt her.

"Olivia is my daughter," Dr. Black finally said. "She ran away from our home in Illinois three weeks ago. We'd had a bad fight and, at the time, I thought she was just being stubborn and would come back when she'd cooled off. But she didn't come back. It wasn't until I'd come to Indy to seek your uncle's help in finding her that I discovered she'd been running for her life from CAMFers. They burned down our house and made it look like an accident. I even blamed her for the fire—" Dr. Black stopped, blinking back tears and putting a hand to her mouth. "I—it was my fault—I didn't listen to her—wasn't there for her. And now they have her." She stopped, overcome with emotion.

I felt bad for her. I knew what it meant to lose someone. But her runaway daughter really wasn't my problem.

"So when did this Grant guy enter the picture?" I asked.

"Grant and Olivia and me," Passion said, taking up the story, "we're all from Greenfield. We went to high school together. When Olivia left town, I went with her, and we went to Indy. Grant was already there attending college at the University of Indiana."

"So, that's why you went to Indy? To stay with him?"

"No, not exactly," Passion said, glancing worriedly at my uncle.

We were getting close to something she thought he didn't want me to know. Good.

"So how'd he become involved?" I pushed.

"It was just weird chance that he came to the Eidolon with Eva," Passion answered. "He didn't know we'd be there, and we didn't know he would be."

"And the Eidolon? What the hell is that?"

"Something Samantha came up with," my uncle answered before Passion could. "A yearly rite of passage for teenagers from The Hold and a chance for their non-Marked friends to support them. Unfortunately, the CAMFers showed up at this one and Samantha was shot."

"Wait, this was the thing Samantha got shot at? The thing that was supposed to save The Hold?"

"Yes," my uncle said, grinding out the word. "They killed most of the attendees and took the rest. We don't know how many others they have besides Olivia and Grant."

"And you were there?" I turned to Passion, a completely new respect for her rising in me. "You survived that?"

"Yes," she whispered, looking strangely unhappy about it.

"What about this connection you have with Olivia? You can feel what's happening to her? How is that even possible?" I knew I was pushing my luck. I could see I was upsetting everyone, Passion most of all, but I had to know. I had to understand all of this if I was going to help Danielle.

"Olivia was wearing a pair of dog tags," Passion said. "They're special. They block minus meters and connect the two of us when one of us is touching them."

"Magical dog tags?" I asked, incredulous. "Where did you get those?"

"I—we—" Passion looked around the room as if she were searching for the answer in the air.

"They're a PSS artifact of unknown origin," my uncle said. He was lying and that meant I'd just reached the end of the information train. They were all clamming up, their faces closed and guarded. Still, the more I was with them the more I'd learn. They all had different lies. It was always that way. One person guarded one thing; another person, something different. Together, they would protect it all, but separately I could break it apart lie by lie, piece by piece. I just had to be patient. And vigilant. I already knew about Passion's PSS blood. Reiny had let that slip easily enough. Obviously, this Grant and Olivia had PSS too. That was pretty incredible in and of itself. Three people from the same small town having PSS? What were the chances? But that mystery would have to wait for later. I'd never been to Illinois before and I had business in Oregon first.

If the CAMFers were holding Olivia and Grant in this compound, then that was probably where they were holding Danielle as well. Help rescue them and I'd get to her.

It was ironic my uncle seemed much more concerned about rescuing two complete strangers than his own niece. Ironic, but not surprising.

"Well, I know Oregon," I pointed out, shoving the blankets off my legs and swinging them over the side of the bed. I had to make myself an asset. My uncle liked people and things he could use. It was why I hated him. It was also his weak spot. "I can probably pinpoint various places a compound might be located if we can get satellite images." I stood up, trying to hide how wobbly my legs were. I hadn't used them much in a while. I'd have to remedy that. "There's a lot of wilderness, but we should be able to narrow it down, especially if you have access to heat signature technology."

"That won't be necessary," my aunt said, exchanging another look with my uncle. "We have people who can find it. And when they do, we'll have to plan our approach carefully. The hostages' safety is paramount, and the CAMFers have considerable power and influence in Oregon."

"Yeah, we wouldn't want to step on any toes," I said. "We could just invite the CAMFers to another Eidolon and hope they come."

"Don't joke about that," Passion snapped, glaring at me, her pale hands balled into fists at her sides. "Don't *ever* joke about that."

"I'm sorry," I said. "But I still don't see how we're going to rescue anyone if our main concern is not upsetting the CAMFers."

"Politics always comes into play," my uncle said. "So does wisdom. As your aunt pointed out, we have contacts in Oregon who can get a message to the CAMFers and arrange a hostage exchange there. They consider the state their turf, so they'll feel more confident and cocky, which will play to our advantage."

"Yeah, and then what? We negotiate with CAMFers?" What could my uncle possibly offer them they didn't already have? Because, as far as I knew, CAMFers wanted everyone on the planet with PSS dead and gone. Then again, if what Passion said about her connection with Olivia was true, they hadn't killed her yet. That meant Danielle might still be alive, too. I clung to that hope. It was my lifeline. Without it, I knew I'd spiral back down into the murky pool of darkness my mind kept returning to. If my uncle thought he could negotiate with CAMFers, he probably knew something I didn't. Who was I kidding? He obviously knew tons of shit I didn't— like what he'd been doing a week ago.

"We negotiate," Uncle Alex confirmed. "And we use force once we have what we want from them. That part of the plan will have to play out somewhat spontaneously."

"Okay," I said. "Do you at least have an idea where this negotiation might occur?"

My uncle's eyes flicked away from me, then came back again. "Warm Springs," he said.

"Warm Springs?" I echoed in disbelief.

Everyone stood staring at me. Passion and Dr. Black looked confused. My aunt and uncle had their poker faces on.

"You're not serious?" I asked, laughing. "You think the Indian reservation that booted you out on your ass after you extorted one of their most sacred beliefs and two of their most legendary shamans is the best place in Oregon to negotiate with CAMFers? You think the tribes of Warm Springs will welcome you with open arms like the prodigal son? You betrayed your own people. They're not going to let you step inside the casino to play slots. They hate you there. They hated you when I was a kid. By now, you're probably the Wendigo they threaten their children with around the campfires at night."

"I think you're overestimating my infamy a little," my uncle said, giving me a fake smile. "The reservation is neutral ground. They can't rightfully turn away tribe members. They won't break tradition. And we do have something to soften our return, I think. Something they're interested in that will open the doors less reluctantly."

"And what might that be?" I asked.

"You," he said.

And there we had it—the reason my uncle had come to my rescue and invested so much quality time and resources into me. He thought I was his key to Warm Springs. The only problem was he was dead wrong. True, I'd lived there with my mom as a toddler and infant, though I didn't remember much of it. Even after my family had defected to The Hold, my mother had frequented the reservation, taking Danielle and me with her when she'd visited my grandparents. She'd wanted us to know our heritage, but she'd also been fighting The Hold's influence over her people, trying to play both sides. The last time I'd been to the reservation was for my grandparents' funeral when I'd been six. And our reception had been mixed. I remembered that much. Even at that tender age, I'd recognized the anger and betrayal mixed with the grief on the faces of everyone who'd looked at us. Later, when my mother wasn't watching, children had thrown stones at Danielle and me and called us names in a language I barely knew.

Despite all that, when Danielle and I had been in foster care, I'd thought about escaping to Warm Springs almost daily. It became my fantasy, my dream of rescue and belonging, maybe because it represented the opposite of everything my uncle stood for. But I'd never gotten up the guts to go back.

I'd tried once, on the day I'd turned sixteen. I'd stolen a car to celebrate and driven the two hours on US-26 from Portland straight into the red and gold high desert of central Oregon. I'd stopped at the brown sign welcoming me to The Confederated Tribes of Warm Springs, Mount Jefferson majestic and white against the skyline behind it, and I couldn't make myself go any further. I'd swung a U-turn in the middle of the road and driven back to a home where the father thought I was a threat to his manhood and the mother was determined to use me to prove it. The day after my birthday, I was arrested for the car theft. The three days in juvie had been a nice respite from them.

"David, are you okay?" my aunt asked, touching my arm again.

"Yeah, I'm fine," I said, stepping away from her. "But this isn't going to work. I'm not your 'in' for Warm Springs. I haven't been there since I was six. They don't know me from Adam."

"Our sources say otherwise," my uncle argued. "I have a contact within the tribe. He can arrange for us to stay at the resort at Kah-Nee-Tah on reservation land. It's a public place, so we shouldn't have any trouble there. I've got a cover story all lined up with me as a CEO rewarding my best sales team with a weekend casino vacation. That allows us to bring a contingent of men, disguised as my employees. And your presence will help. I've been told this is true, and I've been given evidence to support it."

"What evidence?" I still didn't buy it. What could he possibly have that would prove I had influence over the tribes of Warm Springs? None. Because I didn't.

"This," he said, reaching into his back pocket and pulling out a folded piece of paper. He held it out to me and I just looked at him. "Take it," he said.

I didn't want to. Didn't want to find out how far he'd gone to use me this time. But I was also curious.

I took the paper and unfolded it, first one flap, then the second, finally revealing an 8.5" by 11" printed sheet with a picture covering the entire thing.

I stared down at it.

It was a picture of a mural, painted floor to ceiling on a huge wall of the interior of a building. To either side of the painting there were tall windows, bright sun shining in and making the colors of the mural glow.

Flanking the mural wall were desert plants in pots, and a few people sitting in comfortable chairs to one side, like it was the lobby of some hotel or museum.

"What is this?" I asked, the paper in my hand shaking.

"Whoa," Passion said. She'd sidled up to take a peek. "That's you." She looked from the picture to me, awe in her eyes. "That's totally you."

I wish I could have denied it, or shared her enthusiasm, but I couldn't. The mural was, in fact, a giant painting of a guy with a PSS chest who looked an awful lot like me. He was perhaps a tad bit younger than I was, his features slightly more tribal and chiseled. He was naked from the waist up, the cavity of his PSS chest exposed and glowing for all to see, the blue heart unrealistically large, filling the cavity of his icicle ribs like it was trying to break out of them. The landscape in the background was the desert at night, red sand against the deepest blue starry sky. And tucked behind him, almost hidden in shadows, was a small, slender, hooded figure, a child or a maybe a young woman. I couldn't be sure which, but it looked like he was protecting her.

The picture disturbed me. Deeply. Why would the tribes of Warm Springs have commissioned a mural of me? And it had to be me. I was the only one on the planet with a PSS chest. I was pretty sure of that. Who had painted this?

I searched the bottom of the mural for an artist's signature, but there wasn't one.

But there was a title. Scrawled across the bottom in glowing blue letters were the words *GHOST HEART*.

17

OLIVIA

We had to work together to get the ball gag off. I had Grant bend over the cement slab, facing away from me. Then I sat down, my back to his head, so my cuffed hands could work the straps. When I finally felt them give, I slipped my fingers between the leather and his hair, loosening it along his skull. He took a deep breath and blew out, spewing the ball from his mouth. Then he ducked his head, tossing the whole thing off onto the floor.

"Fuck that," he growled, kicking the damn thing into the corner. When he sat up fully, his shoulder brushed mine, warm and solid.

I looked up and found him staring down at me, his eyes swimming with emotion.

"I thought you were dead," he said. "Again."

"I thought you were dead too. I don't think I've ever been so happy to see anyone in my life."

"Me neither," he grinned, and I reveled in it. There we were, the two of us, handcuffed, imprisoned, and recently tortured by CAMFers, and we were grinning at each other like two kids reunited at summer camp. I felt almost high, giddy because I wasn't alone anymore. Grant was here with me.

But suddenly his face grew pained and serious.

"Olivia," he said, looking away. "What happened—what I did at Shades—I was a complete idiot. I never should have—"

"Hey," I said, nudging his shoulder. "Look at me."

And he did, his blue eyes locking with mine.

"You were a complete idiot," I agreed. "And I forgive you. We have bigger things to worry about than a sloppy kiss stolen in the dark."

"Sloppy?" he asked, a smile dancing at his lips again.

"You want to argue that point?" I smiled back.

"No." He said, all serious again. "I just want you to know you're safe with me. I would never hurt you or force you to do anything. And if it came off like that, I'm truly sorry."

"Apology accepted," I said.

The silence grew between us. Maybe he was thinking about Marcus, or wondering what had happened to Passion and the others. But I didn't want to talk about it.

Thankfully, he didn't ask. Instead, he looked around the cell and said, "This is exactly like the one I was in."

"Do you know what level you were on?"

"Not sure, but I'd never taken the elevator until today."

"So, probably the upper level. Were the others up there too?"

"I have no idea. I didn't even know there were others until a couple of hours ago when a guard gagged me, pulled me from my cell, and chained me to them. Did you—do you know any of them?"

"No." I looked down at my feet. After all the isolation I'd endured, all the abuse, it felt surreal having a normal conversation with Grant. I kept wanting to pinch myself to make sure it wasn't a dream. But it also felt freeing and right. "I mean, I remember seeing them at the Eidolon, but I didn't know them."

"Me neither," he said.

"What did they do to you?" I was afraid to hear his answer, but I needed to know.

"They questioned me a lot." Now he was looking down at his feet, at the shackles and chains still attached to his ankles. "Mostly about you. I wish I could say I held out, but I told them pretty much everything I knew."

"Even about the time we made-out in your garage?" I teased, wanting to take the pain in his voice away.

"Well no, not that." He looked up, grinning. "You swore me to secrecy, remember?"

"Yeah, and then you turned around and told Emma the very next day."

"It wasn't the next day," he protested. "I think she wheedled it out of me a few days later.

But that was your fault. The hickey you gave me wasn't exactly subtle."

"Oh my God," I said, shoving him with my shoulder. "I did not give you a hickey."

"Yes, you—wait, what is that?" He craned his neck, looking past me to the far wall.

And that's when I heard it too. The sound of mortar crumbling. The sound of rats that weren't rats.

"It's a friend," I whispered, turning too, just as the tip of a finger broke through again. "Come on," I got up and walked over to the wall, kneeling down.

Grant shuffled after me, kneeling as well, and both of us watched the finger wiggle back and forth as if searching for us.

"Someone is over there? Have you talked to them?" Grant asked, and then, before I could even answer, he was shouting. "Hey! Who are you? Can you help us?"

The finger pulled back quickly, disappearing.

Fuck. Had he scared her away? Had she been surprised to hear his voice instead of mine?

With my hands still bound, I didn't even have a free finger to beckon her back, so I bent down, putting my mouth to the hole. "It's okay," I said. "I'm still here, but I'm handcuffed. And that was my friend, Grant."

There was no response.

I sat up and turned to Grant, "I've talked to her once before," I told him. "But she didn't answer then either." Something held me back from telling Grant about the note she'd sent me. I don't know why. It felt wrong to tell him when I knew she was listening, like a betrayal.

"How do you know it's a she?" he asked.

"Her finger's smaller than mine," I explained.

"Could be a kid, though."

"Could be." But I didn't think so. Maybe I just didn't want to imagine a kid wandering around in the CAMFer's basement next to the morgue.

"Why won't she talk to us?" Grant asked.

"I don't know."

"She could be gagged," he pointed out.

"Maybe." I hadn't thought of that—not until now—but it made sense. "If she is, couldn't we use Morse code to communicate with her? Do you know it?"

"Sort of," Grant said. "I know S.O.S. and that's about it. But it's pretty obvious we need help. Besides, what would we do? Tap it out on the wall with our heads?"

"Dammit!" I leaned my forehead against the rough stone wall. "We need to get these handcuffs off or we're screwed."

More mortar crumbled down next to my foot and something poked through the hole, but it wasn't a finger. It was something metal, and it fell with a soft clink onto the pile of dust on the floor.

Grant and I stared down at the key, small and silver.

"Holy fuck," he exhaled. "Is that what I think it is?"

I scooted around on my ass, fumbling at the key with my fingers and finally managing to pick it up. "Put your back to me so I can try it," I told him.

He turned and we sat, back to back, me trying to stick the tiny key into a tiny keyhole I couldn't see.

Eventually I got it. I felt the key slide into the hole and catch. I gave it a twist and heard a satisfying click as one side of Grant's handcuffs fell open.

"Good," he said, turning toward me. "Give it to me and I'll undo the rest." His warm fingers took the key from mine, and I could hear him unlocking his other wrist. Then, he made quick work of mine.

When I finally turned around, free at last, he was holding both sets of handcuffs.

"Try your shackles," I urged him.

He set the cuffs aside and bent over, giving it a try. Somehow, I wasn't surprised when the shackles fell open with a click.

"What should we do with them?" he asked, tossing them next to the cuffs.

"We should keep them close. Next time they come for us we need to have them on, but unlocked, in case we get a chance to escape. Plus, we don't want them to know we have help." I looked down at the hole in the wall. "It worked," I called softly. "Thank you so much."

Again, there was no response.

"Maybe the key will work for the door too?" Grant said, starting to get up.

"No." I held him back. "It won't." I'd inspected that lock enough to know it was the wrong kind of key. "And the camera," I said, nodding toward it. "We don't want them to see we're free, or that we have a key."

"God, did you do that?" he asked, eyeing the damaged camera and sounding impressed. "Are you sure it even works anymore?"

"I'm not sure," I said. "But I know they can't see us over here."

"Whoever gave us this key," Grant said, nodding at the wall, "isn't a prisoner. How would a prisoner get a key?"

"I don't know," I said. "If she's not a captive, what is she?"

"Hello!" Grant called. "You over there. Who are you? How did you get this?"

"Don't do that! You'll scare her, and she's all we've got." But it was too late. I could hear the rustle of cloth and the soft scuff of her feet as she moved away from the wall. "See?" I huffed at him. "Why did you do that?"

"Because whoever that is over there can help us get out of here. They just proved it," he said, holding up the key.

"Okay. Fine." I snatched it from his fingers, annoyed. "But she's not going to help us if you yell at her. She isn't our genie in the wall."

"Seems like she sort of is," Grant said. "Hello?" he turned back to the wall, calling even louder. "Are you there? Can you help us?"

"Stop it," I hissed. "You've already scared her off. Do you want to call them down on us too? You're acting like a dick again. Just stop it." He was supposed to be my ally, not another liability.

"All right, all right." He held up his hands in a gesture of peace. "I'm sorry. I promise not to yell at your genie." The last part he said snidely, but I just ignored it. Still, I was suddenly very glad I hadn't told him about the hidden note.

"What about this thing?" he asked, reaching out and touching the special cuff on my right wrist. "Will the key work for it?"

"No." I looked down at it too. "It doesn't have a lock. I don't know how it works. They put it on me when I was drugged."

"It looks like it would just slide right off," he said, slipping the tip of his finger between the bracelet and my skin.

"I know." I pulled away. "But it doesn't." It had been an intimate touch, one I hadn't invited, and suddenly I was afraid of Grant again, a terror rising in my chest.

"What's it supposed to do?" he asked, oblivious to my inner turmoil. "And what was all that with you sticking your hand into me? What were they trying to get you to do?"

That's right. Grant didn't know any of this. He'd come to the Eidolon, found out I was alive, made a pass at me, and ended up being kidnapped by CAMFers at the end of the night. He had no real idea what was going on. Or why. He didn't know about my history with Fineman or the things my hand could do. And I really didn't want to have to explain the details of the last month to him. The less he knew, the better for him. Still, he deserved some explanation.

"Back in Greenfield, my ghost hand started doing some weird things," I said. "It reached into Passion Wainwright and pulled something out—and it did that again later—pulling strange items out of people that represented some kind of issue or emotional burden they had."

"You pulled those dog tags and that matchbook out of someone?" he asked, incredulous.

"Well, the tags are from Passion." I didn't need to tell him they'd been blades or why. That was Passion's secret. "And I eventually pulled something out of Fineman. A silver cube. That was in self-defense and I wasn't gentle. Taking it put him into a coma, and pissed him off. Now he's determined to make me put it back into him. Thus, the experiments with you today."

"But it didn't work. Everything you tried to put into me wouldn't go."

"I know, but he's figuring out what doesn't work, so he can figure out what will. You weren't the source of those items, so I was pretty sure they wouldn't go into you. And I was right. But he can use that information to his advantage. He can keep using me as his lab rat to figure it all out." I didn't want to tell Grant about Major Tom, didn't want him to know the many awful things I'd done with my hand. In his eyes, I was still the innocent girl he'd left in Greenfield when he went away to college. That was the girl he had a crush on, but she didn't even exist anymore. That Olivia was long gone.

"So, what happens when you put the cube back into him?" Grant asked.

"I don't know. It's complicated. See, something else got inside the cube by accident. Something from inside someone else. And now he's been tinkering in his lab with everything. I have no idea what will happen if I put it back in him."

"Why not just do it and find out?"

"Because he wants me to," I said, feeling like I was explaining calculus to a baby. "If it's important to him, it's bad for me. For us. For anyone with PSS. That man is crazy, and I won't do anything to help him. *Ever.*"

"Not even if he'd let us go? I mean, it might be harmless. If the cube came from him originally, how could it be bad to put it back?"

"What makes you think he'd let us go?" I asked, staring at Grant, a cold, hard pit of fear forming in my stomach. "Why would you say that?"

"I'm just saying, if it's what they want and they get it, maybe they'd—"

"What did they say to you?" I demanded. "What did they promise you to convince me?"

It had only been a guess, but he looked away when I asked, his eyes flashing guilt.

"Oh my God," I said, the air around me suddenly sterile and cold. "You're on their side. They put you in here with me to convince me to help them." I wanted to grab him and shake him. I wanted to kick him out of my cell and never see him again. But I needed what he knew. All of it. "Who talked to you? Mike Palmer? Fineman himself? Who the fuck talked to you, Grant?"

"Mike Palmer the Fire Chief is here?"

"Yes. I told you before, he's a CAMFer."

"Well, it wasn't him."

"Who, Grant? Who the fuck did you talk to?"

"Olivia, the doctor knows us. He was with your Mom."

"The doctor?" I choked out, my gut tightening into knots. "He doesn't want to help us, Grant. He wants to use us, maybe even kill us. He's the one who orchestrated the massacre up on those cliffs. He killed Nose and Yale and—everyone. He's a fucking monster." I was yelling, almost screaming, tears running down my face, my entire body shaking. Grant's appearance had been a spark of hope, a glimmer in the darkness. But Dr. Fineman had taken that spark and pissed on it. He'd fooled me into hoping and then impaled me with it.

"Hey." Grant was wrapping his arms around me, and I let him. "It's okay. You don't have to help them. I'm sorry. I'm an idiot. Don't listen to me."

I melted into the firmness of his body, resting my head on his chest and slipping my arms around him, gripping him like I would never let go. Sobs shook me as I clung to him. I'd almost forgotten what it was like to be touched for comfort. To receive care instead of violence.

"I just want you to be safe," he whispered into my hair. "That's all I meant. I'm not on their side. I promise you, Liv. I'm only on your side."

I wanted to believe that so badly. Some part of me yearned to give everything over to him and let him decide my fate. Wouldn't it be easier that way? I wouldn't have to think anymore. I wouldn't have to agonize. If I turned everything over to Grant, nothing would be my fault or my responsibility. No one could blame me for anything. He was older and stronger than me. It made perfect sense.

But I couldn't do it.
I couldn't lose myself that way.
Not to Dr. Fineman, or Anthony, or Grant.
Not to anyone.

18

MARCUS

I was up to two walks a day, one in the morning and one in the evening, but my uncle still wasn't convinced I was well enough to travel. Of course, they didn't let me walk alone. Reiny came and when she couldn't, Pete did, as if they were afraid I'd keel over and need CPR of the PSS. Physically, I felt fine. Psychologically, I was a basket case, but I pretty much always had been, so I kept that to myself.

I didn't talk much on the walks, once I'd figured out they wouldn't tell me anything. But I had a lot of time to think. The main thought being that everyone was waiting for me—waiting for me to recover, waiting for me to remember, waiting for some invisible second shoe to fall. My aunt and uncle kept insisting that arrangements were being made for us to fly to Oregon for the hostage negotiations as soon as possible, but I had a feeling it all somehow rested on me.

I hated waiting. Why would someone sit around waiting for bad things to happen? Action was better. At least then you had some say in the matter, even if you fucked it up.

So, when I got the chance to escape from Reiny on our morning walk, I took it. Some guy had stopped us to flirt with her on our boring circuit around the farmyard. Usually she blew the gawkers off, but she must have been interested in this one because this time she didn't. Instead, she stopped and flirted back. After a couple of minutes, it was obvious she'd forgotten I was standing there next to her, which was exactly what I'd hoped for. I took one step back, then another. Neither of them even glanced my way. Four more backward steps, and I slipped around the corner of the gun range building, slinking along the wall to the cornfield out back. I wasn't kidding myself. I knew I wasn't going to get far. But I was tired of being babysat.

The corn was high and ripe for the harvest. The crisp, yellowing stalks towered over my head in neat rows, rustling in the breeze. I ducked into the nearest row and ran. My boots kicked up clods of dirt, and I heard Reiny calling for me, but I was free. I had escaped my uncle and his machinations once again. At least for a little while.

Cornfields in Indiana are fucking huge. I ran until my heart was hammering in my chest and I had to stop to catch my breath, and I still hadn't reached the end of the field. Maybe I wasn't in as good of shape as I'd thought I was. No, the field was just huge.

When my heart quieted down, I listened for the sound of pursuit but didn't hear anything. I knew they were looking for me. It was only a matter of time before my uncle called out the cavalry and tightened the noose again, but it would take a while for him to call in the helicopters and shit.

I turned to the left and ran that way for a while. Might as well enjoy the freedom while I could and explore a little.

At last, the corn thinned ahead of me, spitting me out behind an old barn, probably used to store hay for the cows across the road. There was no one around, no vehicles either, but there were some small tire tracks near the front leading to the road. The barn doors were locked up tight with a big chain and padlock, but a peek through one of the wide cracks in its walls revealed three ATVs parked inside, all with trailers attached and piled high with what looked like camping equipment. There was a fourth trailer packed full, but no ATV with it, so maybe that's what the tire tracks were from. They'd looked to be about the right size.

I circled back around to the doors and inspected the lock. One of those ATVs could get me away from my uncle pretty quickly. He would never find me if I went off-road. But what then? I couldn't get to Danielle on my own. I had no resources. No friends. Going forward with my uncle and my aunt was my only hope for getting Danielle back.

Plus, I needed to know why there was a painting of me at Warm Springs. What did it mean? Maybe my uncle truly had no clue, but I doubted it. If I went to the reservation, I could find out for myself.

I turned around, ready to head into the cornfield and make my way back when I heard something buzzing down the road. I ducked behind a dilapidated shed next to the barn, peering through its wide slats, and watched as the missing ATV pulled up. There was a guy driving and Passion was on the back, her long hair gusting in the wind and whipping around her helmet.

The driver was helmetless and he killed the engine, stepping off the machine. I'd seen him before, milling around the farmhouse. I'd noticed him because he was younger than the rest of the Holders, closer to my age, and he always seemed to be turning away when I saw him, as if he was avoiding me.

Did Passion have a boyfriend and was I about to witness a private moment between them?

Yeah, it was definitely time to go. I turned toward the cornfield again, just as Passion pulled her helmet off, but her voice stopped me.

"Why'd you bring me here?" she demanded of the driver, and she didn't sound happy. "Where did you get the key to the barn?" She didn't even get off the ATV; she just sat there, stiff and angry, her hair whipping in the wind.

"Marcus hid a spare, just in case," the guy said. "And I brought you here because we need to talk, and you know it. Whatever was going on back there was the perfect distraction. No one even noticed us leaving."

Marcus meant me. This guy was talking about me leaving him a spare key. He knew me as Marcus, just like Passion did. I looked him over again, but nothing stirred. No memory. Nothing. I glanced at the barn. Had I been here before? With him?

"Something was wrong back at the farm. Something to do with Marcus," Passion said. "Don't you even care?"

"Marcus can take care of himself." The guy shrugged. "Haven't you figured that out by now?"

I sort of liked him. At least he had confidence in me. Probably more than I had in myself at the moment. Yeah, I definitely liked him.

Passion didn't seem to though. She was glaring at him, her eyes blazing. I'd never seen her angry before and it was kind of hot. "What is that supposed to mean?" she asked. "Are you saying Marcus knew what you told me back in the bathroom?"

Aha, it seemed I'd stumbled onto a conversation about myself and the shit I didn't remember. This should be interesting.

"Yeah," the guy said. "He knew his uncle was in negotiation with the CAMFers over something big, because I told him. And he knew his uncle was in contact with me."

My uncle colluding with CAMFers? Why wasn't I surprised?

"You said you weren't spying for Mr. James," Passion said, her voice almost a hiss.

"I wasn't," Jason said, "but sometimes he sent me messages. Marcus knew that. In a way, I helped him keep tabs on his uncle."

That sounded like something I'd do.

"What messages?" Passion asked, realization slowly dawning in her eyes. "The night at the McMansion when Palmer came and the tapes got changed. That was you covering up a message from him."

I had no idea what she was talking about, but I was getting the gist this guy had been playing both sides of the fence and probably still was.

"What message did Mr. James send you that night, Jason?" she asked, a tremble of fear in her voice.

"He told me to go the Eidolon," Jason said, "and he told me to stop the ceremony before any new initiates jumped. But I didn't tell Marcus the second part. I wasn't sure I was even going to do it. And before you knee me in the nuts again, I didn't know the fucking CAMFers were going to come and kill everyone. I just thought I was stopping the Eidolon, and my instructions were to get Samantha to safety no matter what."

"Get Samantha to safety? She got shot. You let them shoot her."

"No." Jason shook his head. "They didn't shoot her."

"What are you talking about?" Passion protested. "I've seen the wound. I heard the shot right after you left me in the—" She stopped, her face gone deathly white, her eyes wide and haunted. "You," she said, staring at Jason. "You shot Samantha. And he asked you to. Her own father asked you to shoot her."

"He knew I wasn't gonna kill her," Jason said. "Bo had seen me shoot. He knew I could do it."

Holy shit. This was the guy who'd shot Sam, and my uncle had fucking asked him to. And apparently, I had been this guy's friend. Or he'd been mine. Fuck.

But something in his explanation didn't add up. If my uncle hadn't known the CAMFers were coming, why arrange such drastic measures to get Samantha away?

"Take me back," Passion said, her lips pinched together, her nostrils flaring. "You betrayed all of us. They have Olivia because of you."

"Are you kidding me?" Jason laughed, but it wasn't a nice laugh. "I saved her. Fuck, I saved you. I even hid us from the CAMFers and got us back to the Holders and the damn pool so they could fish Marcus out. How is that a betrayal?"

They fished me out of the pool? Wait, had I been at this Eidolon thing? Was that my memory of water and drowning? That hadn't been when I was with Danielle. I had been with Passion and Samantha and this guy.

"How naïve do you think I am?" Passion asked bitingly. "You actually expect me to believe it was just a coincidence that the CAMFers showed up at the Eidolon? Someone told them we were going to be there. Someone with a connection to them."

It was exactly what I'd been thinking.

"And you think it was me?" Jason asked, charging up to the ATV and getting right in Passion's face. "You think I was working for the CAMFers? For my father who turned me over for extraction? A man who was disappointed he wouldn't get to shoot me in the head because there was a better use for me?" He grabbed onto the handles of the ATV and shook it, looking as if he was might vault over the machine any moment and attack Passion. "I am going to fucking kill my father with my own hands, and Mr. James is going to help me do it when he overthrows the CAMFers once and for all. That's what this is all about. This whole thing is a build up to an all-out war between the CAMFers and The Hold. The Eidolon was just a bump in the road."

Passion stared at him, unblinking, unmoving, and as far as I could tell unafraid, which was damn impressive because the guy was fucking scary. He had seriously lost it. If he touched her, I'd step in. I wouldn't let this whacko hurt Passion. But the conversation between the two of them was garnering me more information than I'd gotten the entire time I'd been holed up in the farmhouse, so I didn't stop him. Not yet.

"Yale and Nose weren't just a bump in the road to me," Passion said. "Take me back to the farmhouse. Now."

"No." Jason shook his head, but most of the gusto had gone out of him. "I thought you'd want your things. Your clothes and stuff from before." He gestured toward the barn.

"I don't want it," Passion said stiffly. "I want you to take me back."

"No, get off the wheeler," he insisted, grabbing her by the arm.

"Let go of her," I said, stepping from behind the shed.

He turned, the look on his face something I will never forget—part shock, part shame, part something-I-couldn't-name.

"Marcus," Passion said, looking over her shoulder, her face lighting up. That was all. Just my middle name.

"What are you doing here?" Jason asked, dropping Passion's arm and looking thoroughly confused.

"Did you remember the barn?"

"No," I said. "Just random chance I guess, but I can say it was pretty informative."

"What did you—you heard all of that?" Passion asked, sounding concerned.

"Yep. But don't worry. My brain hasn't exploded or anything yet. And apparently," I turned back to Jason, "I know you." I'd considered him valuable once. If he had a connection to my uncle and the CAMFers, he still was, even if I'd have to watch my back around him. Better to keep your enemies close, especially if you could convince them they were friends. "Nice to meet you again, Jason." I held out my hand. He looked like a handshake kind of guy.

He stared down at it and glanced back up at me. Then he grasped my hand and gave it a strong shake.

"You have PSS and your dad is a CAMFer," I said, squeezing his hand. "God, it must suck to be you."

"At least I can remember shit," he returned the jab as we dropped each other's hands.

"How long have we known each other?" I asked.

"We met a month before the Eidolon. You don't remember me at all?"

"Nope, sorry. Don't take it personally."

"As long as you don't take it personally that I shot your cousin."

I did, but I wasn't going to tell him that.

"Look, I hate to break up this little reunion," Passion said from the back of the ATV, "but I think they're coming for us." She pointed down the road to a cloud of dust rising in the air and heading in our direction. Trucks. Probably several of them.

"What do you want us to do?" Jason asked me. "Because they're about to find our stuff unless we get out of here."

I had no idea what was in the stash in the barn, what evidence there was that my uncle might use against me, but I'd obviously hidden it for a reason.

"Get off," I told Passion, grabbing the helmet from her.

She didn't even hesitate. She was off in a second.

"Put this on," I told Jason, shoving the helmet into his hands. "Take the ATV. With any luck, they'll think you're me. Keep them busy as long as you can. If they catch you, tell them you stole the ATV and went for a joy ride."

He jammed the helmet on, jumped onto the ATV, and fired it up. Again, not a question and no hesitation. They both followed me like it was what they were meant to do. It was weird. The only one who'd ever really listened to me was my sister, and she barely had. But when Jason had asked me what to do, I'd known. And I'd known they'd do it.

Jason peeled out, spitting up a cloud of dust around Passion and me as he turned right onto the road, away from the oncoming trucks.

"Let's go." I grabbed Passion's hand and we ran toward the cornfield.

And we made it, slipping between the tall stalks just before the trucks went barreling by, tearing after Jason.

19

OLIVIA

woke to darkness and thought I must be dreaming. The cell was never dark. It was constantly bathed in the perpetual flicker and buzz of an inset fluorescent light. In fact, the buzz had been getting louder and more insistent lately, like a bug trying to drill into my skull, and I'd begun to think it was a unique kind of torture designed by our captors to break us. Grant thought I was paranoid and the bulb was just failing. I'd suggested where he could shove the light bulb and the word "paranoid." Paranoid was a word reserved for people who hadn't been kidnapped by militant CAMFers. I wasn't paranoid. I was a realist. Except now it looked like Grant had been right and the bulb had gone out.

Slowly, my eyes adjusted, aided by the gentle blue glow of my ghost hand. At least the horrible buzz was gone, silenced at last.

Grant was still snoring, his arm thrown over me. We slept side by side for warmth, and comfort, and safety, the handcuffs and key nestled between us, ready. But Anthony hadn't come back for us.

We thought it had been three days, based on how often some random guard had left trays of food just inside the door. It was hard to know for sure though. It was hard to tell anything abandoned in a cell deep beneath the earth.

Abandoned. Even my enemies had lost interest in me, and it pissed me off. I felt myself losing the will to fight in the absence of anyone to fight against. Anthony's hate had been the wall I'd banged against. Even Dr. Fineman's experiments, as horrible as they were, had taught me things about my ghost hand I wouldn't have learned otherwise. Was it sick to miss that? Was this how Stockholm syndrome started? By feeling betrayed when the bad guys finally left you alone?

No, not alone. I had Grant now. Grant and I, living and breathing within the same four stone walls. Sleeping together. Pissing together. Shitting together. Getting on each other's nerves. Arguing over what we should do if we ever had an opportunity to do anything.

Sharing a tent with Marcus had never been this hard. We'd understood each other's moods and needs without even voicing them. God, how I missed him. I wanted him with me, as selfish as that was. Maybe Grant was my new torture, not the light bulb. That was unfair to Grant. I knew it was. But I still felt it.

He inhaled, loudly, then snorted out and rolled away from me, unpinning me with his arm but also jamming me against the wall. He had rolled onto his stomach, which quieted his snoring, but now I was fully awake.

When I heard the scratching at the wall, I extracted myself from the slab, careful not to wake him.

I crossed the cell, sliding down next to the hole, and I knew she was there. I could hear the rustle of her clothes on the other side. I could feel her presence and relief washed over me. Where had she been for the last few days? Why hadn't she scratched until now? I'd been worried she was gone, scared off by Grant for good. Or that they'd caught her helping us and moved her, or worse. I'd even begun to suspect she didn't exist. What if it was really Anthony, or Palmer, or Dr. Fineman sticking their finger through the hole and laughing at me? *Let's send her a note offering to help. Let's give her the key to the handcuffs and leave her there to die, clutching it hopefully.* I wouldn't have put it past them.

But now she was back, and I believed in her again.

I couldn't call to her. It might wake Grant, and I didn't want him messing things up again. So, instead, I slipped my finger into the hole, accidentally jamming it right into hers.

I felt her jerk her finger away in surprise. There was a soft rustling on the other side of the wall and she touched my finger, gently pushing it back to my side. I bent down, putting my eye to the hole and found another eyeball staring right back at me, the iris dark brown and curious. Then her eye disappeared, followed by more rustling. All I could see was a small blur of light, and then sudden darkness as a piece of paper came ramming toward my eye.

I moved my head and grabbed the paper. It was another page out of *The Bone Road*, page forty-seven this time, with three lines of writing scrawled between the text.

The first line read, *Don't trust the boy.*

I glanced over at Grant. She must be referring to him. He'd freaked her out when he'd yelled at her, just as I'd suspected. Was that why she'd waited to come back until he was asleep and snoring loudly? She trusted me, but not him. Could there be more to her mistrust than just his yelling through the wall? Did she know something about Grant that I didn't?

I looked down at the next line she'd written.

They are coming for you. Soon.

Great. I guess I should be careful what I wished for. There I'd been, pining away for Anthony and Dr. Fineman, and it seemed they were on their way to pay me a visit. Or did she mean someone else? And how did she know? Who was this girl, and what was she doing here?

I glanced down at the last line of her note. *Trust me*, it said.

Um, okay. I'd been doing that, as much as anyone could trust someone they'd met through a wall and only touched fingers with. But I was going to need more. I still wasn't absolutely convinced this wasn't another one of Fineman's mindfucks. What if the warning to not trust Grant was just another way to mess with my head? Then again, I kind of didn't trust him already.

He'd tried to talk me into helping the doctor. Fuck. How could I trust anything or anyone in this fucked up place?

Was this what Marcus had gone through in foster care? This paralyzing fear, this suspicion shrouding every interaction and decision? How had he lived like that? No wonder he'd had so much trouble confiding in me, trusting me. I thought I'd understood before, but I hadn't. His entire life had been this guessing game of how others would betray him. Not if, but when and how. And it had only gotten worse when the CAMFers had taken his sister, the one person he'd ever been able to rely on.

Danielle.

I looked down at the note in my hands and then at the hole in the wall. I remembered that brown eye staring at me through it, curious and vaguely familiar.

Dr. Fineman had sworn to me he still had Danielle. He'd shown me video of her on one of the first days of my captivity. He'd tried to use it to convince me that Marcus was working for him and always had been, that the CAMFers were using Danielle as leverage to bend him to their will. I hadn't believed it. I couldn't. Marcus had not been lying to me when he'd told me his sister was dead. There was no way he could have feigned that agony. He had believed it.

But what if half of what Dr. Fineman had told me was true? What if they still had Danielle and Marcus didn't know it? They could have tricked him into believing she was dead. Or maybe, by some miracle of her power to heal, she'd survived extraction, just like he had. What if she'd woken up to find Marcus gone, escaped away without her? What would she have done to survive? Dr. Fineman had implied that he and Mike Palmer had recovered from their injuries thanks to Danielle's power. Was she working with them, or for them, or was she just trying to stay alive like I was?

I glanced down at the hole again, light and motion catching my eye.

And then her finger came through, but not her normal finger, not a flesh finger.

I stared down at the delicate fingertip of PSS jutting through the wall, and then her entire hand came through up to the wrist. As I stared down, mesmerized, she turned her PSS hand, palm-up, and held it out for me the way someone offers you their hand to hold, an intimate gesture.

Take my hand. Trust me.

I reached out my ghost hand and took hers.

I had only touched someone else's PSS once before. Marcus and I had shared that—my fingers brushing against his chest. This was just as sensuous. It was like hearing Samantha play, the knowing, the being, and the wonder. Sensations rushed over me: well-being, trust, peace, safety, rest. Suddenly, all my aches and pains were gone. I wasn't hungry anymore. I wasn't tired anymore. I wasn't afraid anymore.

Holy crap.

I yanked my hand out of hers.

It was overwhelming, that feeling. It had been wonderful and too much, all at once, like I might implode from the goodness of it.

Her hand was disappearing back through the wall.

"Don't leave," I called. "Are you Danielle?" But it wasn't really a question anymore. "I know your brother. I know Mar—David. Do you know a way out of here?"

There was no answer except the sound of her moving away. Of course she didn't know a way out, or she wouldn't still be here. And yet, she'd somehow managed to get the key to the handcuffs, which meant she wasn't quite as limited in her freedom as we were. Danielle had been here for eight months. She must know this place backwards and forwards by now. If she could help us, we might all get out of this hell hole together. I could be the one to reunite Marcus and his sister, the sister he believed was dead.

I could save her.

We could save each other.

The cell door banged open and Anthony charged in.

I'd been so focused on the Danielle thing, I hadn't even heard them coming.

Them. *Plural.* Because Anthony was not alone. He'd brought a whole platoon of armed CAMFers.

A couple of them grabbed Grant, shaking him out of a dead sleep. He struggled a little at first until one of them backhanded him across the face.

Anthony grabbed me, yanking me up.

I let the note drop from my hands behind me, hoping he wouldn't see it.

They yelled at us, shoving us toward the door. If they noticed we didn't have our handcuffs on or that Grant was unshackled, they didn't seem to care.

I should have known then something was terribly wrong. I should have known by the triumphantly smug look on Anthony's face. But I was still in a daze from finding Danielle and whatever she'd done to me. It was hard to feel fear. It was hard to feel anything except the euphoria welling up into my body from my hand.

They took us up the elevator, down the hall, and shoved us through Dr. Fineman's darkened lab into the interrogation room. The lights were off in there too, but Anthony flicked them on and ordered four of the guys to stand guard outside. "No one comes in," he told them. "No one."

They nodded and left the room, shutting and locking the door behind them, leaving Anthony and four more guards inside, two each holding Grant and me.

Alarm bells were going off in my head by then. Who would Anthony need to keep out? And why?

I looked around the room and over at the two-way mirror.

Dr. Fineman wasn't here.

I couldn't sense his ever-watching presence.

As far as I could tell, it was the middle of the night.

And that was when I realized Anthony had brought us there on his own. He was acting without Dr. Fineman's knowledge or permission. There was a mutiny among the CAMFers, and I was its focal point. Palmer's words to Anthony from days ago echoed in my head. *Something needs to be done.* He had meant something had to be done about me and my hand, and I had a terrible feeling I was about to find out what that "something" was.

Suddenly, the spell woven over me by Danielle began to wear off. Grant and I were in trouble. Serious trouble.

I looked over at him, trying to warn him with my eyes, but he was staring at Anthony who had crossed to the table in the middle of the room. There was a metal case there and Anthony opened it, pulling something out. It was metal too, and long, and looked like a cross between an electric carving knife and a minus meter.

"Bring her over here," he said, gesturing at the chair, and the two CAMFers holding me propelled me toward him.

"What are you doing?" Grant demanded, struggling against the men holding him. "Leave her alone. We'll cooperate. Just don't—" One of the guard's fists came down on the back of Grant's neck, knocking him to his knees, turning his protests to moans of pain.

"Leave him alone," I yelled, trying to dig my bare feet into the smooth floor, trying to stop my forward momentum toward Anthony, and the table, and the device in his hands, but it was no use. There were two of them, and they were huge, and I was nothing. They shoved me forward, one pinning me against the edge of the table, the other grabbing my arm and holding it out across the tabletop, my ghost hand right in front of Anthony.

"Oh, we're going to leave him alone," Anthony said, shoving his ugly face into mine. "But I'm afraid you're not so lucky. You see this?" He held the device up. "Do you know what this is?"

I shook my head, staring at it, almost transfixed by its horrid beauty.

"It's a special kind of minus meter," he said. "See, the original ones Dr. Fineman made were kind of glitchy. They would drain the PSS out of you minus cunts, which was good, but then you'd just keep leaking it out until you died a slow, agonizing death. Now, some of us thought that was just fine, didn't we, Max?" he asked the man holding my arm.

"Yes sir, only good minus cunt is a dead minus cunt," the man said.

"But the good doctor doesn't agree with us. We don't see eye to eye. He wanted to come up with a way to extract PSS without killing the subject. Sadly, he just didn't have the right ingredients to create such a thing, until he stumbled upon some unique blades in a small town in Illinois."

I stared at the thing Anthony was holding. Now I could see that each notch in the blade's serration was a small, sharp, individual piece of metal, all of them carefully welded together to make a whole. Marcus had made something new out of our Passion's blade, something to protect me. Dr. Fineman, sick fuck that he was, had made this.

"How's that for irony?" Anthony said, flipping a small switch on the handle of Dr. Fineman's new invention.

The device began to hum and something red flashed across my vision, a line of light running from the inside of the handle to the tip of the gently curved blade.

"That's the self-cauterizing laser," Anthony said with a grin. "The blades sever the PSS clean through and the beam closes the ethereal wound right up. I mean, it's not just any laser. The doc had to make it special just for this. Of course, we haven't had a chance to test it fully until now."

"He didn't tell you to do this." I locked eyes with Anthony, ignoring the cold fear eating at my guts. "He wants me to put the cube back in him. He wants me to pull other things—"

"No!" Anthony slammed one fist down on the table, waving the machine around wildly in his other hand. "You're too dangerous. He's blinded by his science, but he'll thank me for this in the end. What you do with that hand—it's an abomination. And there's only one way to make sure you never do it again."

There was no more warning than that.

He lowered the blade to my wrist, exactly where my PSS met my flesh.

I have felt pain before. The room with the blades under Palmer's house had been very bad. I thought I'd lost my ghost hand then. That's what it had felt like. But this was a hundred times worse.

I remember hearing Grant screaming, or maybe it was me. I remember bucking against the men who held me, the sensation of the table digging into my chest. I remember seeing the red light and the blade cutting through my PSS like butter. And as it was severed, it wisped away, sucked into a small port at the base of the oversized knife handle.

At some point, the lights in the room flashed in and out and I was racing down a narrow tunnel toward darkness and peace, only to find myself suddenly standing in a golden cornfield with Marcus, the breeze ruffling his hair, an achingly-blue autumn sky hanging over us.

"What's the matter?" he said, tugging me by the hand. He was holding my hand.

"I—Is this heaven?" I asked, totally confused. Since when had I believed in heaven?

"Nooo—this isn't heaven," he said, grinning. "It's a cornfield."

"But how did I—never mind—I need to tell you something." I moved closer to him, slipping my arm around his waist the way he liked me to.

His eyes went wide in surprise. "What do you need to tell me?" he asked, his voice both skeptical and hopeful all at once.

I fixed my eyes on his lips, moving in to kiss him the way I had that first time in his tent.

I could feel his hesitation at first, his body tense, but then he relaxed into it, his lips opening to mine, our tongues touching, his arms pulling me against him.

I pulled away and looked up into those smoldering brown eyes. "I love you," I said.

"Passion, whoa," he said, dumping me out of his arms, and backing into the corn a little. "Listen, I appreciate the sentiment but—"

I didn't hear the rest of what he said. I looked down at my hands. Neither one PSS. They weren't my hands. This wasn't my place. Marcus had just called me Passion and Anthony had been cutting off my ghost hand with Passion's blades.

The cornfield and Marcus flew up into the sky and away as I was sucked down into the dark earth, the cold earth, the dead earth.

Later, someone was carrying me, but it was nothing like when Marcus had carried me and called me babe.

And when I woke, lying on the slab of cement in my cell alone, the bulb in the ceiling had come back on and I could clearly see that the end of my right arm now ended in nothing but a fleshy stump.

I was alone. What had they done with Grant? Had they killed him? I tried to muster up the will to care, but I couldn't.

I didn't want Grant.

I wanted Marcus and the cornfield.

I would give anything to have it back.

Even my hand.

20

MARCUS

'll admit, when Passion slipped her arms around me and kissed me, I wasn't expecting it. I mean, I hadn't gotten that vibe from her, and it wasn't like girls threw themselves at me in general. Danielle had once told me I was too guarded, that I never let anyone in, but she also knew why. When you grow up in foster care, affection is like a dangerous, secret code. You might be reading the signals right. Or returning a hug from your new sister might result in you getting the shit beaten out of you by your new dad. So, yeah, I wasn't a touchy-feely kind of guy.

But I was still a guy.

I was also totally caught off guard.

One minute Passion was fuming at Jason as we fled through a cornfield, the next minute she'd stopped, stock-still, and her expression had completely changed to this adorable, awestruck look. Then, she'd asked me if we were in heaven, and her eyes zoned in on my lips, her hands going around my waist—for a split second, she'd looked like someone else, someone completely different.

So, yeah, I didn't fight it. Why would I?

Until she dropped the love bomb completely out of nowhere.

"Passion, whoa." I pulled out of her embrace and backed up a little. "Listen, I appreciate the sentiment but—"

"Oh, no," she put her fingers to her lips, blinking up at me like I was a bright light. "I'm so sorry. That wasn't—I don't love you. I mean, I like you, but not in that way. You're a nice guy and everything but—no."

"Then what the hell was that? You just kissed me."

"No, I didn't."

"Yes, you did."

"No, I know. I did, but I didn't."

What was that supposed to mean? Was she crazy? Was she using me to get back at Jason? "Oh, well, I'm glad we cleared that up," I snapped.

"No, I mean it wasn't *me*," she said, catching my eyes, trying to communicate some wordless cryptic message. "I don't like guys," she said finally, looking embarrassed. "Samantha and I—we were together before the Eidolon."

"You and Samantha?" I blurted. "But she isn't—"

"Yes, she is," she assured me. "She likes both. But I said something about her father she didn't like, and now she'll barely talk to me."

Sam, my little cousin, was bi? Actually, I wasn't that surprised. Sam had always been enthusiastic about all human beings. She loved people. Period. As closed off as I was, she was the polar opposite. She was also totally blind to my uncle's flaws, which apparently now included having her shot.

But that still didn't explain the whole kiss-you, love-you, now-I'm-suddenly-gay thing Passion was pulling.

"I'm still confused," I said, brushing a hand though my hair. "If you like girls, then why kiss me? You keep saying it wasn't you. So what? You were suddenly demonically possessed by a straight person and they lunged for my lips?"

"Pretty much," she said, giving me that look again, like she expected me to read her mind.

"That doesn't even—" I started to say, and then it all clicked into place. The way she'd spoken and acted and even looked different. The sudden confusion on her face when she'd asked where we were. The familiar way she'd touched me. "It was her," I said. "That girl you can feel through the tags."

"*That girl*?" She was back to being angry Passion again. "She's not *that girl*. Her name is Olivia, and you know it."

"Right. Whatever," I said. "So, she was into me?" I tried to keep the amusement out of my voice, but it wasn't easy. It seemed I'd been a very busy boy over the last eight months. Not only had I been to this Eidolon thing, I'd also collected a bunch of groupies, a barn full of camping gear, and an admirer I didn't even remember.

It was kind of funny.

Except Passion wasn't laughing.

"She wasn't *into you*," she said. "You were into each other. You were in love. You *are* in love."

"No way," I said, the humor suddenly gone out of me. "Not possible. I don't do that."

"Don't do what? Love people?"

"Love them. Trust them. It's kind of a policy I have."

"Well, she broke your policy," Passion insisted. "Olivia isn't exactly a hopeless romantic either, but you both softened around each other, like all your hard edges had been rounded. And if telling you causes your brain to explode, it's exactly what you deserve." She crossed her arms over her chest.

I knew there was no way I'd loved this girl, but obviously I'd convinced Passion I had, and probably the girl as well. What had I been doing?

"And don't tell me you don't love anyone." Passion said. "What about your sister?"

"Yeah, I love my sister, but that's different." Now she was just being annoying. "We only have each other. You wouldn't understand."

"Wouldn't I?" she shot back. If looks could kill, I would've had to reboot again. "What do you even know about me?"

"Nothing," I said. What did she want from me? To confess my undying love for a girl I didn't even know. "I don't remember anything, remember?" I began to pace up and down the narrow corn row.

"That's kind of the whole point. I don't remember Olivia. At all. So don't fucking tell me I love her, okay? Because I don't."

"But you did," she said, her nostrils flaring. "And she loves you. You think it sucks to forget? Try being one of us for a day. We've lost things too. You were our friend. You were our leader. You saved our lives. You knew what the hell was going on with the CAMFers and The Hold, and you had a plan. You always had a plan. At least, we thought you did. We trusted that you did, and you NEVER trusted us, and you led us straight to the Eidolon. Two of my friends died there. Two of your friends. And you don't even remember them. And now what? You sit around like a lump for days feeling sorry for yourself, pining after your sister. I lost my sister too, okay? She died. She drowned when we were twelve. So, don't you dare tell me I don't understand." She stormed off down the row and she was crying. I'd made her cry.

I followed her, feeling like a complete dick. She was right about some things. Yeah, I'd been wallowing in self-pity and been consumed with worry about Danielle. Danielle and I—I had been the only one to ever truly protect her. You think foster care was difficult for me? That was nothing compared to what it was for Danielle. She'd always been a beautiful, delicate girl. And she'd been a healer, willing to take on other people's pain, and guilt, and darkness, always seeing the good in them, even when there wasn't any. Even when they were hurting her. Or abusing her. While I raged against our fate with violence and stubbornness, she suffered quietly, sometimes even keeping things from me so I wouldn't get in trouble trying to help her.

And now she was gone, and I didn't know where, and I couldn't protect her. It was tearing me up inside, and it made it hard to remember that all the people around me were missing something too. They were missing me. Or their friends who had been taken. Or both.

"Hey," I said, catching up with Passion and grabbing her elbow gently to stop her forward march. "Can you stop for a minute?"

"What?" she asked, whirling around to face me.

"I'm sorry, okay? I'm sorry about your sister, and I'm sorry I was a jerk about the Olivia thing. I just don't know what to do with that right now."

"I know," she said, her guard dropping. "Me neither."

"Can I ask you something?"

"Sure."

"When you felt her did you see or feel anything that might give us a clue to her location?"

"No." she shook her head. "It was different this time. I didn't feel where she was at all."

"But if there was anything, even something little that could lead us to where they are—"

"And by 'they' do you mean Grant and Olivia, or do you just mean Danielle?" She wasn't angry this time. Her eyes were just sad, with maybe a hint of pity.

"I mean all of them," I said, but it was a lie and we both knew it.

"You need to think about this," she said, softly, putting her hand on my arm. "For the last eight months, you didn't have your sister and she didn't have you. My sister was my twin and we were close, and when she died I didn't think I'd be okay, you know?

I thought I'd end too. But I didn't. I went on living, and doing things, and meeting people, and changing. And loving. You've had a life for the last eight months, even without your sister. I know you don't remember it, but you did, so it's possible." Her eyes were trying to tell me something, and I looked away. I pulled my arm away too. This was way too heavy of a conversation to have in a cornfield with a girl I barely knew.

"So, if I had such a great plan for defeating the CAMFers," I said, trying to lighten the mood, "you think you could let me in on it?"

"Yeah, well, you didn't exactly share it," she said, wryly. "You tended to keep the rest of us in the dark. That was mostly what you and Olivia fought about. She hated that you didn't tell her stuff, that you wouldn't trust her."

"We fought?" I asked, teasingly. "I thought we were the best couple ever?"

"I never said that." Passion looked up, peering through the corn in front of us.

The wind had picked up and the rustling of the stalks had grown louder. No, it wasn't the wind. Someone was crashing toward us, not just one someone, but a whole platoon.

"Don't run," I said, taking her arm again. There was no point. They were already on top of us.

"Hold it right there!" an armed Holder yelled, crashing into our row, his automatic weapon pointed at us.

In a minute, my uncle's men had surrounded us on all sides.

"So, obviously, I'm free to go," I said, smiling at the one closest to us.

"Your uncle was worried for your safety," he said with a straight face. "This field is unsecured. He was afraid you might run into trouble. We'll escort you both back to the farmhouse."

"I bet you will." I gestured for the guy to lead the way.

They took us back, surrounding us all the way.

My aunt and uncle were waiting on the front porch, Jason standing next to them, the dusty ATV parked to one side. When I looked at him, he glanced away. So much for me being the fine rebel leader Passion had portrayed me as. It looked like Jason had led the Holders straight to us, instead of leading them away like I'd told him to. They didn't seem to have the stuff from the barn though, so maybe he was still playing both sides. Either way, I expected my uncle to chew us all out. But he didn't.

"Good. You're back," he said instead. "We're flying out from a local airstrip in two hours. You have an hour to pack."

"Remember," my aunt added. "We'll be in high desert, but it's still fall, so bring something warm."

"We're going to Oregon? Today?" Passion blurted. "But I've never flown before, and I only have one set of clothes."

"Come with me," my aunt said, stepping down and wrapping an arm around her. "I'm sure Samantha has something you can wear. Let's go get you out of that hideous camouflage."

I watched them walk into the house together, disappearing into the shadows.

"So what gives?" I turned to my uncle. "You're suddenly ready to do this?" Half of me was screaming with excitement, the other half was screaming with fear. This was my uncle I was dealing with. He left nothing to chance.

"The final arrangements in Oregon fell into place this morning," he said. "And you're obviously ready to go."

"You were waiting for me to run?" I saw Jason smirking out of the corner of my eye. Had that whole scene at the barn been a set up? Had they planned for me to hear it?

"I was waiting for you to show some heart," my uncle said.

21

OLIVIA

The scratching in the wall did not come again. Danielle, or whoever she was, had abandoned me. All her promised help, scrawled notes, and tender touches had gotten me absolutely nothing, zilch, nada. They'd taken my hand. Anthony had fucking cut off my ghost hand. My PSS was gone. And so was Grant. They'd taken him somewhere else, or killed him, I didn't know which. The only thing they'd left me with was pain.

Even it was fading, a little at a time, the pain where pain had never been before making way for a far more disturbing sensation; the sensation that my hand was still there. I could feel it. As long as I wasn't looking at that awful, blank, fleshy stump, my ghost hand was there in my mind. I could move it. I could see it. A phantom limb of a phantom limb. So, I did everything I could not to look at the stump. Or when I did, when I forgot and accidentally moved it across my line of sight, I pretended it belonged to someone else. Because it did. That couldn't be me. It just couldn't.

For a long time, I just lay there, trying to figure out what I could have done differently. Could I have stopped Anthony? What decision could I have made that would have prevented me from ending up here—handless and alone? Thinking of the past was comforting. In every memory of myself in my mind's eye, I had two hands. But something kept bringing me back to the present, something hard and sharp, digging into my backside. When I finally rolled over and found the chain mail cuff that had been on my wrist, the one to protect everyone from the hand I no longer had, I hurled it across my cell and laughed. I kept laughing and I couldn't stop. It sounded awful and strange, and it hurt my lungs and my face and my gut. Eventually, the laughing turned to crying and that hurt too.

Maybe I was going mad.

Maybe going mad was the best alternative. Because when my brain began to work again, it thought things like, *This will make my mother happy—the hideous ghost hand gone and just a normal handless girl for a daughter.*

Or, *this was my punishment for reaching into people and pulling things out. I deserved it. I must have deserved it.*

Or worse yet, *Why hasn't Marcus come for me? It's too late now. Everything is ruined. I am ruined.*

I'd seen him in a cornfield. With Passion. I'd gone to

them when Anthony had laid the knife made from her blades to my wrist. I had kissed Marcus and told him I loved him, and he had kissed me back. No, he had kissed her back.

What had they been doing, just standing around in a field together? They were supposed to be rescuing me. I'd told Passion where we were and that Grant was here. I'd told them to come. But what if they weren't coming? What if they were together now?

I knew that didn't make sense. Passion liked girls, and she liked Samantha, specifically. She hadn't kissed him. I had. But he hadn't know it was me. He'd called her Passion, and he'd kissed her back. Why had he done that?

No one brought me food or drink.

It was like they'd forgotten I existed.

Fuck them.

I cannot explain what it means to have a piece of yourself severed from you. Something that has always defined you. Something that makes you who you are. I had been the girl with the ghost hand. Now, I was a girl with no hand. I was stump girl. All my life, I'd felt different and other. Sometimes that had sucked, but part of me had liked it and reveled in it, and I hadn't even know that until it was gone.

Yes, I was having a grand old pity party and no one was invited but me.

There was nothing left to do except drift in and out of a troubled sleep, waiting for someone to come and help me.

Waiting for Marcus.

Waiting for anyone.

*

She came to me in my dreams, a ghost in black robes, floating straight through the wall of my cell like a dark angel. When she settled next to me, I wasn't surprised. That's how dreams are. Strange things happen and they aren't strange. It didn't seem unusual that I could not see her face, except for the glow emanating from deep in her cowled hood. It didn't seem odd that I knew her, or that she knew me. And when she touched me with her hand, I felt warmth flow out of it into my body like a river of goodness, and I heard her voice in my head.

All will be well.

You will be whole.

Your hand will come back to you.

Perhaps in the dream world, all those things were true.

"Please," I begged her. "Help me. Get me out of here."

Soon, she whispered in my mind. *But you have to be strong. You can't give up.*

"No," I argued. "You have to help me."

You have to help me, she said, which made no sense. Why had she come into my dream, if not to help me?

She turned her head toward the cell door, exactly the way Princess Leia does in that holographic R2-D2 message just before she blinks out.

And she blinked out.

My ghost disappeared.

The door to the cell slammed open, and I sat up, groggy and disoriented, as Dr. Fineman barreled in, several guards flanking the door behind him.

He looked me over, his eyes settling on the wrist stump in my lap, and he scowled, rage flaring in his eyes.

"Bring him in," he barked over his shoulder, and two more guards dragged Anthony in between them.

He was bloody, and beaten, and he did not look triumphant anymore.

"Look at her." Dr. Fineman grabbed his hair and yanked his head up, pointing it in my direction. "She was mine. I went to great trouble to acquire her. She was the key to everything I've been working toward for years, and now she is useless."

"She was too dangerous," Anthony croaked. "She killed—"

"Silence!" Dr. Fineman yelled, and one of the men holding Anthony pulled back a meaty fist, pounding him in the ear. I'd received that same blow so many times from Anthony, it had to be karma. Very ugly karma. "She killed no one, you idiot," Dr. Fineman spat. "That unfortunate accident was a result of the amplifications I'd done in my lab, a side-effect I've already remedied. You have no understanding of science or what I'm doing here. You've ruined a very costly investment, an investment worth more than you will ever understand. I needed her PSS and her hand, and now I have neither. I have nothing, and you are going to pay for it." With a horrible glint in his eye, Dr. Fineman gestured to the guard, who pulled out a large, sharp-looking knife from his belt. "What about a hand for a hand?" Fineman asked. "Does that seem fair?"

"No," Anthony cried, staring at the knife in horror. "You can't."

The two guards holding him lifted him by his armpits and dragged him toward me.

I scuttled back, pressing myself against the wall as they pinned his arm and hand to the slab in front of me.

"No," he whimpered. "Please." He craned his neck, trying to look back at Dr. Fineman. "You have her PSS. I used the new device."

"I have nothing," Dr. Fineman glared at him. "You did something wrong. The entire sample was contaminated. Her signature was so muddied I could barely tell what it was, let alone who it was from. It is useless. I will never be able to identify the markers for her powers now. Her ability is lost forever and so is any hope of duplicating it, thanks to you."

A part of me rejoiced at that. They'd taken my hand, but they hadn't gotten what they wanted. Dr. Fineman was royally pissed off about that. His maniacal plans had been ruined by his own guys, by a seed of dissent nurtured by Palmer and brought to fruition by Anthony. Still, another part of me mourned. The power of my hand was gone. Lost forever. No one had it. Not even the CAMFers. My ghost hand had truly and utterly disappeared from the world.

"No, that's impossible," Anthony argued desperately. "I did it right. It worked exactly like you—"

"Enough," Dr. Fineman said, glancing at the man with the knife.

As much as I hated Anthony, I had no desire to see him mutilated right before my eyes. But no one was asking me. One minute the blade was in the air, the next it was slicing into his skin.

I buried my face in my knees, waiting for the screaming I knew would come. I couldn't even cover both my ears with my hands.

The sounds Anthony made weren't the worst of it. Under his screams and moans, I could hear the grunting of the men who were holding him down and the crunch and snap of bone as they severed his wrist. His hand did not come off easily like mine had. The knife did not pass through it like butter. He must have passed out because I could still hear them sawing at it even after he'd stopped making noise.

"Take him away," Dr. Fineman said at last. "And clean up all this blood."

I didn't lift my head to the sounds of them dragging him out. I didn't move a muscle when someone swabbed the blood from the slab I slept on. I was hoping they'd forget about me, these monstrous men. They could leave me down here forever and I wouldn't care, as long as they left me alone.

"What are your plans for the girl?" someone asked.

"She's useless to me now," Dr. Fineman said. "We'll dispose of her in the morning."

"Yes, sir," the voice said, as they closed and locked the cell door behind them.

I got my wish and they forgot me for a while. I don't know for how long. Time stretched on. Or didn't. It had to have been more than one night that I lay there. However long it was, I spent it contemplating my own death. They'd killed Marcus when he was here; he'd just managed to come back. And Marcus had claimed they'd killed Danielle. After what I'd experienced, I was beginning to wonder if the notes and the hand and the ghost were all a part of a delusion I'd made up to cope. Maybe there was no way out of here but to die.

When I stumbled to the wall where I'd hidden the first note, there was nothing there. Either someone had taken it or it had never existed. When I scrambled in the dirt where I'd dropped the second note, I found nothing.

But Grant had heard her. He'd yelled at her and scared her away. He'd seen the key, and we'd used it to together to free our bonds. Unless Grant had been a part of the delusion too. Where were the handcuffs we'd taken off and his shackles? Someone had removed them from the cell, or they'd never been here. What if they'd drugged my food all along, and nothing I'd thought was real had ever happened? Suddenly, the only thing I was sure of was my missing hand and Anthony's, his blood still streaked across the slab I lay on.

I slept fitfully, and once I woke with a start, something flashing across my eyelids, pulsing like a strobe and drawing me back to consciousness. But when I opened my eyes, I saw the fluorescent bulb hanging above me, drab but constant.

And then they finally came for me.

I had wondered how they'd kill me.

Cut my throat? Strangle me? Sever my other hand with a guillotine and let me bleed out? Nothing seemed beyond belief anymore.

So, when Dr. Fineman came in and said, "You are a very, very, lucky girl," I knew I wasn't.

I didn't respond, staring past him. If he was going to kill me, I was going to give him as little satisfaction as possible.

"It seems just when we have no more use for you, someone else does. You've been ransomed, my dear. Well, not truly yet, but arrangements are being made and negotiations will commence shortly."

I didn't believe a word of it.

"Don't you want to know who has saved you?" he taunted me. "And not just you, they've asked for your friend, Grant, too. Two of you for the price of one, really. Such a steal."

I stared at his shoes, the smart Italian ones he always wore. Those pompous shoes.

"There's only one problem," he said. "I'm afraid you're no longer in the condition they might expect. There's the small issue of your missing hand. I imagine Mr. James and your mother won't be pleased about that."

Mr. James and my mother? Was it possible?

"Oh yes," he said, sensing the smallest kernel of hope in me. "They're actually on their way here right now. And it isn't just your mother and Mr. James. All your little PSS friends are coming. At least the ones who are still alive."

He wanted me to ask about Marcus. I knew he did. But I didn't believe any of it.

"You're lying," I said. I'd seen Passion and Marcus in a corn field a day ago. Or had it been two days? They could be on their way. It was exactly what I'd been hoping for. I had to ask him. I had to know.

"Is Marcus with them? I thought you said he was working for you."

"Perhaps he still is," Fineman said, smiling wickedly, delighted that he'd baited me into asking. "There's only one way to find out." He gestured to the guards. "Take her upstairs to one of the empty staff suites and get her cleaned up. She needs a shower, and some clothes, and come up with some way to hide the missing hand. Let them find that out after the exchange, not beforehand. *Beforehand.*" He chuckled. "That amuses me."

"Yes, sir," one of the guards said, taking me by the arm and helping me stand.

I didn't believe it. This was just part of the game before they killed me, to give me false hope.

I still didn't believe it when they took me all the way upstairs and into a wing of the compound I'd never seen before. The hallway was not made of stone. It was more like a long hotel corridor. They opened a door and locked me in a room that looked like an expensive hotel suite, minus the windows, and of course, with cameras in every corner. There was also a queen bed piled high with pillows, a small desk and chair, a lounge area off to the right, and behind another door, a master bathroom with a full tub and shower.

The first thing I did was lock myself in the bathroom. The second thing I did was guzzle down glass after glass of clean, cool tap water.

It was impossible to miss my reflection in the bathroom mirror. I looked terrible. I was skinny, and dirty, and bruised. My hair hung in greasy mats.

My face looked like it was covered in soot. When I was done drinking, I reached up to wipe a dark smudge off my cheek, and there was the stump. I stared at it. My not-hand. My hideous, truncated wrist.

I lowered it, leaving the dirt on my face, and turned away from the mirror, scanning the bathroom for cameras. I didn't see any, but I turned back to the mirror. It could be a two-way. That was just the sort of sick-fuck thing Fineman would do.

I took a couple of towels and tried to drape them over the corners of the mirror, but they kept falling off. Everything was harder with one hand. I tried again and again, finally flinging the towels into the corner and storming into the larger room. I grabbed the wooden chair from the desk and carried it into the bathroom. It had metal feet on the bottom of its wooden legs. I hefted the whole chair up, as best I could, feet toward the mirror, and slammed them into it.

The mirror didn't crack. It just had four small impact-marks, like little decorative stars.

I slammed the chair into the mirror again, pain shooting through my shoulder and making me drop it, one of the metal feet gouging into my right pinky toe when it fell.

"Fuck!" I screamed, shoving the chair away from me. My toe was throbbing and bleeding. "Fuck you!" I yelled at the mirror, flipping it off, loathing it, and yet utterly helpless against it.

I opened the shower door and slammed it shut behind me, sinking down against the cool porcelain of the tub.

At least the glass shower door was frosted, not clear.

I stood up and tried to undress myself, something I'd never done before with only one hand.

In the end, I just ripped at my clothes, tearing and pulling them off, tossing them out the gap at the top of the shower. They were rags anyway, dirty and worn out from all the abuse they'd taken.

When I was naked, I looked down and saw dirt and—something moving—small dots that weren't dirt, jumping around my feet.

I turned on the water as fast as I could.

It felt surreal, like a dream, when that hot water hit me. How long had it been since I'd bathed? Two weeks? A month? I didn't even know what day it was.

The shampoo smelled divine. I rubbed it all over my body, not just in my hair. I lathered and rinsed over and over again, using the entire bottle. It smelled so good I was tempted to taste it, but I didn't. When it was gone, and the bathroom was filled with steam, and the hot water started to run cool, I wrapped myself in a towel and got out. I had nothing to wear, but the towel covered all the important parts and I could always make a toga out of the bed sheet. Thankfully, when I went out into the bedroom, there was a pile of clothes lying on the bed.

That might have creeped me out before I'd been taken, but the CAMFers had done much worse than invade my privacy. Still, I went back into the bathroom and got dressed in the damp shower.

The clothes didn't really fit, but they were warm and clean.

I went back out into the bedroom and sat on the bed.

This was really happening.

They weren't going to kill me.

They wouldn't waste clothes and shampoo on someone they were going to kill, would they?

Maybe they would. Just to be cruel.

I pulled a pillow into my arms, hugging it to me, and curled up on the end of the bed, trying not to shake or cry or fall asleep.

I failed miserably on all counts.

22

OLIVIA

I opened my eyes to see Mike Palmer sitting on the edge of the bed.

I didn't move. I was fresh out of fear, or shock, or whatever it was they were trying to make me feel. I just stared at him.

"I'm not going to hurt you," he said. "I know you're not likely to believe me, but we don't have much time. I've shut the camera feed down. We have about ten minutes before it comes back up. So, this is going to have to be quick, and you'll have to piece some of it together on your own."

I didn't say anything. I had learned not to say anything. My mother would be so proud.

"I am not a CAMFer," he said. "I mean I work for them, yes, but that isn't where my true loyalties lie. When I was in Greenfield, I reported to both The Hold and Dr. Fineman about you, but my main objective was to keep your father's painting out of the hands of the CAMFers. That's why I burned down your house. I never expected you to stay inside so damn long. I ended up having to call the fire department myself. That was when I knew you were going to be a royal pain in the ass."

This was another trick of Fineman's. He wasn't done with me yet. He would never let up, unless I killed him. I was going to have to kill him.

"Then," Palmer continued, "when you bumped me back to your camp, I knew the whole lot of you were trouble. That kind of power doesn't go unnoticed. By either side."

"You expect me to believe you work for Mr. James and The Hold?" I couldn't bite my tongue any longer. "You shot Marcus!"

"I shot Marcus in the chest," he pointed out, "because I knew he could reboot, and I couldn't blow my cover."

"No," I shook my head. "I tortured you with my ghost hand. I saw you piss yourself with fear."

"You saw me piss myself," he said, shrugging. "It's not that hard to do. I was playing the part I was trained to play. Why do you think I warned you against going to Shades? You were never supposed to be there. Your presence in this compound has complicated everything we've been working toward. Plans cultivated and set in motion for years, thwarted by one stubborn, impossible girl."

"Oh gee, I'm sorry, did I mess up your diabolical plans to rule the world? They must not have been very fucking good if one girl could mess them up so easily."

"You call this easily?" he asked, looking down at my wrist stump.

I pulled it to my chest and glared at him.

"There is a war coming," he said, ominously, like an actor in some cheesy action film. "It has been coming for a long time, and you're a wrench in the works if I've ever seen one. But a wrench is a tool I can use."

"Whatever you think I'm going to do for you, you're wrong," I assured him.

"No, I'm not," he said. "Not if you want to save the people you love. The people coming to get you, and the people already here in this compound." He held out his hand to me. There were two crumpled notes in it, two pages of *The Bone Road* with handwriting scrawled between the lines.

"You found those in my cell. So what? You think that makes you my friend? Maybe you were the one who wrote them in the first place. One thing I know for sure; you convinced Anthony to cut off my hand."

"Yes, I convinced him to do that," Mike Palmer said, totally flooring me. "It was the only way Dr. Fineman was ever going to let you go. You really think he'd be trading you off to Mr. James if you still had your hand?"

"So, you were just doing me a favor?"

"I did what I had to do, and now it's your turn. Mr. James thinks he can win this war. So does Dr. Fineman. Neither of them can, but they're too stubborn to ever admit it. I should know. I've worked for both of them for years. But there are bigger stakes than ever before, and my allegiances have changed. I'm working for someone else now, a third party, shall we say, and she needs this from you."

"She?" I asked, staring at him.

"You've met her," he said, glancing down at the notes. "I could have written those, but I can't stick my hand through a stone wall."

Danielle. He was saying he was working with Danielle on her behalf. No, I wasn't taking the bait. He could have made her write the notes and reach through the wall.

"Even if I believed anything you've said," I told him, "which I don't, what the hell do you think I can do? I lost my ghost hand thanks to you. I have no power. I have nothing. I'm the one who needs help."

"You haven't lost anything." He looked down at my stump again. "You just think you have."

"Um, no, I really don't have a hand," I said, shoving the ugly thing at him, and that's when I saw it flash. My missing ghost hand pulsed into existence, a strobe of PSS. And then it was gone.

I stared down at it, waiting for it to do it again.

And it did.

A hand, flashing into existence, then out again.

"What the fuck?" I said, looking at Mike Palmer.

"It's coming back because you shared PSS with her," he explained, "but I'm not sure why it's flashing."

The flashing reminded me of Marcus's chest when it rebooted. Marcus, whom I'd shared PSS with as well.

"Anyway," Palmer said. "The important thing is it's coming back, and you can control it."

"No, I can't." I held my new flashing wonder-wrist out to him. "It's random."

"No. You have to be able to control it," he said, looking worried. "Try thinking of it as a light switch you can turn on and off with your mind."

"But I can't turn light switches on and off with my mind."

"Practice," he insisted. "There's no surveillance in the bathroom, and you have to get this. If Fineman sees it, he'll never let you go. And you can't just turn it off. You need to be able to turn it on, too, because you're going to need that hand. Now, I have to go," he said, looking at the cameras nervously. "Whatever happens, whatever it looks like I'm doing, I'm trusting you not to blow my cover. Do you understand? If the CAMFers come out on top, I need to be with them. I'll need to protect her."

"No—what am I—"

"Use your power," he said, getting up from the bed, "and trust your hand. It knows what it's doing." He was moving toward the door. "Think about everything you've learned from The Hold, and everything you've learned here, and be ready to use it. I'm counting on you being a royal pain in the ass one last time."

Then he opened the door and was gone, shutting and locking it behind him.

I looked up at the camera and then down at my hand.

Off, I told it, and held my breath.

*

Later, a CAMFer brought me food. Really good food: spaghetti with garlic bread and a fresh Caesar salad. I'd managed to keep my ghost hand off since Palmer had left but, after I ate, I locked myself in the bathroom, stepped into the shower, turned my back, and practiced. *On. Off. On. Off.* It took some concentration, but I could control it. I could even hold it on for longer than a flash. At first, only for a minute or two, but the increments got longer and longer the more I practiced. My hand was back, cooler and more versatile than before, but how was that even possible?

Palmer had said my hand had come back because I'd shared PSS with Danielle, whose ability was healing. That made a certain kind of sense. I'd also shared PSS with Marcus, who could reboot. Maybe my flashing hand was some sort of combination of the two. So, at least that much of what Palmer had said seemed true. Telling me the bathroom had no surveillance seemed oddly convenient though. Had they seen me try to break the mirror and sent him to divert my attention away from it? Either way, this new hand was all I had to work with, and I was going to have to figure out how to use it.

As for the rest of the crazy shit Palmer had been spouting about being a double agent who now worked for Danielle, or the big war coming and me saving the world, I was skeptical.

Some of it was mildly plausible, but I was seriously having trouble wrapping my head around Palmer being a good guy who played a bad guy, or who played both. If that were true, how could I ever trust him? No, I was a pawn to him like I'd always been. He'd actually said it; I was his tool.

So, if he was lying, then what was really going on? This could be one more elaborate mindfucking experiment arranged by Fineman. Or maybe the doctor truly was trading me and Grant to Mr. James and my mother. Either way, I had very little control over the situation. If there actually was a big, nasty, war coming, and I ended up in the middle of it, I'd deal with it then.

Except Palmer had warned me to prepare. He'd said to utilize everything I'd learned from The Hold and from Fineman.

"What have I learned?" I asked myself, my voice echoing a little in the shower.

"Hello? Anybody here?" a voice called from the outer room. I knew that voice.

"Grant?" I yelled, throwing open the shower and charging into the bedroom.

He turned toward me and I threw myself into his arms. "You're okay," I said, burying my face in his shirt so he couldn't see my tears. "They didn't hurt you."

"No," he said softly, lifting my head in his hands, his eyes darting to my stump. "But they hurt you. Olivia, your hand…" He wrapped his fingers gently around my wrist and pulled it between us. "I'm sorry I couldn't stop them. I tried. I tried to break away."

"It's okay," I said, touching his cheek, seeing the sorrow etched across his face. He was cleaned up, just like I was, and smelling great, his hair still slightly damp and curling at his neck. He had on fresh clothes too.

But nothing could wipe away the haunted look in his eyes. Did he see that same look in mine?

I glanced over my shoulder at the cameras.

"Come with me," I said, taking him by the hand.

Once we were locked in the bathroom, I turned to him, making sure my body was blocking the view from the mirror. "There are no cameras in here. We can talk. And I need to show you something." I held out my stump and turned on my hand.

"Holy fuck!" he said, his eyes wide. "How did you—I thought they cut it off."

"They did, but it's coming back. At first it was just random flashes, but now I can sort of control it." I showed him by turning it off, and his eyes went even wider.

I thought about mentioning Palmer, but in the end, I didn't. I knew what he'd told me sounded crazy. I didn't need Grant to tell me that, and I still wasn't sure I could trust Grant completely. I wasn't sure I'd trust anyone completely ever again in my life.

"That's amazing. You are amazing," Grant said, grabbing me, picking me up, and twirling me around. Then the twirling slowed, and I was sliding down the front of him; the hard, defined, warm, front of him, his arms strong around my waist, his eyes blue and intense.

My feet touched the ground and I stepped back quickly, out of his arms, looking anywhere but at his face. "I'm glad you're okay," I said. "Did they tell you we've been ransomed? They're letting us go, supposedly. But it's hard to believe."

"Yeah, they told me. I wasn't sure if I could believe it either. But it looks legit, right? Why else would they clean us up, and feed us, and put us in a fancy room together?"

"It could be another trick to lull us into submission and get us to help them."

"Except they don't know you have your hand back, do they?" he asked.

"I don't think so." Again, it all hinged on Palmer and whether he was telling the truth.

"I think they're really trading us," Grant said, hope in his voice.

"Me too," I said, looking up at him. "But we should work on some kind of plan, you know, just in case."

"Yeah, okay," he agreed. "What did you have in mind?"

"I'm not sure yet," I said, but an idea was forming in my head, swirling around and colliding with all the things I'd seen and done and heard about PSS since that first day I'd met Marcus in my Calc class. It was a terrible, wonderful, horrifying plan that would involve testing the boundaries and functionality of my new ghost hand on the only resource the CAMFers had given me.

Grant.

"No, this isn't right," I said, stepping away from Grant and flashing my hand out of existence.

We were in the shower together, towels draped over the door in case Palmer had been lying about the mirror. Grant was sitting in the desk chair, his shirt off, and I was standing in front of him, but I couldn't do it. I had never used my hand on someone I cared about on purpose, unless you counted the time I'd touched Marcus's chest. This was too much like that, intimate and sensual and terrifying. And it was too much not like that, because it was Grant, and I didn't love him that way.

"Liv, it's going to be fine," he said. "You're not going to hurt me."

"I could, though," I stepped back, overwhelmed with fear. My brilliant plan to reach into Grant didn't seem so brilliant anymore. "I'm just—I'm second guessing myself."

"Okay, talk me through it again. Talk yourself through it," he encouraged. "Why are we doing this?"

"Because I have this theory about the things I pull out of people," I said. "I think my hand can sense PSS, sort of the way Samantha can hear it, and I think the burdens come from within the PSS itself."

We'd been over this already. Grant and I had been locked in the suite together an entire day and night. We'd slept a lot, the deep dreamless sleep of the exhausted, and we'd devoured the meals delivered to the room. We'd also talked this out until we were blue in the face, and I'd practiced turning my hand on and off until it was almost second nature. Based on everything I thought I knew about PSS and my hand, this should work. But what if I was wrong?

"So, that means you couldn't pull something out of someone like me, who doesn't have PSS?"

"Well, we aren't positive you don't," I pointed out. I knew he'd gotten this the first time, and he was just humoring me. "The Hold discovered that a lot more of the population has PSS than we ever imagined.

PSS isn't rare. It just goes undetected. For example, you could have the tiniest bit of PSS, even just a single cell of it, but I don't think you do, because I don't have the urge to pull anything out of you. When Dr. Fineman made me try to put the matches into you, I didn't feel any pull or resonance. Even when you were being a douche at the Eidolon, I thought about putting my hand into you because I was ticked off, but there was no real urge. And don't you dare apologize again." I held my hand up even as his lips began to move. "I know you're sorry. The point is when I reached into Fineman, it felt the same way. There was no compulsion. I had to make myself do it. And at first, my hand couldn't find anything. Pulling the cube out of him was like pulling something out of thin air, and it didn't have a power because it didn't come from PSS. It was just a blank, like a place-holder. The cube, by itself, couldn't do anything, but when combined with Jason's bullet it blasted us three days and three miles away."

"The bullet was like an instrument, and the cube was like its amplifier," Grant said.

"Exactly. And the ironic thing is most of the CAMFers probably have PSS, and they don't even know it. I mean, I've pulled stuff from some of them, and I've felt the resonance." An image of Major Tom flashed into my head, and I shooed it away. Had Dr. Fineman known then what I was just figuring out? Did he know many of his CAMFers had hidden, internal PSS?

"That could mean PSS has been around a lot longer than we've realized," Grant said. "It could have been a mutation that started out on a cellular level and just kept getting bigger and bigger. And it wasn't until it started manifesting outwardly, that anyone took notice."

"You might be right," I said. Every time we talked about this, we came up with new realizations and discovered new ramification. "It could actually be rarer not to have PSS than it is to have it. If that ever got out, it would seriously screw with both The Hold and the CAMFers. It would change everything."

"So, it seems I'm the rare one now," Grant said, giving me sad puppy dog eyes. "Which sucks because I've kinda always wanted to have PSS."

"No, you don't. Trust me." I brushed my fingers across his face, trying to erase that look.

"Well, at least I get to have you reach into me," he said, biting playfully at my fingers.

"Don't." I yanked them away, frowning. "This isn't a joke."

"I know," he said, growing serious. "Maybe I'm scared too, okay? But we need you to do this. If you find a cube or a blank or whatever in me, it would give us something powerful to use in case they don't trade us. In case something goes wrong."

"I know," I exhaled. "I'm not going to pull it out. I'm just going to feel for it. Better to keep it inside of you, in case they search us. But if we know it's there, and we get into trouble…"

"See, that makes perfect sense," Grant said, smiling. "You're not going to hurt me. You're just going to feel me up a little. I want you to do this, Liv. I really do."

"But I haven't reached into anyone since my hand came back, and when I pulled the cube out of Fineman, it put him in a coma."

"Yes, but you said you tried to hurt him, that you did something else with your hand. That's probably what caused the coma, not taking the cube."

"I don't know. I might kill you or something right before we get rescued. That would totally suck. It's too much of a risk."

"No, it's not," he said, grasping my stump and raising it gently to his chest.

This was crazy. I shouldn't reach into Grant unless I absolutely had to. Except that was the way I'd always thought about my hand, and look where it had gotten me? Other people had used me and my hand. Hadn't I sworn to myself if they ever let me out of that cell, I would show them exactly what my hand could do?

"Okay." I took a deep breath and looked down at Grant's face. How could I have doubted him? It was obvious he trusted me enough to put his life in my hands.

On, I thought to my ghost hand, and it flashed into existence.

I reached out and slipped it into Grant's chest.

It wasn't harsh or scary or painful. The inside of Grant's psyche was smooth and soft, like down inside a silk pillow.

He tipped back his head and closed his eyes and his lips parted, letting out a gentle sigh.

It was so fucking hot I almost lost myself. I almost forgot about my theories and my hand and jumped onto his lap, wrapping my legs around him.

But then my hand was touching something, all corners and edges, and I was grasping it, mapping it in my mind with my fingers. I had felt it before.

A cube. There wasn't any question.

I pulled my hand back, slowly out of him, trying to ignore how aroused I was, and I wasn't the only one.

He was panting a little, and there was other evidence.

"Are you okay?" I asked, my voice all wobbly.

"Yeah." He exhaled and opened those baby blues, staring up at me. "That was—what did you feel?"

"A cube," I told him, avoiding the real question.

And the real answer.

23

MARCUS

The four-hour flight to Oregon on my uncle's private jet gave me a lot of time to think. Of course, they seated me next to Reiny, my eternal medicinal watch dog. In fact, it was obvious all the seating arrangements had been carefully orchestrated too keep us younger passengers in line. Pete sat next to Passion. My aunt was sitting with Olivia's mom. My uncle and Samantha had a seat together, while Jason was in the back with my uncle's small security team: Bo, Butch, and Bruce.

The plane had once been a small commercial plane that my uncle had bought and converted, adding larger seats but keeping them in the usual two-to-a-row seating arrangement.

When we took off, I could hear Pete joking with Passion across the aisle from me. He was trying to distract her, but it didn't seem to be working. She was pale and clutching the arms of her seat. Then I saw her reach into her carry-on and pull out a magic eight ball. She rolled it around in her hands, and her face grew calmer as she and Pete bent their heads over it like a couple of kids, asking it inane questions.

I turned to Reiny to comment about it and found her fast asleep, curled up in a little ball against the window shade, her head against a pillow and a blanket pulled over her. She certainly deserved a rest. She'd been taking care of me almost non-stop since I'd arrived at the farmhouse, and it had been a pretty thankless job. I mean, I certainly hadn't thanked her. I'd been more of a royal pain-in-the-ass.

And she hadn't just been my nurse. She'd treated everyone at the farmhouse at one time or another. For example, right before we'd left for the airstrip, she'd given Samantha and Jason a shot. It was some kind of vaccine booster, she'd said, against a childhood disease cropping back up in Oregon thanks to the anti-vaccine movement. Then she'd explained that Passion and I didn't need it. Our blood work had shown we already had the antibodies.

I hoped my uncle was paying her well. I mean, even with his loss of The Hold, he still had jets to fly off in and plenty of money to burn.

Seeing Reiny next to me, asleep and small and not poking me with anything, made me wonder what her story was. Why was she working for my uncle? What was her connection to The Hold and PSS?

She was clearly too old to have it, but maybe a family member did. A younger sibling, perhaps? Or maybe it was simply medical curiosity. She was Native American though, and we were headed to Warm Springs. Coincidence? I doubted it. In all her days of caring for me, she hadn't let anything slip about her tribe or her background. Had she been excited about this trip? Definitely yes, but I'd figured we were all excited about getting out of that damn farmhouse. Maybe Reiny had been excited about going home. Maybe she was my uncle's tribal connection. If she was from Warm Springs, she must know something about the *Ghost Heart* painting.

I turned to wake her, thinking I could pump her for information while she was groggy and more susceptible to questioning. I reached out my hand, ready to shake her shoulder, but I kept hearing Passion's voice in my head. "Try being one of us for a day," she'd said out there in the cornfield. "We've lost things too."

I dropped my hand and let Reiny sleep, but I couldn't shake that scene with Passion. Man, she'd been pissed and given me a piece of her mind. I'd been thinking about what she'd said, too, about what the last eight months must have been like for everyone else. It was time to consider it. It was time to get out of my own damn head.

For me, those eight months had been like falling asleep and waking up again, like no time had passed. There'd been a few surreal dreams, more like hallucinations than anything else, but I knew I'd dreamed of Olivia. I remembered it—a girl with a ghost hand who wasn't my sister. It was somewhat of a relief too, because some of those dreams had been—well, let's just say they hadn't been "brotherly."

So, I'd had a girlfriend, or a fling or something. Passion claimed I'd been in love, but that was hard to believe. I mean, don't get me wrong; I liked girls. I'd been with plenty of girls. But I didn't really believe in love. Maybe my parents had been in love. It was hard to remember, and if they had been, ultimately, it had killed them. Besides, how could you love someone you didn't trust? And I'd learned not to trust anyone, not fully. It was more important to protect yourself. Self-preservation and love were mutually exclusive. I had a strong instinct to survive, even my PSS echoed that inclination. So, yeah, I couldn't believe the whole love thing.

Which raised the question of why Passion was so convinced otherwise.

The answer seemed obvious; I'd been faking it. I'd told Olivia I'd loved her, and she'd told Passion, and they'd both believed it. The only reason I could think of for doing that was if I'd thought it would somehow help Danielle. In the long run, maybe it had. I was currently flying toward my sister because of the connection between Passion and Olivia, so apparently, my plan had worked. Not too bad for someone with no memories of what the fuck he'd been doing.

I wanted that to make me feel better.

But it didn't.

The rest of it, though, the stuff Passion had said about me being their leader, about them trusting and following me, about my campaign to take out the CAMFers, that was almost harder to believe than the love thing.

Was that really me? Was that who I'd become?

I wasn't a leader. I just wanted to find my sister. I just wanted everyone to leave us alone and let us live our lives in peace.

So, what had changed?

What had happened to that David to turn him into Marcus?

Something had. Something big everyone kept veering around and avoiding in their slow unveiling of my life and actions from the last eight months. Passion had been hinting at it in the cornfield when she'd suddenly gone soft, touched my arm, and told me about her sister's death.

I wasn't an idiot. Some part of me knew what it was—the thing no one would tell me. I just didn't want to face it. I'd happily veer away from it with them as long as they'd let me. Because if I wasn't flying toward Danielle, if I wasn't saving my sister, I didn't know what I was doing or how to do it.

I looked around the plane. What had the last eight months been like for each of these people I was traveling with? Sam's life had been unraveling, her parent's marriage and The Hold dissolving in front of her. What about Passion? What had she been through to inspire all those scars on her arms she tried so hard to keep hidden?

And this Jason guy? Apparently, his dad was a CAMFer who'd wanted to kill his own son. If that wasn't bad enough, my uncle was using the kid so hard he'd convinced him to shoot Sam. That was fucked up.

Then there was Olivia's mom. I hadn't gotten to talk to her much, but her daughter had run away. They'd lost their home. Now Olivia was a hostage of the CAMFers, and even if we got her back, there was no way she was going to be in good shape. I knew what they did to people.

My uncle's voice rose, and I glanced to the front of the plane where he and Samantha were sitting. They were arguing, but all I could really hear was the murmur of angry voices. I didn't envy Sam. She loved him. He was her father. That had to suck.

My uncle's version of the accident had shaken me more than I'd like to admit. I'd gone over and over my memories of that night, but they were only glimpses and broken flickers, like a badly preserved home movie. I had been a child, scared shitless, hunkered down in the back seat of our car, trying to comfort Danielle and be the brave big brother. My parents had been scared too, and that had scared me even more. My mother, in the passenger seat, kept glancing behind us. She said we were being chased. She said something about my uncle. Then there had been a bright flash of light, and the wailing, mammoth, cry of a train whistle barreling down on us. And then nothing.

Was it possible my uncle hadn't been the villain that night? Had I manufactured him into one, slowly, over minutes and days and years of bitterness and grief and abandonment?

Fuck. Did it even matter?

He'd abandoned us. He should have never made that promise to my mom. She was wrong to ask him.

He could have protected us, loved us, been there for us. What had she been thinking?

She'd been trying to protect us, even if she hadn't understood how it would all pan out.

Even if she'd been horribly wrong, she'd loved us.

My uncle did not love me.

I was his tool, nothing more.

"Would you like a drink?" a voice asked softly.

I looked up to see a pretty flight attendant holding a tray of drinks. My uncle knew how to travel in style.

"Sure," I said. "Got anything alcoholic?"

"How old are you?" she asked flirtatiously, her eyes roaming over me. "You don't look old enough."

"I'm definitely old enough," I said, surprising myself by flirting back.

"Okay," she looked over her shoulder to make sure my uncle wasn't watching before she handed me a glass of beer. "My name is Layla," she said, her fingers brushing mine as I took it. She must have been in her early twenties, and she was hot as fuck, all legs and boobs and ass. "If you're old enough for a drink," she said in a hushed voice, leaning over so I could see the beautiful bounty of her cleavage, "maybe you're old enough to join the mile high club."

She had to be joking. I mean, she was just flirting with me. She didn't actually mean—

"Excuse me," Reiny voice interrupted, shocked and angry. "What the hell do you think you're doing? This is Mr. James's nephew."

And that was the end of that.

Layla disappeared as fast as I'd ever seen anyone disappear. In fact, I worried for a little while that she'd thrown herself out of an airlock, but when we got off the plane, I glimpsed her face peering out from the pilot's cabin like she was afraid she was going to get fired if anyone noticed her.

Probably the only reason she didn't get fired was that Reiny had taken my beer and guzzled it down in pure fury. And shortly afterward, she'd fallen asleep again, but not before she'd played big sister a little more.

"You, Mister," she said. "If I hadn't interrupted her, you wouldn't have gone for that, would you?"

"No way," I said. "I'm already a member of the club anyway."

"You are not!" She pinched my arm playfully.

And when we landed in Portland, I still wasn't, thanks to Reiny.

The resort at Warm Springs known as Kah-Nee-Tah rose out of the burnt-red dirt of the high desert tablelands of central Oregon. The building was designed in the shape of an arrowhead. The two long sides were open-air corridors with the rooms stacked in three stories along them. Each room had a small balcony looking outward and over the sparsely vegetated hills and valleys, lined with small trails for tourists to enjoy. The inside courtyard featured a huge swimming pool, fed by the local hot springs, which actually had to be cooled to eighty-nine degrees so visiting families could enjoy it year-round without scalding themselves. Thus, the name Warm Springs.

That was what the brochure the front desk clerk handed me said, anyway.

What I saw were my people. My people answering phones and checking in patrons. My people cleaning rooms and bussing tables at the two restaurants. My people cooking, and carrying luggage, and managing the casino. People who looked at my face with a question in their eyes. Do we know him? Is he one of us? Why does he look familiar?

I felt a camaraderie of genetics and appearance and ancestry I hadn't felt for a very long time, if ever. At the same time I felt like an imposter, like someone was going to stop me and call me out at any moment for pretending to be something I wasn't.

If my uncle and Samantha felt the same, they didn't show it.

Reiny, on the other hand, was swept up in a chorus of greetings and hugs and welcome as soon as she stepped through the doors. I guess that answered my question about her connection to the tribes. As a group gathered around her, I could see them casting curious glances in my direction, curious, yet cautious. Respectful, yet guarded. It was awkward, but it helped remind me I was a stranger here. These weren't my people. We might share DNA, but they didn't know me, and I didn't know them.

Reiny came over and introduced us to her brother, Lonan, one of the managers of the resort. He was probably the one who'd sent my uncle the picture of the mural and arranged for our accommodations.

In between room assignments, instructions, and the handing out of key cards, I stepped away, descending down into the main lobby, the huge mural, *Ghost Heart*, rising to the ceiling on one wall. There was no placard with it explaining who had painted it or why, no artist's signature anywhere on it.

I was still staring at it when a little girl skipped up to me and said, "Hey, that looks like you."

"Molly, come here," her mother told her. "Don't bother him."

"But that big picture is him, Mama. He must be famous," she said, skipping her way back to her parent.

"That's not him, sweetheart," the woman explained. "See, he doesn't have a hole in his chest. That's not a real person in the picture. It's a make-believe hero, like Superman. It's not real—it's just a story."

"But how do we know he doesn't have a hole in his chest?" the girl insisted, pouting and looking at me over her shoulder as her mother pulled her away by the hand. "He has his shirt on."

"Shush now," the mother hissed as they disappeared down the corridor.

"David," my uncle said, striding up to me, his eyes scanning the mural carefully and succinctly, like a man appraising something he doesn't want you to know he wants to buy. "Let's go. You and I are sharing a room."

"You're not serious," I said. "Shouldn't you be rooming with your wife?"

"Don't be an ass," my uncle said, my jab obviously hitting the mark. Maybe he and Aunt Chloe really were on the rocks. Or, their "issues" were the perfect excuse for him to babysit me personally now that we were so close to whatever prize he was after.

"I won't, if you won't," I said to his back as he strode away.

And I followed him because, ultimately, whatever my uncle was up to, I needed to be there.

It was time to stop running.

It was time to be the guy Passion had told me I'd become.

24

PASSION

"**C**an you put that thing away?" Samantha asked. Well, it wasn't exactly a question. More like a command. "It's giving me a headache," she added, coming in from our room's little balcony.

"Um, okay." I wasn't sure how a magic eight ball could give her a headache, but I tucked it into my camo jacket pocket anyway. I was sharing her room. I was breathing her air. I was even wearing her clothes, but I'd insisted on keeping the jacket because it had pockets big enough for the eight ball. "I'm just so nervous," I added. "Aren't you?"

"Of course I am," she said, plopping down on the queen bed opposite mine and staring at the clock on the nightstand between us. "They're late.

He said we'd be leaving around five, and it's 5:09."

"I know," I said, just as the clock rolled over to 5:10. I didn't point out it was still technically *around* five, or that her father did whatever he pleased no matter what he'd said, just like she did.

I didn't want to fight with Samantha. I wanted to make up with her. I wanted things back the way they'd been before I'd opened my big, fat mouth about her father. I certainly wasn't going to tell her what Jason had told me, because it would utterly destroy her. So, when I'd heard we were rooming together my hopes had soared, only to be dashed the moment we were alone. She was still pissed at me. She had barely spoken to me the entire afternoon and evening.

The unspoken tension between us had become so unbearable that, for a few hours, I'd gone exploring the lodge alone, checking out the Warm Springs pool, the little souvenir shop, the restaurants, and the mural of Marcus. I'd hoped to find something about the mural somewhere, maybe in one of the lodge brochures or in a book in the shop, but no such luck. In fact, when I asked the shop clerk about it, I got a very vague but polite answer. "It's a legend of our people," she said. "A sacred legend." I could read between the lines of her emphasis on the word sacred. It wasn't for tourists like me. It wasn't for white people.

Of course, I hadn't been alone while I'd explored. Butch, from Mr. James's security detail, had tailed me the entire time. Still, I'd gotten away from Samantha's silent treatment for a little while. I'd also noticed more people checking in, a huge flush of new guests, mostly men, all trying to look like vacationing sales reps and failing miserably. I recognized a few of their faces from the camp at the farmhouse. Mr. James must have reserved every available room at the resort for his undercover entourage.

"It's almost dark outside," Samantha complained, getting up and walking to the balcony doorway again. The balcony was small, but the view wasn't. Laid out before us was a vast landscape of red soil, low shrubs, rolling hills, deep gorges, and flat mesas, all slowly being painted in pinks and oranges as the sun went down.

"It's beautiful," I sighed.

Samantha turned just as there was a knock at the door. "Come in," she called, giving me a look.

Pete entered, his eyes immediately going to our feet. "Good. You both have decent shoes on. Because it looks like we'll be hoofing it."

"Hoofing it as in walking?" Samantha frowned.

"No, hoofing it as in hoofing it. We're taking horses," he explained. "That's the best way to get where we're going."

"Horses? Cool," Samantha said, grinning widely. "But where exactly are we going?"

"Neutral ground," Pete said. "Someplace deep within the reservation. That's all I know."

"Okay," I said, standing up. Today I'd flown in a plane for the first time and survived. Now it looked like I was going to get my first horseback ride too.

Horses should not let humans ride them. They just shouldn't. There is no reason I can fathom that an animal so large, powerful, and skittish would let another animal jump on top of it, boss it around, yank its head this way and that, and kick it in the sides. There is no logic to this.

When you are riding a horse, its muscular body moving between your legs, when you are feeling the fullness of its otherness and selfness, you know this completely. You know what you are doing should not be, that it is some kind of horrible mistake, a temporary anomaly of nature which could, at any moment, reset itself back to the rightful condition that horses are wild, and humans are the things that go flying off the backs of them.

That is what I kept thinking as I rode a smoky-colored horse named Asher along a dark winding trail under a starry sky. Thankfully, Asher followed the horse in front of him, and the horse in front of him followed the one before him, and so on, their warm breath huffing into the cool night.

Our group consisted of Reiny and her brother, Lonan, up front as our guides, plus all of us who'd been on Mr. James's plane. Samantha, her parents, and Dr. Black rode up front right behind Reiny and Lonan. Then came Pete and me, Marcus and Jason, and finally Bo, Butch, and Bruce, taking up the rear. Reiny and Lonan's horses didn't stay in the rut of the trail like the rest. Their horses didn't even have saddles or reins. It was weird. I'd always thought of Reiny's natural environment as an ambulance or a hospital room, so modern and stark and technical. And I'd first seen Lonan behind a hotel desk, checking in customers. Now, I could see this was where they belonged, this land.

Maybe Reiny had always been a healer of some kind. Maybe Lonan had always welcomed visitors to the reservation. They were true to themselves wherever they were.

My horse stopped in the middle of the trail.

Jason's horse, behind me, didn't even skip a hoof beat. It went right around us.

"What's the hold up?" Marcus asked, smirking, as he went by too.

"I don't know," I said, tapping Asher gently in the sides with my heels.

Then I heard the plop and the phhtt of exiting gas as my horse dumped a load in the middle of the trail. It was steaming. I could actually see the steam rising up from it, and he wasn't done yet. There was more plopping and farting happening.

"Hey," Butch protested mockingly as his horse stepped around us. "What are you doing? We're supposed to take up the rear. Get it? Take up the *rear*?"

A lance of pain shot through me. That was just the sort of cheesy butt joke Nose would have made about Yale. God, I missed them.

"It isn't me," I said to Bruce, swallowing my pain as his horse meandered around us too.

I turned and looked in front of me.

The rest of the party was cresting the hill ahead of us.

"We'll wait for you," Bo said, his horse skirting mine.

Finally, Asher was done and probably about ten pounds lighter. He must have felt it too, because he suddenly leapt forward, charging up the hill.

I lost hold of the reins and grabbed the pommel of the saddle. I was bouncing all over the place, up and down, side to side, holding on for dear life. I could feel myself sliding toward the ground, but I dug my feet into the stirrups and pushed myself up.

Asher crested the hill, stopping short so fast I almost flew over his head. Then, he stomped around, sidling up between Reiny and Pete's horses and blowing a raspberry with his big hairy lips.

"Asher, be good," Reiny scolded, pushing him away with her foot as he tried to crush my leg between him and her horse. "Are you okay?" she asked, grabbing the dangling reins and handing them to me.

"Yeah, I think so. He just got really frisky all the sudden."

"Good job staying in the saddle," Pete said.

"The horses don't like this place," Lonan said, coming alongside us. "The people don't either, for that matter."

I looked down the hill, following Lonan's gaze.

In the valley below us, lit up by bright lights on its exterior, was the strangest building I'd ever seen. It was round and flat with a glass dome rising out of the middle of it like some kind of weird observatory. The rest of it was made of stone, making it look both ancient and modern all at once. It didn't appear to have any windows, except for the dome, and I couldn't see a door. The ground surrounding it was strange too—all barren looking, as if it had been scoured clean of foliage or life of any kind. All that was left were a few twisted tree stumps, black and charred, as if someone had taken a blowtorch to them. I glanced back at the building and noticed a dark slit in the exterior wall facing us. Maybe it was some kind of door or entrance.

"What is that?" I asked Reiny.

"That's The Roundhouse." She glanced sidelong at Lonan as she said it. "At least that's what we call it when we're being polite."

"And when you're not being polite?" Pete asked.

"Then we just call it The Zit," Lonan answered, smiling grimly and glancing toward the group, his eyes finding Mr. James. "It doesn't belong here," he told me in a hushed voice, obviously not wanting the other man to hear. "It never has. It's a festering boil, but it will be lanced soon enough."

"Let's go," Reiny said, gesturing for us all to follow as her horse ambled down the hill.

At the bottom of the steep incline we all dismounted, and Reiny, Lonan and Mr. James moved away to have a brief discussion. They kept their voices low, as if they didn't want the rest of us to overhear, but sound carried easily in the desert.

"What if we have a medical emergency? Mr. James said to Reiny. "He's your patient. How can you just leave him like this?"

"You have Pete," she said. "You hired me to nurse him back to health, and I did. And I brought you here. The rest is on you. That was always the deal. Once this is taken care of," she gestured at The Roundhouse, "the tribes will consider your other requests."

Go, Reiny. Way to put Mr. James in his place.

I looked at Marcus. He had definitely heard. Samantha and Jason too. They were probably wondering the same thing I was. What deal had Mr. James struck with the tribes of Warm Springs, and how were we all going to help him pay for it?

Reiny and Lonan were leading the horses away. I hadn't even gotten a chance to say goodbye to them or Asher. Reiny turned once, looking back at us, her eyes finding Pete and nodding at him before she and her brother mounted their horses and rode into the darkness, leading the other animals behind them.

"She'll be okay," Pete said, his voice thick with emotion. "She's a smart woman."

What was going on? I wanted to ask Pete, but Mr. James was already ushering us forward. "Come on," he said. "We've been out here too long already. We need to get inside." He was right. We were exposed. The three Bs were looking nervously up at the hills and taking defensive positions around us. The whole group must have felt it because we picked up the pace, approaching the recess in the strange structure, which I could now clearly see housed a large metal door.

"What is this place?" Dr. Black asked, sounding appalled. And no wonder. It was like approaching a spaceship or an ancient ruin at the bottom of the ocean. Except for the lights and the security cameras in the corners. Those were decidedly modern and of human origin. "Please tell me they aren't keeping my daughter here," she added, her voice hushed and terrified.

"I don't know where they've been holding her," Mr. James said, putting his hand on her shoulder, "but this is where the exchange will take place. If she wasn't here before, she is now."

"And why is that here?" Samantha asked angrily,

pointing to a symbol on the door. It was a blue circle with a pair of hands clasped in the middle of it. I had seen it before at The Warren Gun Club. It was the symbol for The Hold.

"When we get inside, I'll explain," Mr. James said, stepping up to a large security panel next to the door and beginning to punch a code into it.

"No," Samantha said, inserting herself between him and the panel. "Tell us now. We deserve to know what's going on before we set foot inside this place. This building belongs to The Hold, and I've never even heard of it before—"

"Samantha," her mother said, joining the fray, her voice a warning. "Your father will answer your questions when we get inside.

"I'm surprised at you," Mr. James added. "You're putting everyone in danger by—"

"*I'm* putting everyone in danger?" Samantha interrupted, laughing bitterly. "Oh, that's rich coming from you. You wouldn't tell me on the plane how you knew Jason, or what you'd hired him to do, but I'm not an idiot. Passion overheard the two of you talking, and I know it had to do with the Eidolon. Does mother know? Does she know you had full knowledge the CAMFers were coming that night?"

Mrs. James was looking confusedly between her daughter and her husband.

Great. The James's family shit was about to hit the fan, and I was definitely going to get pulled into it.

"I said we'll talk about this when we get inside," Mr. James said, trying to push past his daughter to the panel.

"No!" Samantha cried, whirling around and jabbing random numbers into the keyboard. "You owe me an explanation." The panel began to flash red, but she'd already turned around to confront her parents again. "Both of you. I know you've been lying about everything, even your breakup. Why would you do that to me? Why would anyone do that to their daughter?"

I glanced to my right at Marcus, wondering what he made of all this, but he wasn't even paying attention. Instead, he was staring at the big metal door with The Hold symbol on it. No, he wasn't just staring. He was fixated on it, and something was wrong. His body was perfectly still, his muscles rigid, but his eyes were flicking back and forth, right to left, really fast, like someone dreaming with their eyes open.

"Hey, are you okay?" I asked, reaching out to touch his arm.

He flinched and looked down at me, his eyes normal again except for the confusion and desperation in them. "I—I remembered something," he said, his voice a hushed whisper.

"What?" I whispered back, hope soaring in me. "What did you remember?"

"This place," he said, looking up at the building again. "I've been here before, but the door was different. And the approach. They brought us in from the other side." His eyes rose to the landscape beyond The Roundhouse. "They brought Danielle and me here. This is where—" He stopped, his eyes focusing on something up in the hills I couldn't see.

Did he remember the rest of it? Did he remember his sister was dead?

The stone wall next to us made a strange ping, rock crumbling off of it to the ground.

"Get down! Get down!" Bo yelled, as he and his brothers drew their guns, returning fire.

No, please, God. Not this again.

 Dirt was spraying up all around my feet, the hiss of bullets whizzing past me in the dark.

I threw myself forward into the door recess, smashing into Samantha and her parents and Dr. Black, who had already taken refuge there. They pulled me in among them, and I turned to see Marcus still standing out in the open.

Thankfully, Jason was charging toward him, a gun in his hand. He barreled into Marcus, propelling him forward.

My hands joined the ones grabbing Marcus and pulling him in, and Jason followed soon after, quickly taking up a position at one of the outer corners of our hidey-hole and returning gunfire.

Mr. James was crouched near the door's security panel, jabbing at the buttons, but it was still blinking red. He turned, casting a look of fury at one of the security cameras, and yelled, "Override it you fucking idiots! Get this door open, now!"

I looked out across the desolation of the moonlit desert.

Butch and Bruce were shambling toward us, Pete held between them, slumped and unmoving. Bo was running behind them, still laying down fire.

Not Pete, please not Pete.

When they were almost to our little nook, Jason and Marcus ran out and helped them drag Pete in. There was blood, lots of it, pouring from a gaping hole in his neck. The three brothers scrambled to stanch it with hands and pieces of their own clothing.

Marcus looked at me, then wiped the blood from his hands onto his shirt.

The gunfire had slowed, just a few occasional shots ringing out, a reminder we were pinned down and outnumbered.

Behind us, the door hissed and began to lift, causing those of us plastered against it to jump forward in alarm.

Light shone out, blinding me as I turned to see what new danger might accost us from inside.

Mr. James stepped around me, striding into a huge warehouse-like room, bustling with people and computers and equipment.

"Get these people inside!" he bellowed, as forms ran forward, grabbing us and helping us into the building. There were men with guns and a medical team put Pete on a handheld gurney, whisking him away.

"What the hell was that?" Mr. James demanded, striding up to a guy in uniform, more furious than I'd ever seen him. "This is a guaranteed neutral zone. We came for peaceful negotiations. I have my wife and daughter with me, for God's sake. Get the CAMFers on the line now, and mobilize all our troops immediately."

Apparently, Mr. James didn't like being shot at any more than the rest of us.

25

MARCUS

I remembered things. Things I didn't want to remember. I remembered this building, the strangeness and familiarity of it all at the same time. I remembered what it was like to be trapped inside the trunk of a cop car and how, even with the noise and vibration of the axles grinding under me, I could still hear Danielle crying softly in the back seat where they'd thrown her after they'd hurt her.

That had been my fault, because I'd stolen a car. Because I'd promised to take my sister to Warm Springs for Valentine's Day, or at least drive by the sign and remember Mom and Dad the way we did sometimes. Just sit and remember together. But we'd never made it to the sign. I'd been speeding a little, racing along the flat desert highway at night, because that kind of road was made for speed. Then, suddenly, there were flashing lights behind us, and a siren, and for a split second I could have made a different choice. I could have tried to outrun them and gone on a high-speed car chase. But I looked over at Danielle's terrified face and I knew I couldn't do that to her, not to the girl who still had night terrors about the crash and always wore her seatbelt. She would never forgive me, and it would just get us in more trouble anyway. So, I'd let the cops pull us over. CAMFer cops. Rapist cops. Cops who had pulled their guns as soon as they'd seen Danielle's hand.

I'd tried to distract them. I'd tried to deflect them from her and onto me, screaming that I had PSS too, telling them about my chest, but they didn't take the bait. They weren't interested in me until later. Until they were done with Danielle and realized they might be able to get something more out of both of us.

That's when they'd thrown me in the trunk and driven us here, to this valley and this building, but from a different approach and to a different door, just like the one in front of me but with no Hold icon on it.

I had gotten my sister and myself back onto the reservation at last, ironically.

It was coming back to me in bits and pieces of memory, like a jagged jigsaw nightmare. What they had done to us.

Now, here I was again, only this time my uncle had brought me, and we'd just been shot at. Pete had been wounded badly. My aunt and Dr. Black had cuts and bruises on their faces and looked like they needed medical attention themselves. Bo and his brothers had gone off with some military-looking guy, rattling off information about the forces we'd encountered outside. The room I was standing in looked like some kind of war-zone headquarters mixed with a LAN party.

"What is going on? What is this place?" Samantha demanded, slipping out from under my aunt's protective arm and confronting my uncle again. Sam, undaunted, and in a rage was a terrible, wonderful thing to behold. "You said you'd tell us when we got inside. So, we're inside."

"Samantha, this is hardly the time," Aunt Chloe said, trying to pull her back.

"No, she's right," my uncle said, looking at my aunt. "You and Sophie should see the medics and get those cuts taken care of. You can fill her in, and I'll talk with the kids."

The kids. He sounded like such a dick when he was trying to act all nurturing and fatherly.

"Okay." My aunt put her arm around Dr. Black, who looked in shock, guiding her away.

My uncle's eyes swept over the rest of us: me, Passion, his irate daughter, and Jason, the guy in his back pocket. "Come with me," he said. "There's a room we can use for some privacy over here."

He led us to a typical conference room dominated by a long table with rolling office chairs around it. We all sat, except for my uncle. I didn't know about the rest of them, but I was bracing myself to be served up a full plate of bullshit.

He turned to Samantha. "You asked me what this place is, and it's difficult to explain, but I'll do my best.

Essentially, this is where The Hold was born." He was addressing us all now, his voice taking on a nostalgic tone as he geared up for a mini-sermon on his favorite subject. "Here, a group of people first gathered who believed PSS was the next step in humankind's evolutionary process. They built this structure as a sort of temple, a research facility, and a commune. Unfortunately, not long after the group formed, there was an event that divided it, causing a philosophical split, a parting of the minds, if you will. One faction wanted to revere and honor those with PSS, accepting it as a spiritual mystery to be consecrated, not analyzed. The other faction thought the prerogative should be scientific research and utilization. One side saw PSS as a gift, the other as a resource to be controlled. And so, the two factions parted ways, and the purpose of this facility changed. No longer a headquarters, it became more of a neutral zone, a way for each side to always keep the other in check. The building itself, owned by both sides, was divided exactly in half, each half owned and utilized by one of the factions, with a neutral zone in the middle."

"The Hold and the CAMFers *share* this building?" Samantha asked, appalled. "They work together, and you never told me? You lied to me my entire life?"

"I didn't lie," he protested. "But I couldn't tell you. Only a small, select number of people on either side know this facility exists. And we don't work with the CAMFers. We have our side and they have theirs. We're completely separate entities," he said, glancing at me.

If he expected me to be shocked, he was going to be disappointed. At least, I wasn't surprised by the part about The Hold and the CAMFers sharing the same origins. I'd always know they were two sides of the same coin. But the thing about them sharing the compound? I hadn't known that. Still, I wasn't shocked. I was just royally pissed.

"They held us here," I said, my eyes drilling into him. "They tortured us."

"You remember?" he asked, sounding surprised, maybe even alarmed.

"It's coming back to me." My hands balled into fists under the table. "And you knew it. You let them."

"No," he said, adamantly. "I had no idea you and Dani were here, or that they'd taken you. My men tailing you—they lost you that night. I thought you'd just stolen a car and run off again. I didn't find out otherwise until weeks later, after you'd gotten away. Even then, I wasn't sure what had happened to Dani. I've been trying to find out ever since, to build a case against them. I even tried to negotiate her return." His eyes flicked to Jason, only for a moment, but I saw it. "They claimed they didn't have her," he went on. "That they'd never had either of you."

"That's bullshit," I said. "You knew it was bullshit."

"Yes, I did," he admitted. "But I had to be able to prove it, and I couldn't. My hands were tied."

"Your hands were tied?" Passion echoed, her voice flaring with anger. "What does that even mean?"

"There are guidelines," my uncle explained. "Rules by which the two sides interact to keep conflict at a minimum. Members of The Hold are strictly off limits to the CAMFers. But Dani and Marcus weren't officially under Hold protection—"

"Wait," Samantha jumped in. "So members of The Hold are protected, but anyone else is fair game? I can't even believe I'm hearing this. What about the fucking Eidolon? They shot members of The Hold there. But you knew they were coming, didn't you? You baited them into coming so you could gather evidence against them, save the day, and show everyone you were a better leader than John Holbrook? That plan sort of backfired, didn't it? You risked everything, and lost it. You risked me," her voice broke as she said it. "You let innocent people die just to save your position."

"That's not how it was," he said firmly, but I could hear the desperation creeping into his voice. "I had security at the park. I had Leo and an entire team ready to stop them and gather evidence. But he turned on me. He—eliminated his own team. He'd been your driver for years. He was one of my best men. I never suspected—"

"You never suspected he was a double agent?" I jumped in. "You just told us The Hold and the CAMFers are so intertwined they're practically a human centipede. And you still think you can tell where your head stops and a CAMFer's ass starts? You're delusional."

"Watch it," he warned me. "Have some respect."

"Yeah, that's not gonna happen." I smirked. "Your own men screwed you. You let the CAMFers massacre innocent members of The Hold. You arranged to have your own daughter shot off a cliff, because you know, that's great parenting. And then you completely lost control of everything. What's not to respect?" God, I loved to see him squirm like this. Finally, everyone was seeing what I'd always known about him.

"What?" Samantha blurted, her face white as a sheet.

Fuck. I'd gotten carried away and forgotten Sam didn't know about the shooting.

Passion was staring at me, her mouth hanging open, her head shaking a horrified "no."

Even Jason was glaring at me, his hand on the table flicking a quick middle finger in my direction.

"You shot me?" Samantha turned to Jason, her voice trembling "And you arranged it?" She looked back at my uncle, tears spilling down her cheeks.

"Samantha," he said, full desperation in his voice. "It isn't what it sounds like. I was just keeping you safe."

"No!" she yelled at him, standing up and backing away from the table. "You are not who I thought you were. Not even a little. Everything you taught me about The Hold, about protecting the Marked, it was all a lie. This is just about power for you. You're some kind of narcissist or sociopath or something."

"Everything I've done," he insisted, "has been to protect you and The Hold and the Marked. Why do you think your mother and I risked our marriage to sway them? The Hold was going to split over CAMFer aggression even before the Eidolon. Can't you see what's going on around you? I brought an army here, and so have the CAMFers. There is going to be a war. The truce between the two factions is over. They made sure of that the moment they took David and Dani. In fact, I think it's what they've been pushing for even before that. But it's complicated. There are things hanging in the balance you have no understanding of."

"Oh, I understand completely," Samantha spat. "You weren't protecting other people. You were protecting yourself. I don't want to have anything to do with you or The Hold ever again. I don't even want to be in the same room with you," she finished, walking out and slamming the door so the walls shook.

The room filled up with silence.

My uncle stood there, staring after her, his face a mask of mixed emotions.

He must have known Sam would find out about the shooting. If he'd really wanted to hide it, he would have eliminated Jason. So, he'd wanted her to find out. That was the only explanation. My uncle was a smart, diabolical man. He'd know what was going to come out in this discussion with Jason, Passion, Sam, and I all in the same room, and not just the shooting, but all the dirty laundry about The Hold and the CAMFers and this building we were in. Sam's sense of justice was fierce, and always had been. She wouldn't get over this for a very long time. My uncle knew that. Of course he did. Which meant, for some reason, he'd upset her on purpose. He'd intentionally created a distance between himself and his daughter. The question was, "why?"

And I still didn't know why he'd brought us to this building in the middle of a valley in the middle of a war. He didn't give a rat's ass about hostages, I knew that much. If he hadn't cared about Dani and I being here, he certainly didn't care about Olivia and Grant. Maybe they were already dead, and the whole hostage thing had just been a ruse to get us to come with him. And then there was the deal he'd made with the tribes, the thing he'd been arguing with Reiny about. No, he wanted something here, something he'd only hinted at. There was a reason he hadn't moved against the CAMFers until now. Something had changed to destroy all those years of stalemate between the CAMFers and The Hold. Something big.

Whatever it was, it was in this building, still barely holding the two sides together like the nucleus of an unstable atom.

And my uncle had come to take it.

"Sir," a man said, sticking his head in the room. "Sorry to interrupt, but the CAMFers are insisting on meeting with you immediately."

"And what about them firing on us out there?" he asked angrily. "What are they saying about that?"

"They denied responsibility, sir." I could tell the guy was embarrassed even relaying that information. "But we'll have proof soon enough. Our men are moving into position as we speak."

"Then it's time," my uncle said. "How is Pete? What's his condition?"

"Serious but stable, sir."

"Good. Tell Bo and his brothers to meet us in the corridor."

"Yes, sir. I'll let them know," the guy said, shutting the door behind him.

My uncle turned to me. "You're coming too." It wasn't a question. "Otherwise, you won't believe a word I say about what goes on in there. And Samantha will believe you. I need an objective witness, and you're about as objective as they come."

Jason stood up. Apparently, he was coming as well.

"And I'm coming," Passion said, a look of determination in her eyes. "Olivia and Grant are my friends. I want to be there for them."

"Very well," my uncle said.

When he didn't argue I knew it had been his plan all along to take us. Us and not Sam. Which meant he was leading us into serious danger, and he knew it.

"She shouldn't come," I said, wanting to protect Passion from my uncle's schemes. "They'll have minus meters. Think of what that would do to her. She has PSS blood."

Passion was glaring at me, but she'd thank me later. She didn't understand him the way I did. She didn't know what he was capable of.

"She'll be fine," he dismissed my concern. "You'll all be fine. Minus meters are the least of our worries."

Easy for him to say. He didn't have PSS.

"This is finished today," my uncle said. "The CAMFers just don't know it yet. Our military force is three times theirs. We can take this compound and everything in it, but we must secure the hostages before they realize it and get desperate. Timing is key. This is about psychology, not brute force. So, we have to keep our heads. You going to be able to do that?" he asked me.

"Yes," I said, noticing the sweat beading on his upper lip. My uncle didn't get nervous. Whatever was about to happen, he knew it was a gamble, a high-stakes gamble with the CAMFers. And if this was his poker game, Jason and Passion and I weren't his fellow players.

We were his chips.

26

OLIVIA

Six armed CAMFers led by Dr. Fineman escorted me and Grant down a long hallway. They'd searched us, but not handcuffed us. They'd also put gloves on me, the right one rubber-banded around my stump and stuffed with something to make it appear, at least from a distance, like I still had a hand. They'd also made us put on black hooded robes, exactly like the ones we'd worn at the Eidolon.

"Oh, put up the hoods," Dr. Fineman said, looking smug. "It makes you seem so mysterious." He was mocking us, reminding us he'd killed our friends, and we were powerless against him. Even as he traded us away, he wanted us to carry that fear with us, to wear it like a mantle. I could see the gleam in his eyes.

He thought we were subdued, all the fight gone out of us.

Grant and I did our best to look the part, heads bowed, feet shuffling, eyes straight ahead. Little did the doctor know, I had an ace up my sleeve, or rather, an entire hand up my sleeve, plus Grant's cube at the ready. Of course, I had no idea what would happen if I used it, and I'd need something to combine it with. That part might get a little tricky. There was no guarantee any of the guards had PSS. They were too far away for me to tell and, for this to work, I'd have to get close enough to reach inside one of them. Still, if I had to use Fineman like a hand puppet and pop him back into a coma, I would. Whatever would free Grant and me, I'd do it.

We arrived at the end of a hallway, standing in front of a metal door with seriously heavy security on it. There was a large camera over the door trained on us and two video monitors up there as well. The left monitor showed what must be the other side of the door, just a cut of a small portion of the room beyond, with someone on the other side guarding it and facing away from us. The monitor on the right showed a hallway exactly like the one we were in with a door identical to the one in front of us, but we weren't up there on the screen. That other hallway, the mirror of ours, was empty.

On the door there was a huge security panel and Dr. Fineman punched a code into it. He also did some kind of thumb and retina scan, and the door still didn't open, but part of the security panel slid aside, revealing a keycard slot. Then, he reached up and pulled out a keycard strung on cordage around his neck. Still, he didn't put the card in the slot. He just stood there, holding it and looking up at the monitor on the right, waiting for something and tapping his foot impatiently.

"Where are they?" he demanded, turning to one of the guards. "You said they were on their way."

"They're here, sir," the guard said, pointing above the door.

I looked up, and the empty hallway on the right monitor wasn't empty any longer. Alexander James walked up to the door and looked up at the camera. And he wasn't alone. Marcus was next to him.

Marcus, his dark eyes peering down at me, curious, suspicious, cautious, mesmerizing.

Marcus alive and upright and real.

My eyes darted to the camera above our door. Could he see me? If their camera fed into our hallway, ours must feed into theirs.

But when I looked back at the monitor, he was glancing over his shoulder, saying something to Jason and Passion who'd just come up behind him. There was no audio feed though. I saw their mouths move. I saw Jason nod. I saw three more figures join the group, but their faces were out of camera range, an escort of burly, headless bodies. They weren't female, I could tell that much, so I was guessing my mother hadn't come. I was simultaneously disappointed and hugely relieved by her absence. If I was going to do something awful with my hand, I'd rather she not see it.

I glanced at Grant. He was grinning at me.

This was really happening. The CAMFers were letting us go. We were going to be free.

Dr. Fineman held his keycard up to the camera.

In the monitor, Mr. James drew a similar keycard from around his neck and held it up.

Dr. Fineman reached out and pushed a button on the security panel.

Mr. James appeared to be doing the same.

Our security panel's screen began to flash red numbers, counting down from ten like it was preparing for a shuttle launch.

Dr. Fineman held out his keycard.

In the monitor, Mr. James held out his keycard too, poised to use it.

I was getting a bad feeling in the pit of my stomach. This was a lot of security. There was no way it was all for us. I glanced over my shoulder, back down the long hallway we'd just come down. It had no doors except this one, a single door with massive security. What was behind it?

I looked up at the left monitor. That had to be the room beyond this door. And on the right monitor were Mr. James and my friends, standing in a hallway like this one, also leading to a door which led into that room. What the hell was going on?

The red number flashed from 1 to 0 and the door made a loud buzz as Dr. Fineman inserted his keycard into its slot.

The door swung open.

Dr. Fineman stepped across the threshold and I followed, Grant behind me.

Mike Palmer stood guard just on the other side.

He was the one I'd seen in the monitor with his back turned. Dr. Fineman stepped past him, not giving him a second glance.

But I stopped, pausing right next to him. "CAMFer pig," I said, loud enough for Fineman to hear.

"What did you say?" Palmer spat, reaching out and grabbing me by the elbow.

I could feel Grant behind me, tensing up. I could hear the guards, caught back in the hallway, shuffling nervously.

"Let go of her," Dr. Fineman turned, frowning at Palmer. "She is nothing. She is useless, and you have something more important to attend to. One thing. One priority. Do you understand? I chose you for your dedication to the cause, and you'd better not disappoint me."

"No, sir." Palmer dropped my arm and looked properly reprimanded. "I won't."

"Go then." Fineman waved him away. "It's time. You know what to do."

"Yes, sir," Mike Palmer said and he stepped away, opening up my view of one of the most amazing rooms I'd ever seen. It was so huge and expansive, I'm not even sure you could call it a room. It was more like a cathedral or a conservatory, its domed glass ceiling hanging far above us in giant, precise hexagons, the stars winking in and out in the night sky beyond them.

I craned my neck to take it all in and my hood fell back. Screw Fineman. I wasn't putting it back on.

"Holy shit," Grant exclaimed softly next to me. "What is this?" He was looking up too, his head and hood thrown back.

But no one answered him.

Dr. Fineman just led us further into the room, a pompous smile on his lips.

The entire inside of the dome was open, with no interior walls, and it was dimly lit, so the effect of the night sky was all the more dazzling. In the middle was a huge empty area, a giant circular mosaic of floor tiles mapped out in intricate detail. The rest, closer to the outer walls, was decorated with a series of folding screens placed strategically throughout to mark off various sections and block them from view. There were furnishings, too. Off to one side was what looked like a library with shelves full of books, comfortable seating, and a few lamps. Mike Palmer disappeared from view behind one of the library screens. For a moment, I thought I heard the murmur of voices, but it was hard to tell. The acoustics in the dome were weird, sound bouncing off curved walls so I couldn't be sure what direction it was coming from.

Despite its open and massive architecture, the dome felt like a private, individual space, like we'd invaded someone's home uninvited. And it was hard to measure the length and breadth of it all. Was it a hundred feet across? Two hundred?

Whatever the distance, my eyes didn't have any trouble finding the door on the other side, exactly opposite ours.

It had a guard too and was already open, Mr. James stepping through, his eyes landing on me immediately.

My heart soared. I'd never thought in a million years I'd be so happy to see that man. But I was.

There was movement behind him and Marcus stepped in.

I didn't expect it, but my knees started to buckle, all the strength suddenly gone out of them.

Grant grabbed my elbow, holding me up. "Hey, it's okay," he whispered. "We're going to be okay." He was comforting me, but he was also warning me not to mess this up. I had to hold it together. If we were going to walk out of here, I had to be able to walk.

Or Marcus could carry me.

Fuck. That didn't help. That made me want to fall on the floor even more.

I locked my knees and stared at Marcus, hungry for him, willing those beautiful brown eyes to look at me. Instead, they swept the dome, surveying it just as I had. What would he see when his eyes found me after so much distance and time and agony?

Finally, he looked down from the dome, his glance flicking to my face but avoiding my eyes. He inspected me, coldly, calculatingly, his face devoid of all emotion. And then he was done with me, his eyes moving on to Grant.

I stood, stunned. I felt like I had been smacked, hard. Like my whole body had been thrown to the ground, the air slammed out of me. What the hell? How could he look at me like that after all I'd been through, after all we'd been through together?

No, that wasn't fair. Of course he'd come to a meeting with his uncle and the CAMFers wearing his poker face. He would never show them what he wanted, even if it was me. That look had been for them. I'd get my look later, when all this was over.

His glance had already left Grant, falling on Dr. Fineman, still cool, calm and collected. I'd seen Marcus rage against this man before. I'd seen Marcus try to kill him. Now he simply looked at him, no hatred flaring in his eyes, just curiosity mixed with caution.

I tore my gaze away from Marcus, my heart plummeting, my hope dissolving. Something was wrong. Horribly, horribly, wrong. I can't explain how I knew, but this was a different Marcus than the one I'd known. It was in the way he stood, and looked, and saw. It was in every cell of his being. And I could only think of one explanation for that. Danielle was here, a captive of the CAMFers. I'd seen her. I'd felt her. She'd healed me. Even then, even when the evidence was overwhelmingly against Marcus, I still hadn't believed it. Because I hadn't wanted to. Because I'd needed him. I'd needed the hope of him to keep me alive. It's what had gotten me this far. The hope of seeing him again, of connecting with those eyes and seeing love in them.

I was such an idiot.

Passion stepped through the door and her eyes found me and Grant, full of concern and relief. Then she glanced at Marcus and back at me, like she was trying to tell me something. Did she know what I'd just realized? Had she figured it out?

Jason came in behind her, followed by the three guys from the Warren Gun Club. What the hell were they doing here?

Jason's gaze found me, and he looked relieved too. There was more feeling in those eyes than I'd seen in Marcus's, and that's when it hit me again.

Marcus didn't care about me. At all. It had all been a lie. And the rest of them must not know, or why bring him here? Why play right into his hands? Shit. What would he do? Had he promised to deliver us all to Fineman in exchange for Danielle?

"Come along." Fineman strutted forward, leading us to the big mosaic circle in the middle of the dome.

Grant and I followed like obedient dogs, but the guards stayed near the door, as did the guys from the gun club on the other side.

Mr. James reached the outside of the circle first and stopped, Passion, Jason and Marcus stopping a few feet behind him.

Dr. Fineman strode right into it, leaving Grant and I at the perimeter, waiting as well.

"I see you brought Passion to me, as agreed," Dr. Fineman said, smiling maliciously. "And I brought Olivia and Grant. Shall we make the exchange and be done with it?"

No. Please, no. Mr. James couldn't trade Passion for us. She'd never survive the CAMFers.

Passion looked as stunned as I was, her confused eyes glancing from Mr. James to the doctor and back again.

Marcus looked pissed, but not surprised.

"Let's cut the crap," Mr. James growled. "You know very well I'm not giving you Passion, nor did I ever intend to. Just like you never intended to enter peaceful negotiations with The Hold. You fired on us out there. You shot at innocent women and children entering the compound on our side."

"Your side?" Dr. Fineman asked, quirking an eyebrow. "I wasn't aware you had a side anymore, Mr. James. I believe you were officially relieved as leader of The Hold six days ago and have no authority or permission to be here in any capacity. Which makes you and your little group nothing more than trespassers, I'm afraid. And as criminal trespassers, I'll be taking you all into my custody."

"And I'm afraid you're horribly misinformed." Mr. James took an official-looking piece of paper from inside his jacket and held it out. "This is a court-ordered eviction notice from the Confederated Tribes of Warm Springs for the CAMFers and The Hold. Our right to access and maintain this facility has been terminated, which technically makes all of us trespassers. Oh, except for me and my eviction team. You see, the tribes have appointed me temporary server and executor of the eviction, which I can do since I no longer have any official affiliation with The Hold. And since you brought unauthorized armed forces onto reservation land and fired upon civilians, the eviction takes effect immediately."

"An eviction?" Dr. Fineman asked, smirking. "How quaint. Next thing I know, you're going to say you've come to repossess my car. You think this matters?" He gestured dismissively at the document in Mr. James's hand. "Your paperwork and your legalese and your connection with the tribes? We are no longer under your thumb or the agreements made between the Hold and the CAMFers concerning this place and its occupants. Surely you understood this after I took your niece and nephew, after I stormed your daughter's little party. But in case you're still confused, let me show you how serious I am." He waved a hand at the nearest partition. "Bring her out," he called.

Mike Palmer stepped out from behind the screen, shoving a slender figure in front of him, her face hidden deep in the cowl of her hood. But I knew who it was. It was hard to miss the gentle glow of the PSS fingertips peeking out from her left sleeve. *Fineman had put her in a robe too? God, he was a psychotic bastard.*

Palmer had one arm wrapped around her, pinning her arms to her side, but his other hand was up near her throat, holding something, pressing it against her.

It was the device Anthony had used to cut off my hand.

And it was humming, the red laser line bright against the shiny black cloth of her robe like a stripe of blood.

27

OLIVIA

"**D**anielle—" Marcus shouted, a strangled cry suddenly cut short as two CAMFers grabbed him from behind. Even as they forced him to his knees and handcuffed him, a gun held to his head, Jason, Passion, and Mr. James were being taken and bound as well.

CAMFers were pouring from behind partitions. There must have been fifteen or twenty of them.

The three guys from the Warren Gun Club were throwing down their weapons and putting their hands up.

No. This could not be happening.

I looked back at Palmer and his hostage. He'd told me he was working for Danielle, that this was all to save her. He'd told me no matter what it looked like, I couldn't expose him. Was this what he'd been talking about? Was it some kind of diversion?

"Don't hurt her, please," Marcus pleaded. "Take me. Do whatever you want to me. Just don't hurt her."

"What a nice little offer," Dr. Fineman said, strutting around the circle like a peacock. "But I'm afraid there's been some kind of horrible mistake on your part. This isn't your sister, Danielle. No, I distinctly remember killing her right in front of your eyes. Surely you haven't forgotten? It was very memorable. But, oh wait, now I recall something. One of my little spies informed me you've had somewhat of a traumatic brain injury, and you don't remember at all, do you?"

Wait? What? If that wasn't Danielle, who the hell was it? And Marcus had been injured? He'd lost his memory?

I tried to catch Passion's eyes, to find an answer there, but she was glaring at Jason for some reason.

"You killed her," Marcus wailed, thrashing and struggling against the men holding him, his eyes fixated on Dr. Fineman, awash with grief and hate and rage.

It hurt to see him like that, to witness him relive the most painful moment of his life, bound and exposed to his enemies. If he'd forgotten Danielle's death, what else had he forgotten?

Oh, God. He'd forgotten me. That's why he'd looked at me that way when he'd first come in.

I tore my eyes from him, back to Palmer. He was still holding his hostage, but he'd lowered the cutting device, his arm relaxed a little, and he gave me a look. But what did it mean? Did he expect me to use my hand now, when everyone who'd come to rescue me was being held at gunpoint? We were surrounded by CAMFers, and no one was within reach except Grant. I had to have something to combine with his cube. If I was going to do this, I needed another resource to pull from.

And Marcus had forgotten me.

"Yes, I killed her," Fineman said, bending down to loom in Marcus's face.

"Leave him alone," Mr. James growled, trying to lunge forward, but the CAMFers holding him wrestled him back.

"Well, her powers were limited, so it wasn't a huge loss," Dr. Fineman said, turning to Mr. James. "Your niece's PSS was a mere novelty, but I took her sample and replicated it. And its healing properties have come in handy."

"Fuck you," Mr. James spat. "After today you will never hurt another child with PSS."

"Really?" Dr. Fineman asked. "You're going to stop me? How, I wonder, when I hold all the cards? I hold you and your pitiful little group of PSS adolescents. I hold this valley, as you noticed when you came in. And I hold this dome and everything in it, including her." He gestured at Palmer and the robed form. "Shall we introduce everyone, do you think? Is it time to let them know how much you and I truly are alike?"

"You're not going to get away with this," Mr. James said calmly. "I have troops moving in even as we speak, taking back the valley and the compound. You hold the dome now, but you're surrounded and outnumbered. You're trapped, doctor. You might as well give up."

God, I hoped that was true.

"Give up?" Dr. Fineman smiled wickedly. "I think not. After all, I have you. Surely your own men won't attack when it would certainly result in your death. And I have her." He gestured to the captive in Palmer's arms. "The Hold would never move against me as long as I have her, would they? Pull back her hood," he ordered Palmer. "I think it's time we let The Hold's little secret out of the bag."

The girl in Palmer's arms didn't struggle. She didn't make a sound. She just stood there, stoically, as he reached up a hand and tugged back her hood, revealing her face.

I stared at her, and I couldn't breathe.

She wasn't Danielle. She wasn't anyone I had ever met, but I knew her face almost better than my own. I had looked at it so many times, studied it, memorized it. I'd imagined myself meeting her all my life, though never like this.

And her face, it wasn't exactly like my father had depicted in *The Other Olivia*. Here were the same delicate, pixie-like features that made her look so eternally young, but it was more beautiful and incredible than his painting. First, because it was real. Second, because it wasn't completely PSS. Instead, her face was marbled, flesh and PSS swirled in an almost symmetrical design across it. She had a PSS mask around her eyes, and it drifted down over her nose and around her mouth, but her forehead and cheeks and chin were flesh. Her hair, most of it brown, was peppered with stands of PSS like filaments of light, which seemed to have a mind of their own, dancing around her head. Even her neck and throat had a strip of PSS, running nearly straight down the middle and disappearing into the collar of her robe. And out of it all shone piercing, deep, intelligent, brown eyes.

My sister. The Kaylee. *She was real.*

And I wasn't the only one in awe of her.

A hush had fallen over the entire dome. Even the CAMFers had fallen under the spell of that face.

She was looking at me. We were seeing one another for the first time. No, not for the first time. I had seen her once. We had met. In a cell deep in the basement of the compound. We had touched fingers and hands through a stone wall. She had slipped me notes. She had come to me in a dream and told me everything was going to be all right.

"Kaylee," I said, and in my mind the words echoed after it. *We will always love you.*

"She can't answer you," Dr. Fineman said, jerking me back to reality. I had almost forgotten where we were and the horrible situation we were in. "Her vocal chords are PSS, so she's incapable of speech. But yes, she is Kaylee, your sister, brought here to this compound by Mr. James when she was only seventeen days old."

I slowly turned and stared at Mr. James.

"Olivia," Mr. James said, 'You know you can't trust this man or anything he says. You know what he is. How he twists everything."

"How I twist everything?" Fineman laughed. "So, you deny that you took this girl from her hospital crib and brought her here to live in this dome, never to experience freedom, never to step outside, never to know her family?" He turned to me.

"If you don't believe me, ask her," he said, pointing to my sister.

Our eyes met again, Kaylee's and mine, and she nodded.

I turned back to Mr. James. "You lied to my parents," I said. "You told them you were looking. You pretended to try and find my sister when you knew where she was all along, because you had taken her."

"Everything I did was for her protection," he said, no guilt in his eyes. "Your parents had no idea what to do with her or how to protect her. Here she's been safe, neither side able to exploit or use her. She's not a prisoner. No one has experimented on her. She's had everything she could need or ask for. You have to understand, this was the only way to keep the peace between the two factions. From the moment she was born, both sides were bent on annihilating one another for control of her. And I wasn't in charge of The Hold then. I did what I was ordered to do. Even so, I knew it was the only solution. By bringing her here where neither side could use her, we've saved thousands of lives, including hers. And the peace has held for over two decades."

"Peace?" I said, choking on the word. "You call this peace?"

"It was," he argued, talking quickly. "But then nine months ago, Kaylee began to manifest her powers. He knows we can't hold her here much—"

"Silence him," Fineman ordered, and the guard holding Mr. James pulled out a ball gag and shoved it over Alex James's head, strapping it tightly. Even with a red clown nose in his mouth, the man still somehow managed to look dignified, and his eyes were on me, as if he expected me to save him. As if he expected me to save them all.

Next to me, I felt Grant tense up, bracing himself for me to pull out the cube, but what could I combine it with? The CAMFer soldiers were too far away. They'd stop me before I got to them. They'd shoot me, or worse yet, they'd shoot one of the other hostages. I was too afraid. I was shaking. I couldn't do it.

Fineman was looming over Mr. James. He thought he'd won.

I turned and found my sister's eyes, calm, accepting, and hopeful.

Palmer was looking at me too with a bit of regret, almost an apology, as he raised the bladed knife, still humming, and pulled it across my sister's throat.

Her head fell back and she slumped in his arms, blood and PSS welling from her neck and flowing down the front of her robe.

"No!" I cried, and Grant grabbed me, holding me up, pulling me to his chest.

Mr. James thrashed against the CAMFer holding him, moaning loudly around the ball gag in his mouth.

"You see, now no one will have her," Palmer said, looking down at the limp form in his arms. "Not the CAMFers. Not the Hold. Her powers were manifesting far beyond anything anyone could control. She was too dangerous. It was only a matter of time before we couldn't hold her at all."

What had he done to her? Oh, God, what had he done?

Her PSS wasn't going into the knife. It was running down the front of her, dripping to the floor, pooling with her blood. She was dying. Mike Palmer had pretended to be my ally so I wouldn't stop him from killing my sister right in front of me.

On. I thought, sinking my ghost hand straight into Grant, my glove flopping to the floor. It was all one motion. I didn't think about it. I didn't even need to feel for the cube. I knew exactly where it was, and I had it out in a second, tossing it to my left hand. Then I pulled back the front of my robe and slipped my ghost hand into my own chest.

What do you feel when you reach into yourself? Your own strength, and weakness, and humanity. Your own frailty and might. Your own life-force, pulsing and eternal. You feel light and you feel darkness, darkness you must embrace and find and use, because it's a part of you, a crucial part of you. You cannot exile the darkness. You must cup it in your hand and know it.

I felt something, my fingers touching my own burden, grasping it, holding it.

I pulled my ghost hand from my chest, and I looked down at what I held.

It was a stone, small, rounded, and smooth, and etched across it was my father's name, Stephen Carlton Black, followed by the dates of his birth and his death.

It was a marker. The gravestone he'd never had. The span of a good man's life nestled in the palm of my hand.

Dr. Fineman was yelling. He was waving for his men to take me. He could see what I'd done, and what I was about to do. He was staring at my ghost hand, terror in his eyes.

But it was too late. He couldn't stop me.

I pressed Grant's cube and my father's stone together. *But what did I want? What could I possibly wish for that would correct the great mess my life had become?*

I wished for a different world. One where the CAMFers and The Hold didn't need to exist. One where my sister and my mom and I could be together without fear. One where Marcus could trust and love someone. One where kids like Nose, and Yale, and Jason, and Passion could live unmolested, and free, and empowered. I wanted to know, without a doubt, who I could trust and who I couldn't. Wanted to have the people who truly cared about me surround me like a family. I wanted the most ridiculous, outrageous, unrealistic justice for myself and everyone I cared about, and I honestly didn't think that was too much to ask.

But nothing was happening.

Two of Dr. Fineman's men charged me.

I banged the cube and the rock together like a cavewoman, feeling some great terrible pressure of desperation building inside of me.

I looked over at Grant, frantic, and he opened his mouth to say something, but I never heard the words. I never heard them because something pulsed out of me, a wave of energy like an explosion or a tsunami, rolling through the air away from me in all directions, hurling Grant into the distance and sucking the sound right out of him.

One minute he was standing next to me, the next he was gone, winked out of existence.

And it wasn't just Grant.

It was everything.

I turned, looking for my sister, for Palmer, for Marcus, but no one was there. Not Fineman. Not his CAMFers.

I was standing in the middle of the dome in the center of the tile mosaic alone, and all the furnishings and trappings and contents were completely gone. Without the lamps and inner lights, it was dark and growing darker by the minute. I looked up, through the glass dome, and realized that even the stars were fading, winking into darkness from the outer edge of the sphere inward, as if some great telescope was shuttering closed over the entire universe, over me and all I'd ever known.

And then everything went dark. Including me.

28

OLIVIA

A rock pressed into my cheek, and another smaller one dug into my back. I sat up, but it was too dark to see my surroundings clearly. In fact, it was pitch black except for the glaring white light in the distance, which made it even harder to see anything else.

Was I dead? Was that the light at the end of the tunnel everyone talked about? Was I about to see my dad, or God, or the poor sister I'd just let die?

No, I didn't believe in any sort of afterlife except becoming dirt. And I definitely wasn't dirt yet.

The ground under me was gritty like sand though, and the air was cool and unmoving. There wasn't any sound either, which was creepy, like being in a tomb or a cave. Yes, it felt exactly like being in a cave, all still and enclosed and deep.

When I was ten, my parents had taken me to Meremac Caverns in Missouri, and we'd gotten a tour of the caves. In one of the deepest chambers, the guide had made us all turn off our helmet lights and stand there in the darkest dark any human being has ever experienced. I remembered that feeling well. I must be in a cave, and that glaring light was the opening in the distance. But how the hell had I gotten here?

I sat up slowly and carefully, my head spinning a little. The last thing I remembered was being in the dome at the compound at Warm Springs.

There was a rustling sound behind me and I freaked out, scrambling back, pressing myself against the rough, cool wall of the cave.

I heard the snap and hissing flare of a match being struck, and there was Mike Palmer's face lit up in its glow. He cupped his hand around the match and the light grew in intensity and size until he was suddenly holding a large torch. He held it out, sweeping it back and forth, revealing dark forms strewn across the cave floor, lumpy rounded shapes, not rocks, but bodies. Shit. What was I doing in a cave full of dead bodies with Mike Palmer?

This had to be a nightmare. *Wake up*. I told myself. *Wake up now, Olivia*.

Palmer swept the torch my direction and stopped, his eyes landing on me.

For a minute he just stared, as if he wasn't sure what to say.

I moved to a crouch, preparing to flee toward the cave entrance if he made a move toward me.

"For God's sake, turn on your hand," he said. "Help me find your sister." He gestured at the bodies. "She's here. She has to be here."

"Fuck you," I spat. "You killed her." He'd also just made me feel like an idiot. I'd completely forgotten I could turn my new ghost hand on and off. Apparently, it defaulted back to *off* when I was unconscious. But I didn't turn it on yet, just to spite him. And I still wasn't sure this wasn't a dream.

"I didn't kill her," he scoffed. "We just made it look that way. It was all part of the plan to free her. We couldn't just escape. The CAMFers and The Hold had to believe she was dead, or they'd never stop looking for her. We had to make it look like the end of her and when we did, I knew you'd use your hand. It would be the only thing left to you. What did you wish for, though? What did you think of?" He bent down and flipped over the body nearest him. I could see by the light of his magic torch it wasn't my sister. It was Passion.

"Oh, God." I moaned. "Is she dead?"

He put a finger to her neck. "No," he said, already up and moving to the next body. "She's just knocked out like we were from the displacement. You didn't kill anyone. Your power doesn't do that. But this is very important. I need you to tell me exactly what you wished for when you used your hand."

What had I wished for? I'd been so conflicted and confused and desperate. The moment seemed like a blur. It had been an ache in my heart more than any coherent thought. It had been a messy tangle of numerous needs and wants. "I don't know," I stammered as Palmer shone his torch down on Grant, lying face up, and bent to check his pulse. He'd said I hadn't killed anyone, but I guess he wanted to be sure. "There were so many things. I wanted the world to be different. I wanted to be safe. I wanted to know who really cared about me."

"Did you wish for your sister to be safe, to be with you?" he drilled me as he stepped away from Grant and on to another form.

"Yes. Maybe. I don't know."

"Dammit! I need you to know, girl. If she isn't here, we've lost everything. Do you understand? She *is* everything. I was counting on you to get this right, this one thing I couldn't do. If you've messed it up—" he stopped, looking down at the form he'd just turned over with his dusty booted foot. It was my mother.

"Oh my God," I said, jumping up and scrambling across the rocks and dirt to her. "Mom." I grabbed her shoulders and pulled her head into my lap. "Is she okay?" I asked, looking up at Palmer. "Please, tell me she's okay." I brushed my left hand across her head, feeling the soft downy prickle of the stubble there. Her hair was starting to grow back. Why had she ever shaved it?

Palmer crouched next to her, across from me, and put his big, dirty fingers on her pale, slender neck as he held the torch over us. "She's fine," he said, after a moment. "Just unconscious. But we have a problem. She wasn't in the dome with us. She shouldn't be here. If you displaced your mother here, with us, that means you could have displaced Kaylee somewhere else.

And that's bad." He stood up and resumed looking around the cave, waving his torch back and forth frantically. "Wait a minute," he said, and my eyes followed his, seeing the slender feminine form tucked in a corner at the back of the cave.

He rushed over to it, his torch shining down and revealing Samantha James's face. He didn't even bend down and check her pulse, as if he didn't care. He turned to me groaning, "What did you do? How could you bring *her*, but not your sister?"

"This is a dream, isn't it?" I said to him. "Your match turned into a torch. My mother is here. And you keep telling me I've messed up, but I have no idea what you're talking about."

"No, it's not a dream." He rubbed his free hand across his face. "You were supposed to displace us. Me, and you, and Kaylee. That was the plan to get her to safety. She told me it would work. She was sure. But she's not here," he gestured around the cave.

There were no more forms. We had Passion, Grant, my mother, and Samantha, but not my sister. I had sent her somewhere else. And what about Marcus and Jason and Mr. James? What about all the other people in the dome and the compound? When I'd displaced people before, I'd always been touching them. That's how I'd displaced Palmer the first time I'd ever done it. That was how I'd displaced a whole group of us when we'd escaped Dr. Fineman's lab back in Greenfield. But I hadn't been touching anyone this time. They could have been scattered to the four winds for all I knew. Fuck. What had I done?

"She could be outside," Palmer said, hope in his voice as he strode past me and walked toward the mouth of the cave, his body blocking out much of the light. Between that and him taking the torch, I was thrown into darkness again and finally had the wherewithal to light up my ghost hand. It cast a gentle glow across the face of my mother and she moaned, her eyes fluttering open.

"Olivia," she sighed, her eyes opening wider, welling with love and relief. "You're all right." She reached up and stroked my cheek. "I love you so much. And I'm so sorry—so sorry for everything."

"It's okay, Mom." I smiled down at her. "Everything's going to be okay.

"So, you're saying my other daughter is alive. Kaylee is alive?" my mother asked, the firelight dancing across her shocked face. "And Mr. James was the one who took her? And she was at the compound, but now you don't know where she is because Olivia can teleport people en masse and move them through time, but she can't control exactly where they go?"

We were all sitting around a campfire Palmer had built on the rocks just outside the cave. He hadn't found Kaylee anywhere nearby. He'd searched for an hour. And then the sun had set, which meant I'd probably displaced us in time as well as distance. Unless we'd been unconscious for almost twenty-four hours.

After Palmer had returned from his search, there'd been a lot of helping people get oriented and trying to explain where we were and why. Then, he'd built the fire, all the while throwing me passive-aggressive looks of disappointment, which I was getting fucking sick of because I already felt bad.

"That pretty much sums it up," Palmer said, sitting down on a rock.

"But how did you ever gain The Kaylee's trust?" Samantha asked. "And why help her if you're a CAMFer?"

"I'm not a CAMFer," he said, sounding insulted. "I'm a free agent. I work for whoever pays me, and both sides have been paying me for a long time. I was assigned to the dome when Kaylee first arrived. Before that, it was just a job, you know, I figured if I could make a decent paycheck on other people's hate and distrust, why not? But that girl, she gets under your skin. I've never met anyone like her. So, I kept going back to the dome between assignments. Then I was gone for a long time, in Greenfield." He glanced at me and my mother. "And I began to understand where Kaylee had come from, and how I might be able to help her."

I looked around the fire, wondering if anyone was buying this. Mike Palmer the nice guy. Mike Palmer with his heart on his sleeve. *Really?*

"After I left Greenfield," he continued, "I was assigned back to the dome, with occasional assignments elsewhere."

Like Indy and the McMansion, when he'd left us the matchbook. The magic matchbook he still hadn't explained to me.

"But mostly I was at the dome, and things were beginning to get dicey. Kaylee was manifesting powers, and she wasn't very good at hiding them. She doesn't understand deceit. So, I knew I had to get her out. I had to get her free from both groups before they figured out what was going on. That's where Olivia and her hand came in. I knew what she could do. I'd experienced it myself. And Kaylee has an innate sense of how PSS works, and how it can be manipulated. But we never imagined Olivia would displace the entire population of the compound randomly. We thought the closest people to her would end up in the same place."

"I'm sorry, okay?" I said, looking around the fire. "I did it wrong. I lost my sister."

"It's not your fault," my mother said, stroking my back. "You did the best you could."

"Maybe it wasn't random," Grant said, from across the fire. "There might be a pattern we're just not seeing yet."

"Maybe," Palmer said. "I just hope to God Kaylee didn't end up with a group of CAMFers. The Holders would be better, though not by much."

I saw Samantha cringe at that comment, but she didn't try to dispute it.

"You have to understand," Mike said, "Kaylee is completely innocent. She's never set foot outside the dome. She knows nothing of the outside world or how to survive. She can't even speak. If she's with others, she won't be safe. But if she's displaced alone, somewhere out in the wilderness like we are, she won't even survive."

"What about her powers?" Passion asked. "You said she had powers. Couldn't she use those to protect herself?"

"I doubt it," Palmer said. "She can soothe people with her touch, like calm them and take away their stress. She can do what Olivia does, pull things from people, but the objects have different properties. Kaylee can't use them to do anything, but the people she pulls them from can."

So, that explained the matchbook. Kaylee must have pulled it from Palmer, which meant it had been a pretty ballsy move for him to give it to me in Indy with no guarantee of getting it back. How did it work though? Could I have used it? Probably not. But that was so cool, my sister and I having similar powers. I guess it made sense. And the thing about calming people, that was kind of what my mom did for a living.

"But I don't get why those powers put her in danger," Samantha said. "Why would both The Hold and the CAMFers go to war over that?"

"Because she'd just begun to manifest a new power," Palmer said. "She'd started passing through walls and solid objects."

Yeah, I'd seen that one myself, as well as her ability to restore my PSS, which would be a huge threat to the CAMFers. But I had a feeling Palmer wanted to keep that one tightly under wraps. I wasn't going to mention it. I still hadn't told the group about Anthony cutting off my hand, mainly to protect my mom from the horror of it. Everyone just seemed to have assumed my hand had developed a fancy new "on and off" feature.

"She was only just mastering moving through things," Palmer explained, "and I tried to get her to keep it a secret, but she isn't good at secrets. Then Dr. Fineman started acting strange, and I knew someone must have seen her passing through something on camera and told him. He was scared. He was pushing the limits of his agreement with The Hold. He started talking about how dangerous she was, how she had to be taken care of. That's when I knew I had to get her out. For good. So, I convinced him we should kill her in front of Mr. James and crush The Hold once and for all. Not really kill her of course, that was all fake. And I hoped Olivia would do the rest."

"You could have been way more specific when we had our little chat in the security suite," I said, still pissed at him. "My power isn't exactly made-to-order on a good day. And that was not a good day. Not even a little."

"Olivia's right," Grant said, coming to my defense. "You left her completely in the dark and expected her to pull off this miracle for you. She had no idea what was going on, and what she did do probably saved countless lives. Plus, she got us all the hell out of there, which was more than anyone else could have done."

Thank you, Grant.

Even with the fire it was getting cold, the bitter cold of the high desert at night. We'd figured out that much about our location, based on the landscape and the plant life. We were still in the high desert, but Palmer didn't think we were on the reservation anymore. He thought we were somewhere further east.

"I agree," Samantha said, turning to me. "You prevented a war between the CAMFers and the Hold, and that's huge."

"I'm proud of you," my mother said, slipping her arm through mine, her fingers entwining with my ghost fingers. It was both intimate and startling, considering how she'd once reacted to my PSS. But so much had changed since then, including my hand. I'd been keeping it on, because it kind of freaked her out still that I could make it disappear and reappear at will. "I'm still confused about a lot of things," she admitted, "but that isn't one of them."

"She didn't prevent the war," Mike Palmer pointed out like the Eeyore he was. "It's delayed at most. If one of them has Kaylee, the other side will find out soon enough, and all hell will break loose. If neither of them have her and they all think she's dead, there's nothing holding them back any longer. There is going to be a war. It's inevitable."

"Nothing's inevitable," I said. God, he was such a downer.

"Fine, so she delayed it. Give her some credit," Passion piped up, shivering and sinking her hands deep into the pockets of her camo jacket. But then she got a funny look on her face and began digging around in them frantically, as if she'd lost something.

"What's wrong?" Samantha asked, frowning at her. They were sitting next to each other, but they weren't close the way I had seen them before. They weren't together. Something had happened while I'd been with the CAMFers. Something had created a rift between them.

"My magic eight ball is gone," Passion said, looking close to tears. "The one I found at the river."

A magic eight ball. The one I pulled from that CAMFer? What were the chances?

"It probably fell out when you got displaced," Samantha said, still sounding annoyed. "Or it got displaced too. It's just a stupid kid's toy anyway. What's the big deal?"

"It's more than that, okay?" Passion said, getting up and glaring down at Samantha. "I found it after the Eidolon, and it means something to me."

"Okay, I'm just saying there are more important things right now than—"

"You know what?" Passion interrupted. "You don't have to be such a bitch all the time. You're not the only one who's ever been hurt by their parents, and I'm done being your personal punching bag." Passion stormed off into the dark, but she didn't go far. Palmer had told us to stick close, at least until morning. There were coyotes out here and other things that could eat us. But she moved as far away as she safely could, sitting on a rock, her back turned to the group.

I thought about going to her, but I hoped Samantha would. She was who Passion really wanted.

Samantha didn't look sorry though. She was practically fuming. I imagine she didn't get called out for being a bitch very often.

The night was quiet, the fire crackling, and it wasn't hard to hear Passion when she began to cry, her sobs coming in hiccupy gasps like the sound of something deeply broken.

I couldn't sit there and let her hurt alone. I started to get up, but my mom squeezed my elbow, stopping me.

Samantha stood up, her face and demeanor completely changed. She stepped over the log she'd been sitting on and walked over to the rock, wrapping Passion in her arms. They clung to each other, whispering into each other's hair.

I looked away, wanting to give them privacy, my heart happy that at least something had been reconciled on this cold, strange night.

"So, what do we do now?" my mother asked, looking to Palmer. "How do we get out of here and back to civilization, so we can find my other daughter?"

"Well," he said, "first we make it through the night, probably by huddling together around this fire. Then, in the morning, we hike out of here. It shouldn't be too far to the nearest road or township. We're in Oregon, not Alaska. Then we go to Portland. I have friends there who will help us. They should be able to tell us what's happened since the displacement at the dome."

"Yeah, these friend of yours?" I asked, knowing the way he liked to flip-flop between groups. "Are they CAMFers or Holders?"

"Neither," he said. "Just traffickers of information. That's all. They're hackers, and they don't take sides. Plus, they may be able to help us find Kaylee. So, if you can get some rest, you should. We may have a long trek ahead of us tomorrow."

I looked down at the hard ground and the meager fire. I was hungry and thirsty and exhausted. My sister was missing and so was Marcus, and according to what Passion and Samantha had explained, he had no memory of me and our relationship. He'd lost it at the bottom of the pool at the Eidolon. That all seemed pretty grim, but at least I wasn't in a cell, and I wasn't a prisoner of the CAMFers. I had my ghost hand back, and my mother was next to me, proud of me, unafraid of me.

So, I was pretty sure I'd sleep like a baby.

And that's exactly what I did.

29

KAYLEE

The dome of the world was bigger than I'd ever imagined. The sky was immense, touching the bottom of the floor on all sides as far as I could see. And I could see so far. I could see farther than I could comprehend seeing. It didn't end, my eyes straining and not reaching. The world didn't end. It was amazing and wonderful and terrifying, the largeness of everything. The shapes and bumps, the rocks and hills and trees, the green lumps and scratchy things dotting a landscape I'd only ever imagined in my dreams. It made me feel so small, like the ants that had sometimes found their way into my little sphere, my little world. The ants I'd studied and shared my crumbs with and pretended I was the god of.

I was the ant now. I was the tiniest speck of humanity in a colossal world.

I think I would have cried if I'd been alone. But I wasn't.

There was a boy with me. One of the ones who had come into the dome to retrieve my sister. The sad one. The broken one. Well, all of them were broken, but this one most recently and in such an unusual way. He wasn't awake yet, but he was alive, splayed out on the floor—no, ground—that is what the outside floor was called. *Ground*. I needed to remember that. I needed to work on my vocabulary, using all the wonderful outside words I'd learned from the books in my library. Because the more words I had, the more I could write, the more things I could express, and the more world I could hold in my mind.

Mike had been worried I wasn't ready, that my brain would explode with all the new experiences and sensations. Sensations like *wind*. Wind was the air touching me now, caressing me like a friend or a lover. Wind was the air alive and sentient. Or maybe this was *breeze*. Wind was something else, stronger, something I'd get to feel later. And *gust*? That was something stronger again. None of them was a draft, though, the dead, stale shambling of air inside the dome. *Draft*. It even sounded dull.

The wind breezed in the boy's hair, his dark, luscious hair, flopping over his face, revealing long thin lines of white along his skull where something had injured him. Scars. I had one on the back of the flesh part of my hand. I'd jabbed myself with a pencil, digging the sharp point in deep, feeling the pain.

When they'd asked me why I'd done it, I didn't explain. I didn't tell them I'd just wanted to know pain. I'd wanted to give it to myself like a gift. And the scar had just been an unexpected bonus.

Maybe the boy was hurt. Maybe he was hurt so badly and he would never wake up, and I really was alone in the big wide world. What would I do then? And who would stop me?

But then he moaned and rolled over a little, revealing a surprise underneath him.

It was a black ball buried in the earth, only half of it sticking out because the boy had been on top of it, pressing it into the soil.

I reached out and touched it, feeling the PSS essence of it. Not an ordinary ball, then. It had come from inside someone. And not just that. There was something other about it. It had a hidden treasure, like an Easter egg of energies. A riddle, wrapped in a mystery, inside an enigma. I'd read that in a book once. It was from one of Mr. Winston Churchill's speeches. This enigma was tied to the boy in front of me.

I could see the way of it. He'd stored something inside the ball to keep it safe. Maybe he wasn't broken. Maybe he knew something I didn't. Maybe he was wise.

I rolled the ball in my hands, noticing the white circle with the eight in it. Or was it the sign for infinity? On the other side there was a black circular glass indentation, something blue swimming upward toward me.

I almost dropped the ball I was so startled when the words appeared.

"Where the hell are we?" the boy demanded, sitting up and grabbing my arm, looking around frantically as if he thought the wind or the sky might attack us.

We're in the world, I thought to him. *You should know that. You're from here.*

It was easy to talk into people's minds when they touched me, but not many people had ever touched me. Mike had, and he knew. And my sister knew because I'd talked to her, except Mike didn't know that. He'd warned me never to do it. Told me to always write instead. He said if I talked into people's heads they'd want to kill me, but that was silly. I could make them not notice. I could make them see my lips moving, like I just had with the boy. He didn't even realize I was speaking right into his mind.

Mike had been afraid of everything. He'd said if I went out into the world alone everyone would want to kill me, and here I was. Alive. Unless the boy did want to kill me. He looked a little like he might.

Are you going to kill me? I asked him.

"What? No. Of course not," he said, dropping my arm and looking down at the ball in my hands.

"Where did you get that?" He glanced around. "Where is everyone? What happened?"

I reached out and touched his arm, calming him a little. *My sister did it,* I told him. *She sent us away to save us. She sent everyone away, and separated the sheep from the goats, and now we have to save ourselves.*

"Your sister?" His eyes fell on me, really seeing me for the first time. "Who's your sister?"

Olivia, I told him, proudly.

"Of course." He got up, pulling away from my hand. "I should have known she was the sister of the mythical icon The Hold worships. Man, I know how to pick them."

I'm not mythical, I corrected him, but he didn't hear.

"I'm going to pretend this all makes sense," he said, looking down at me. "At least for now. Come on. We should find some shade before we get sunstroke. Put your hood up. That will help. We'll shelter in those trees, and maybe I can find us some water, and hopefully we can figure out where we are."

I got up from the ground, pulled my hood up just as he'd said, and slipped the black ball in my robe's inner pocket.

Then I followed the boy into the world.

THE END

Coming Fall 2015:
Ghost Hope, Book Four of The PSS Chronicles
Go to www.ripleypatton.com
for more details

If you enjoyed this book, please support the author by leaving a review right now on the venue you purchased it from.

ACKNOWLEDGEMENTS

I'd like to thank the universe, so bright and bursting with story. I'd like to thank my husband, Pete, and my two wonderful children, Soren and Valerie, for empowering me to be what I was meant to be. Soren, especially, helped me mold the end on this one and he made me promise to tell you he was right. I just didn't know it yet.

I couldn't have done this without my amazing PA, Samantha Hansen. She does all the hard stuff so I can write, and she never complains. In addition, my awesome Street Team, Ripley's Rebels, handles more PR and encouragement than I can quantify. Had I known what quality people I would meet when I became a novelist, I would have done it sooner.

To all those who supported the *Ghost Heart* Kickstarter, both familiar and strangers, thank you for backing book three. I don't think you'll be disappointed.

And last, but never least, to the amazing team that makes the story into a book: Scarlett Rugers for her wonderful cover designs, Lauren McKellar and Jennifer Ingman for tireless editing, and Simon Petrie for his precise and efficient formatting.

Thanks to all of you, I have a career I love, working with people I adore, and who could ask for more?

ABOUT THE AUTHOR

Ripley Patton is an award-winning author who lives in Portland, Oregon with one cat, two teenagers, and a man who wants to live on a boat. She has also lived in Illinois, Colorado, Georgia, Indiana, and New Zealand.

Ripley doesn't smoke, or drink, or cuss as much as her characters. Her only real vices are eating M&Ms, writing, and watching reality television.

To learn more about Ripley and read some of her short fiction, be sure to check out her website at www.ripleypatton.com. You can also sign up for her monthly e-newsletter there to keep up-to-date on The PSS Chronicles and win cool prizes.